BAD TRAFFIC

PATRICK WEILL

WEILL & ASSOCIATES

CLAIM YOUR FREE PREQUEL SHORT STORY!

By signing up for my readers club, you'll not only receive an award-winning Park and Walker prequel short story, but from time to time you'll also get spam-free emails from me, in which I may send my personal book or author recommendations, let you know about any discounts or new Park and Walker books I have written, or possibly deliver another exclusive short story. You can unsubscribe at any time and I won't sell or share your email address. You can scan the following QR code to join.

I hope you enjoy reading *Bad Traffic* as much as I loved writing it.

Pat Weill
Queretaro, Mexico

Dedicated to the real Murciélago.

CONTENTS

1

MURCI AND NAYELI

The Mexican sun beat down on their backs like a cruel taskmaster. Both of their bodies were bronze-hued and wiry, but only his had jagged, knotted scars, many of them relatively fresh. She didn't know how he'd gotten them. Like a soldier home from the war, Murci wouldn't talk about his time in the United States. Though his return meant a problem for the family, Nayeli was glad her big brother was back; it had been a long two years without him.

"¡Ánimo! You can do it, sis. Another half hour and we'll eat," he said, driving his digging stick into the drought-hardened soil so it stood up on its own. Then he stepped behind her to massage her neck and shoulders.

Nayeli closed her eyes and nodded, drawing inspiration from the back rub, but her brother's words were of little consolation. She didn't need to hear that she could handle the work; she alone had been tending to the small, heavily mortgaged plot of land while he'd been away. And she was too upset to care about food.

The siblings went back to preparing their family's cornfield for planting, Nayeli with only slightly renewed determination. As she labored, her efforts went from plodding and reluctant to wildly fast. She plunged her tool harder and harder, moving quickly down the row until exhaustion forced her to take a knee. Looking back down the line, she realized she'd broken up more soil in fifteen minutes than she normally did in double that time. Her eyes burned, then brimmed over with tears that cut through the dust as they rolled down her cheeks. She hung her head and wished her problems would wither and die like neglected crops. As her dizziness subsided and her breathing returned to normal, Nayeli came to two conclusions: one, her problems would never go away on their own, and two, it was she who was neglected and in danger of drying up. She and so many others.

Murci draped an arm over her shoulders and used his other hand to wipe her cheeks dry. "Don't give up, Naye," he said as he helped her up and walked her home.

He was right. The only sensible thing to do was to keep fighting against the family's desperate financial situation, which was even worse now that Murci wasn't sending dollars home. Nayeli wondered why he'd given up and come back. If it had been her, she would have stayed until she'd earned enough money to make a difference. A small part of her wished he hadn't returned.

On their way back to the rental they called home, Nayeli and Murci trudged past the farmhouse they used to live in. The one their father had built. The one where they'd lived all their lives until only recently. Neither turned to look at it. From there to the new house, Nayeli counted ten semi-feral dogs roaming the unpaved roads in search of food scraps or trash bags; without exception, the animals' ribs were jutting out like those of starving concentration camp prisoners.

***

"I went to the butcher shop today to buy a chicken, but Pablo had raised his prices *again*," Mamá said at the main meal of the day, which she always served at four p.m. In the center of the table, she set down a cloth napkin folded around hot tortillas. Her body still healthy, her copper-colored skin unblemished but for the worry lines on her face, Mamá had been blessed with good genes. Like a new taxi driven all day and all night, she'd held up well, though Nayeli often wondered how much longer that would be the case.

It's not the butcher's fault," said Papá, whom Nayeli had helped move from his bed to the rough-hewn wooden table. His hands were large, but like the rest of his body, they were nowhere near as strong as they'd been only five years before. Dark, sickly circles marked his eyes and his once-commanding voice came out in a whisper. "It's the greedy companies that control everything."

"Everything including the government," Murci added, rolling a tortilla in his palm and biting off a third of it. "Just like in the United States."

Nayeli stopped her spoon halfway to her mouth. "Just like everywhere," she said. "I wish money had never been invented. What this planet really needs is another meteor shower."

"Did you go to the police station today, son?" Papá asked, as if he hadn't heard her.

"Yes, sir. Boot camp starts on Monday."

"Good," the farmer replied, his eyes coming alive with pride. Nayeli wished her father would look at her like that, but that's just how he was. He'd never change.

"And you, honey?" Mamá asked, finally sitting down after everyone else had their soup. "How's school going?"

Nayeli reached for another tortilla, refusing to wish that it were meat, which she hadn't tasted in over a month. Her eyes darted around their dwelling, with its uneven concrete floor and the corrugated iron roof.

"Everything's fine, Mamá," she replied, not mentioning the flyer she'd seen at school and the appointment she had that night.

***

One of the many good things about Murci being back was that Nayeli was freed up to focus on her studies. A few days back, she'd found herself with some free time after class, so she'd strolled over to an announcement board and scanned the notices stapled there. One of them read as follows:

> Seeking female students to work in the U.S. as housekeepers or
> nannies. 9 dollars per hour with free room and board. Study for
> your GED at night. College scholarship opportunities available.

College in the United States of America? Just from what she'd learned in books and on the internet, Nayeli's English was already passable. She was sure she could succeed in such an environment. With the advertised wage and no expenses, she could literally lift her family out of the mire. While mulling over the pros and cons of this tempting opportunity, she recalled a recent conversation in the cornfield.

"Gringolandia's not a good place," Murci had said. "It's a rotten apple that only looks good from the outside."

"Right," she'd replied, squinting in the sun as she turned to look at him. "A rotten country where you can earn twenty times what you get here."

His features hardened. "You don't understand. It's a dangerous place for people like us."

"I'm almost fifteen. And I do understand, maybe better than you think."

"I'm five years older than you, and I've been there, and you haven't. Trust me, you don't want what they're selling."

Life in the States couldn't be as bad as Murci always made it out to be. In Nayeli's view, he just wanted her to stay home so he could order her around like he always did.

She'd eyed the flyer and pursed her lips for a moment. Then torn it off the board and hurried to catch the bus.

***

The following morning, Murci was not surprised to find Nayeli missing from the room they shared. As far as he knew, she'd gone to visit a friend the night before and had most likely stayed the night. But as the morning wore on, the family became alarmed. Mamá placed a call and learned that she'd been lied to. Nayeli had not gone to visit her friend.

Murci searched through his sister's belongings for any clue to her location. When he found the flyer in her backpack, he knew what had happened, and it made him sick. He also felt responsible, since she'd gone in search of the money he wasn't sending home.

His parents wanted to wait for a day or two, hoping the job offer was legitimate, that she'd call or come back after changing her mind, but Murci knew better. He immediately called the number on the flyer but was told he had the wrong number. Later that day, he asked a female friend to call and feign interest in the ad. She was given an appointment and directions to a house on a hill not far from Murci's house. He knew which one it was. As a boy, he'd visited 'Beltran Manor' many times, usually because he'd been dared to knock on the door to what everyone said was a haunted house.

As he came up the crest, the massive home loomed majestic, but once inside, his face puckered at the disarray that infected every square inch of it. There was an acrid odor; rotting pests under the furniture, perhaps.

His face was red and his voice loud when he thrust the flyer in the Beltrans' faces. "My sister's missing and I found this in her stuff. Have you seen her?"

"No, we haven't," Mrs. Beltran replied, looking innocently down at the ad. "We haven't had a visitor in months."

"Is this your phone number?"

"That's Diego Lopez's number," Mr. Beltran said. "He's my cousin's friend. Needed a place to stay for a while."

"No visitors except for Diego Lopez you mean," Murci snapped, eyeing the woman again. "I had my friend call. She was told to show up here right now, at five o' clock. Lopez wouldn't be hiding here somewhere, by any chance?" He fought the urge to search the premises without permission.

For a long time the Beltrans gave no reply. Then they exchanged a glance. "I don't know what to tell you," Mr. Beltran finally said. "Lopez stepped out a few hours ago. If you leave me your number, I'll tell him to call you."

Murci's pulse leapt as he glared at his neighbor. "I think you know more than you're letting on."

Not a small man, Mr. Beltran stepped forward until their faces were inches apart. "Did you just call me a liar, boy?" he bellowed. His breath smelled like he'd just gobbled up a big bowl of shit.

Murci was not a boy. He drew his father's pistol from under his shirt and jabbed its muzzle into the man's fat gut. "Back up, *cabrón*," he hissed through clenched teeth. "Tell me where my sister is or I'll kill you right now."

"They took her to San Diego," Beltran whimpered without delay. "That's all I know, I swear to God."

Not long after that, Murci was busy securing a duffel bag to the back of his motorcycle. The job offer had clearly been bait, but Nayeli was young and naive. *That's what they look for,* he seethed to himself. His transportation ready, he hurried into the house to his father's room. The elder man sat up from his bed.

"I'll bring her back, Papá," Murci said. "I swear."

"I know you will, *hijo.* I believe in you."

As they embraced, Murci closed his eyes and asked God to keep his dad alive until he returned. If he returned. Then he strode back outside where his mother was waiting by his bike. With tears spilling down her face, she gave him a long hug, a quick kiss, and blessed his journey with the sign of the cross.

With a final wave, Murci straddled the black machine, fired it up, and gave the throttle an aggressive twist. The nimble two-wheeler leapt forward and carried him away, roaring and snarling through the night, matching his own fury as he made the long trip north. *Whoever did this is going to hell,* he vowed. *And I'm going to send them there.*

2

SEASONING

The previous evening, Nayeli had arrived at Beltran Manor at the specified hour.

"Hellodear! You mus' be Nayeli," a middle-aged woman welcomed her sloppily. "ImissusBeltran. Comeonin."

As Nayeli stepped into the messy, foul-smelling abode, she noted that Mrs. Beltran held in her hand what was decidedly not her first drink of the night. Through a cloud of smoke, she spotted two men seated at a table littered with empty beer cans. Between them, an ashtray brimmed with crumpled butts.

"Nice to meet you, Nayeli. I'm Samuel Beltran," one man said, hefting his bulky frame out of his chair to shake her hand. He nodded over his shoulder to the other man. "And this is Diego Lopez. He runs the work-study program."

Lopez also rose and offered his hand. His eyes appeared more focused than those of his hosts.

"Hello, Mr. Lopez," Nayeli said eagerly.

"Great to meet you, Nayeli," he replied with a friendly smile that matched her enthusiasm. "Please, take a seat while I get you an information packet."

Mrs. Beltran staggered to the table and cleared away the beer cans and the ashtray. Then she set a plate of greasy quesadillas and a glass of lemonade on the table. "Hereyagohoney," she said. "Illgetsomenapkins."

Nayeli nodded obediently. Ironically, she'd later remember thinking it would be better if the woman drank some of her own lemonade in lieu of another alcoholic beverage. She gulped down half the contents of the glass, her throat parched after the dusty uphill walk. Soon after that, her memory of the visit turned spotty. She knew Lopez had come back and shown her some papers, but that was the extent of it.

The next thing she knew, she was sitting in the back of a car with no driver. The cloth upholstery was black and clean, and there was a strong, sickly-sweet odor of air freshener. Mr. Lopez pulled open the door to her left, letting in a blast of cool air that sharpened her senses. He held it open for another girl about her age, who slid in beside her.

"*¡Hola! Me llamo Marcela.*" The newcomer's eyes sparkled with a blend of excitement and nerves. As Lopez shut her in, Nayeli slumped back into a sleeping position and her irresistibly heavy eyelids fell closed again.

She heard Lopez say, "Don't worry, Nayeli's just tired. Here, have some lemonade."

At some later point, the exchange was made in a dark, deserted parking lot, empty but for a waiting black van. Lopez pulled to a stop and got out. A handsome man came forward to give him a wad of cash, then carried the semi-conscious girls to his van one at a time.

Nayeli was shaken awake when the van jerked to a halt. The only indication as to how much time had passed was that the sun was now high and hot. She was drenched in sweat. Their handler pulled open the sliding door. He was handsome all right, but his fine Latino features twisted in anger as he and two other men half-helped, half-dragged the girls up the steps into a pink mansion.

Once they were all inside, Handsome locked the front door with a key and said, "You may call me Martinez. Let's get you settled in." Although he spoke politely and in their own language, his actions were rough and his grin disconcertingly eager. They took the girls up a grand marble stairway with an intricately carved wooden handrail that was dusty, scratched, and discolored.

They came to a wide landing, then headed into a hallway with several closed doors on one side. Martinez opened the closest one and motioned for Marcela to go in, saying, "I'll be back for you." Nayeli and Marcela exchanged worried glances as he pulled the door closed and the two goons stood guard outside.

Martinez pushed the next door open and gestured for Nayeli to enter first. The space was bare except for a queen-size bed centered along the right-hand wall. A dark-blue fitted sheet covered the mattress and a folded blanket lay at the foot end.

"Before we leave for the United States, you'll be staying here for a few weeks," he told her as he pushed the door closed. "I'll be taking care of you." Then he pulled a set of keys from his pocket and locked the door.

Nayeli was afraid to meet his eyes, but when she finally did, cold dread flooded her body. She'd been kidnapped. But why?

"Your trip north is going to cost us a lot of money," her captor went on, his gaze hard and unwavering. "So you'll have to work off that debt, starting right now. Your job is to keep me happy."

When her eyes flitted to the only exit, he slapped her. Hard. And glared at her until she dropped her gaze to the floor. Then he recited her home address and her parents' names, saying he'd have them killed if she didn't unzip his trousers. That's how he coerced her into manipulating him to orgasm. Before that, Nayeli had never even kissed a boy.

"Not bad," he said matter-of-factly when it was done. "But you'll have to learn to do it better. Sexier, if you know what I mean. I'll show you how."

After he'd gone, Nayeli slid down the wall to the floor and wrapped her arms around her knees. She sat for a moment, trembling, staring straight ahead. Then a cry escaped from her mouth, and she covered it with her hand so no one could hear her sobs.

It later dawned on her that Martinez earned his living by supplying girls to places where men pay for sex. She wondered what would have happened if she'd called his bluff, refusing to comply despite his threat. Maybe he'd have called in the goons. She banished the image from her mind.

Murci had been right all along.

Over the following weeks, Martinez forced Nayeli, Marcela, and a few newer girls to perform unspeakable acts. If they refused, he'd hit them, and if they didn't do it in a pleasing way or showed resistance of any other kind, they'd go without food and water for as long as it took to adjust their attitude.

One evening, all the girls were in a common room zoning out in front of the television when Marcela spoke up. "At least he hasn't gone all the way," she said from one end of a couch. "I wonder why not."

"It's because he's not all bad," another girl replied from the same sofa. "Today he gave me a twenty-dollar bill."

"I hate to say it, but it's not because he's nice," Nayeli explained. She tilted her recliner forward and set her feet on the floor, facing her fellow prisoners. "I bet he gets paid more to deliver virgins. Think about it. They can charge a lot more for your first time."

Marcela pulled a blanket over her bare shoulders. Like Nayeli, she was trim, with skin the color of coffee and cream and straight black hair that hung past her shoulders. Yet she was more fragile, both in body and in spirit. On several occasions, she and Nayeli had cried together and talked for hours, discovering they had more in common than they thought. Born in dusty *pueblos* only a few kilometers apart, they knew many of the same places and even some of the same people.

"*Buenas noches*," Martinez called out from the broad, open archway. When he strode into the room, three men with greedy grins took his place. This filled Nayeli with a growing sense of panic. "Tonight you'll be doing something different," he said, his gaze scanning all of theirs. He switched off the TV and stood before the rough semicircle of fourteen-year-olds. It was the first time Nayeli had seen him in formal clothes. His gray suit and pants were crisply pressed and his hair was slicked back with some kind of product. "By now you all know I'm not the only man you'll have to work for. So we might as well get this over with. Come on in, guys."

His companions strode forward and stopped beside him in a row. Uninvited to do so, one of them pointed quickly to Nayeli, but Martinez shook his head. "She's off limits," he said, then jerked his chin toward Marcela. "And that one's not ready."

This left three girls and three visitors. The men made their choices like captains picking teams on the playground. Knowing better than to disobey, the teenagers led them upstairs by the hand as they'd been trained to do. Nayeli and Marcela were now alone with Martinez.

"Would you like to stay up for a while?" he asked. "You'd better be in your rooms at eleven, though."

The girls shared a wary look. Of course they wanted to stay up. It was the first time they'd been offered this privilege, but Nayeli couldn't tell whether Martinez was being kind or playing a cruel trick. Either way, it was an opportunity she could not afford to waste. After he'd gone, she plopped down on the couch beside Marcela and grabbed her hands. "This is our only chance," Nayeli hissed in a quiet voice. "Once we're over the border, it'll be harder to get back home."

"I don't know," Marcela whispered back. "What if he catches us?"

"He probably will," Nayeli admitted. "But I'd rather die than keep on doing what we're doing."

Marcela took a minute to make up her mind, but she nodded in the end. Nayeli searched her new friend's eyes to make sure she meant it, then led her into the darkness of the kitchen without switching on the lights.

"I've already checked the whole house out," Nayeli murmured. "Every door is locked. All the windows too, except for that little one." She pointed to an older window above the sink, which she figured must have been forgotten when the house was remodeled for malicious purposes. Then she hopped up onto the counter and pushed on the pane of glass. Squeezing herself through the opening feet first, she dropped down to the dimly-lit backyard patio. There were no signs of life save for a swarm of mosquitos. She batted them away, then wheeled around to help Marcela, but as she reached for her friend's dangling legs, something hard smashed into the side of her head and that was all she knew.

***

"That's why I was off limits," Nayeli moaned. She didn't sit up to address Martinez since she knew her head would explode in pain and cause her to throw up on the floor again. "Last night was a test."

"Correct," Martinez replied, kneeling beside her bed. Still in his gray pants and white dress shirt but no jacket. "I knew you were smart, and now I know you're brave." He was busy scooping up her vomit with a dustpan and knocking it into a trash can. "Too brave, actually. We're leaving for the border tomorrow and I don't want anything to happen to you up there." For the third time, he glanced remorsefully at the bloody goose egg on the side of her head.

Nayeli was confused by this sudden display of concern. First the crazy bastard kidnapped and abused her. Now he cared about her, but not enough to set her free? Involuntarily, her stomach clenched and her throat widened. He heard her gag and looked up just as a second measure of putrid, chunky sludge spewed forth, catching him full in the face. He wiped his eyes and mouth with both hands, shook the mess into the bin, pulled out a handkerchief, and cleaned himself up.

"You won't eat or drink until I drop you off."

Nayeli rolled over to face the wall.

***

It took two days in the van to reach the gateway to Gringolandia. There would be no work visa, of course. The five of them were kept bound and gagged for the entire trip, and the cargo area was not supplied with windows. Before the vehicle rolled to a stop at the border crossing, Martinez warned the girls not to make any noise. Even so, a couple of them kicked the walls and let out muffled cries for help. Surprisingly, they were waved on with no questions asked. As the van left the dry, barren land and the ruined streets of Mexico for the well-irrigated greenery and the wide, perfect pavement of San Diego, Nayeli came to the frightening realization that she was caught up in a criminal operation with a budget large enough to bribe its way past the law.

After leaving the rest of the girls at different stops, Martinez took Nayeli and Marcela to an establishment known as Western Nail Spa. A heavy-set older woman opened the door and took charge of them from then on.

The front room had manicure and pedicure stations and a price list on the wall. "Follow me," said the woman, whose breathing became increasingly labored as she led the way to an office that reeked of stale cigarette smoke. She stepped toward a chair behind a desk and dropped heavily into it, then flicked her chin toward a pair of stools. "You may call me Mama," she said in English as the girls sat down uneasily. Her raspy speech gave her away as a chain smoker. She wore bright red lipstick and a floral dress, in stark contrast with her cold, dead eyes. Eyes that had seen it all. Her short, curly hair was dyed brown to hide the gray.

Nayeli suspected that Mama had been beautiful once. Not anymore. The madam scowled as she reached for a pack of cigarettes, fired one up, and tossed the box to a young man standing in the doorway. It was a good throw and a better catch. The young Latino's forehead, cheeks, neck, arms, and knuckles were covered in crude tattoos. His hard eyes sent a clear message: he was not to be crossed.

"I'm the manager here," Mama told them. "And this is Beto, my assistant. We'll be in charge of you now."

Beto cupped his hands as he lit one up, then drew deeply and blew out a toxic cloud. "Come with me," he said in Spanish, but with an accent Nayeli couldn't place. They followed him up a staircase, at the top of which there was a locked door that opened onto a hallway with many doors on each side. Like in a hotel, but the rooms were closer together.

"This is where you'll work and sleep," he said, opening two adjacent doors to reveal a pair of minuscule rooms that looked like jail cells, each with a massage table, a mirror, and little else. "The bathroom is down the hall. To show you my heart's in the right place, I'll give you the afternoon off, but you'll start tomorrow morning. Any questions?"

Marcela raised a shy, shaky hand like a girl on the first day of school. "Will we have to . . . to . . . do . . . everything?"

"Oh, right," their inked-up handler said. "No, only what you're already used to." Then he shot them a smirk. "When your big day comes, we'll let you know."

The young man headed back down the stairs, but not before he engaged the lock with a heavy click that echoed in the empty hallway like the end of the world. Nayeli's features puckered into a frown, her lip quivered, and her eyes stung with tears. What would Mamá, Papá, and Murci think of her?

Marcela held out her arms and Nayeli stepped into a long hug. Both girls heaved and shuddered as they wept.

3

— · —

MARCELA

A Customs and Border Protection officer waved Murci forward to the first position in line at the San Ysidro inspection station. Murci met the white man's gaze as softly as he could. It wasn't easy to do.

"Passport and visa. Take off your helmet."

Murci knew the man would let him through, so while his face and documents were being scrutinized, he ran through the route he was about to take: straight up I-5 to the third exit ramp. It was the cheapest motel he'd been able to find, but it wasn't cheap at all.

Without a word, the officer eyed the next car in line as he handed the documents back. Murci popped his helmet on, shook his head in disbelief, and rolled the throttle back. He lifted his feet and slowly motored away, navigating through a brightly lit zig-zag section of road defined by orange barriers and cones.

Both sides of the border were guarded by several types of troops. On the south side, agents of the Mexican National Guard were deployed in significant number in order to deal with the migrant camps. As Murci crossed the border, he saw U.S. Marines and Army soldiers, who he knew were posted there in response to a variety of national security issues. He averted his gaze, having made up his mind to stay out of trouble at any cost.

Soon he was on I-5, racing down a wide stretch of unblemished pavement. *The gringos don't know how good they have it.* He thought of the deep, dangerous potholes that always appeared after a single storm on the few paved roads of his home town. Mexican contractors, after being awarded generous contracts by their government cronies, would reputedly line their pockets even further by using substandard materials and methods, resulting in infrastructure that needed to be rebuilt every year. *Not that there's no corruption here*, he reminded himself as he dropped from fourth into fifth gear and reached cruising speed.

The cool night air whipped into his jacket as he followed the freeway and found his motel. Soon he staggered into a small, musty room and set his bags down. A sour odor wafted out from under his shirt, but he was too tired to bathe. He breathed and stretched, working out two days' worth of kinks from his lean, compact body. Then he drank from the tap and removed his boots and lay down on the bed. As he did, doubt waged war with his exhaustion. What if he couldn't find her? That was more likely than the one-in-a-million shot he was taking. Before he fell asleep, he was consoled by a memory, the first of several times the siblings had found themselves in danger.

"Murci, Murci, look at me," eight-year-old Nayeli had called from the bare back of a horse on a sunny morning. Her delightful little smile was one of pride in her skills.

"You're a natural, Naye. Let's go for a ride," Murci at thirteen had said, mounting a different horse. Their long black hair swished in tandem as sister and brother rode through the fields, crossing the river that cut through their little town. A few years later, when big business diverted this source of irrigation, many families' livelihoods would be devastated, since climate change would cut the number of rainy months from four to two. Then to one.

For the time being, however, life was good. Their father was strong and he made an honest living farming a broad swath of fertile land. Most of which he'd end up selling. Half an hour out of town, they came to a deep canyon. Murci's horse galloped along the edge while Nayeli rode next to him on the safer side. Then something white sailed by in a gust, a plastic bag perhaps, spooking the horses. Murci's bolted away from the ridge, while Nayeli's drifted toward it, losing traction, stumbling, leaning precariously over the side of the cliff. As the frantic animal scratched in vain for purchase, its fate now decided, Nayeli shot out her tiny arm. Murci locked onto it and pulled hard. She made a daring leap that could have killed them both.

With his little sister cradled safely against his chest, Murci took her back across the river and the green fields. Soon their family's farmhouse rose up in the distance. He closed his eyes to draw a calming breath. When he blew it out and opened them again, he was lying on the bed in the cheapest motel room in San Diego.

He stood and stretched, then snatched his phone off the nightstand. A texting app told him she hadn't checked her messages since she'd been taken. He left her a text below the ten he'd already sent.

The shower water came out cold. Shivering as he dried his hair with a paper-thin towel, he was pleasantly surprised at how quick the process was. He'd had long hair since he was little, but one of the last things Nayeli had done before starting off for Beltran Manor was shave it off, giving him a military-style crew cut for the police academy. Murci blinked back tears, hoping his parents had no idea what had happened to her.

Unfortunately, he had a very good idea. Currently twenty years of age, he'd been to brothels before. He knew about human trafficking and exploitation. Indeed, he himself had been subjected to a form of slavery in the United States, though it wasn't something he liked to talk or think about.

Murci tried to breathe easy until the sun came up but couldn't calm himself. He was so angry he felt an impulse to trash the room. Instead, he paced the floor, stopping every so often to perform push-ups and sit-ups. Then he did a handstand, executing thirty shoulder presses in that position while supporting himself on the wall with his feet. When he dropped his legs and righted himself, he checked his phone again. The gun dealers would be open for business in an hour.

At the first of three establishments, despite his poor command of English, he learned that he could only buy a rifle or a shotgun since he was under twenty-one. He'd have to study for a test, and then there'd be a ten-day waiting period. But Murci didn't want to wait two weeks, and he wasn't thrilled about the idea of a long gun, either, since they're hard to conceal.

At the second store, he was told that it would be better to travel to the neighboring state of Arizona, where he could purchase a pistol from a private party with no background check.

At the third gun dealer, Murci learned nothing new but he did get a combo deal on a lock pick set and a survival knife with a thick, eight-inch serrated blade. If he found her, she'd be guarded by men with guns, so he'd have to find a way to arm himself properly. But he was low on cash, and the knife would do for now.

He blasted into downtown, now with a reassuring bulge in his boot. His destination was the Mexican consulate and then U.S. Immigration and Customs Enforcement to see if they had any record of her entry or status in the U.S.A.

He opened up the throttle, screaming into the bayside downtown area.

Let's see what the gringos have to say.

***

The first rays of sunlight filtered through a bent set of Persian blinds. Nayeli and Marcela examined their reflections in Nayeli's mirror, preparing for their first day of what was being referred to as work.

"I don't think I can do this," Marcela said. Her arm shook as she passed a brush through her wet hair.

"What do you think will happen if you don't?" Nayeli asked.

"Get your asses down here right now!" Mama screamed from downstairs.

Nayeli hastened to put her things away. She and Marcela marched downstairs into the kitchen, where several girls and young women were gathered around a table. Sullen expressions were the norm, and only half of the girls looked up as Nayeli and Marcela sat down next to each other.

Breakfast was plain oatmeal and a cup of water. No sugar at all. "It's to keep you thin," Mama explained, handing them each a bowl of lukewarm gruel. "You don't want to know what I was fed when I was a working girl. If I was fed at all. Maybe that's why I like to eat," she speculated, smiling as she patted her belly with both hands. No one laughed or even acknowledged the joke.

"Mama give us short, supposed-to-be-cute names. So I'm Yekaterina or Kati, from Russia," said a light-skinned, light-eyed, stern-looking girl seated across from Nayeli.

"*Y yo me llamo Cristina o Cristi*," said the girl to Marcela's left. Her creamy brown skin looked just like theirs. "*De Nicaragua*." It was a relief to hear someone speaking Spanish.

"Cho is Cho," said the Asian girl on Nayeli's right in halting English. "Myanmar."

"So you'll be Marci," Mama told Marcela, hovering over the table like a kindergarten teacher. Mama wore the same floral dress she'd had on the day before. It was two sizes too small. "I don't know what to call you, though," she said, eyeballing Nayeli. "Let's go with Nina for now. Eat up, everyone! Cristi, tell the new girls what they need to know."

With that, Mama stormed out of the kitchen and down the hall toward her office.

"The only good thing about this place, if there is one," Cristi told them in their native language, "is that you'll learn English fast. A lot of the men don't speak Spanish, so Mama has an English-only policy with us. She won't speak a word of Spanish to you. Now, you'll have up to eight sessions a day, seven days a week. Your job is to give a five-minute back rub while selling different kinds of happy endings. Make sure you collect the money in advance. Beto will be outside in case of emergencies, but you'll have to make a lot of noise to get him to come in, and you'd better be in danger."

"What about them?" Nayeli asked, eying three girls wearing white spa tunics taking their bowls to the kitchen.

Cristi followed her line of sight. "Girls who don't rock the boat can work in the front room doing nails," she said. "That means less time upstairs and one day off."

"Hurry up, ladies," Mama called out from her office. "Ten minutes. No more talking."

This was it. Nayeli had been dreading this moment. Neither she nor Marcela had serviced any other man besides Martinez. Eight sessions a day? That piece of news went a long way toward explaining the silent, sullen atmosphere they were sitting in. As she felt her instinct to fight, flee, or freeze grip her body, she was struck by what some of the older girls had said, that they'd been there for years. Years? Nayeli wasn't even sure she could make it to the end of this first day. Quelling an urge to make a run for it, she glanced at the open doorway. There stood Beto, leaning against it, his strong, illustrated arms crossed over his chest. He was blocking the way to the front door and to the more discreet side door through which, she'd been told, the clients always came in to the building.

As if he'd read her intentions, Beto held her gaze and shook his head. Clearly, her handlers were ready for any trick she might try to pull. Then a wheezing sound turned her attention back to Marcela, whose eyes were bulging out in alarm as she struggled to breathe. Cristi told her to put her head between her knees and stroked her back in a motherly fashion while Nayeli scooted closer to hold her hand.

"Want to know how I get past the day?" Kati asked from across the table once Marcela had recovered to some extent. "I am two Katis. One for work and one for after work. They don't know each other."

"Wash up now, girls," Mama called out again. "Time to get to work."

Before long, Nayeli found herself standing like a statue in the middle of her room, her gaze fixed on the door. The time had come for her first session. Her heartbeat thundered in her ears. The wait stretched on and on. At last, there came a knock at the door and a man sauntered in. He was middle-aged, overweight, and didn't smell so good. His face was a mixture of guilt and greed.

Nayeli drew a calming breath and tried to do as she'd been taught, but as the encounter progressed, she was unable to go on. "I can't . . . do it," she told the frustrated man, choking back tears. "I'm sorry."

Beto had to deal with the angry customer, which resulted in his adding one hundred dollars to Nayeli's debt and beating her feet and ankles with a stick until she begged him to stop.

***

Mama nodded a greeting to Beto as he plodded into her office. He always came in for last-minute instructions before things got rolling. He took a slouching seat on one of the stools, his eyes droopy and red. Mama had never smoked marijuana, but she knew all the telltale signs. She rolled her eyes, gave an exasperated shake of her head, and spoke to him in their native language. "Make sure Marci and Nina are okay," she told him. "Stand by their doors more than those of the others. After the morning sessions, I need you at the Castlefield."

"Yes, ma'am."

She flitted her eyes toward the door in dismissal, so Beto rose to leave, but he froze as a body plummeted past the window. A heavy thud was heard along with a series of sickening crunches. With a groan, Mama lifted herself out of her chair and lumbered over to look out the window. It wasn't the first time this had happened. They watched the life drain out of Marci's eyes, fixing them in an eerie reproach. Then Mama turned to Beto, who looked dopey and apologetic. It was his job to make sure the roof access door was kept locked at all times. She figured he must have gone up there to smoke weed and forgotten to lock it when he was done.

***

One minute earlier, all the girls had trudged upstairs to get ready for the first session of the day. Marcela didn't care about learning English fast. For her, the only good thing about her predicament—if there was one—was Nayeli. Marcela loved her new friend as she might have cared for an older sister. Without Nayeli, she wouldn't even have made it this far, but the strong bond between the girls wasn't enough; Marcela had made up her mind to take her own life. No tears streamed down her cheeks as she pushed open the roof access door and stepped out onto the rooftop, and she didn't slow her pace as she neared the edge. Panic screamed at her to stop, but she'd known that would happen and she was ready for it. She kept her arms at her sides and tipped forward into a headfirst fall. Her hands shot out involuntarily as she dropped, so when she hit the ground she dislocated her elbows and shoulders in a series of cracks and crunches and also broke her neck. The pain was unbearable but mercifully short. As she took her last breath, she looked up at the window and gazed into Mama's and Beto's guilty eyes.

She hoped her family would understand.

4

THE HONDURAN CONNECTION

O fficer Jeff Walker was sweating under his body armor and the sturdy poly-cotton blend of his police uniform. As he patrolled the curb at San Diego International Airport, his nostalgia took him on a trip down memory lane, back five years. At that time, he'd been a beach lifeguard, wearing only shorts as he sat in the tower. Cool and comfortable. Surrounded by scantily clad Barbie dolls. Zooming around on his motorcycle. But now he worked for the Harbor Police. He'd thought it would be an exciting job, catching crooks and cleaning up the community, but all he'd done thus far was work as a canine handler.

His partner's name was Lulu. An eight-year-old black Labrador retriever, she was a powerful beast with long hair and sharp fangs like those of a wolf, yet her demeanor was nonaggressive. The two of them formed what is referred to as a canine team, and their duty was to conduct airport surveillance as a means of high-visibility deterrent patrol. In other words, Walker spent his days living up to his last name: walking around. Doing nothing. Not once had they discovered an explosive device and he reckoned they never would.

The lawman pulled his handkerchief from his pocket, lifted his cap, wiped his brow, and surveyed the vicinity. He and Lulu were outside the baggage claim terminal, near the road where arriving travelers got picked up by friends or family. Across the street stood a large parking lot, then another road, and beyond that San Diego Bay, though it was tough to spot. This was a major change from the perfect view of the coast that he'd taken for granted at his previous job.

Lulu rubbed her flank against Walker's leg, possibly after sensing his discouragement.

"Good dog," he said, stroking the top of her head from her nose to her floppy ears. "Good job."

Enjoying the attention, the animal closed her eyes. She folded up her hind legs and sat, making honest eye contact and beaming at Walker with an eager, open-mouthed expression that could only be described as a smile.

A few yards ahead, a white SUV pulled to the curb. Walking toward it was a large, dark-haired traveler in a white suit. The big man opened the passenger door and plonked himself down. As he shut the door, Agent Laura Potter, a young U.S. Customs and Border Protection agent, and her German shepherd walked past. Her narcotics detection canine pulled her insistently toward the white SUV and scratched at the rear door.

"¡*Vámonos, Martínez*! Let's go, *cabrón*!" the white-suited man commanded the driver as his window slid shut.

Potter's dog's behavior constituted probable cause, Walker knew. Both canine teams ran to block the vehicle's path.

"Step out of the vehicle with your hands up!" Potter commanded with a hand on her holster.

Walker pulled his Glock but kept it pointed at the ground. Through the windshield, he could see the driver was a well-dressed Latino with slicked-back hair. Close to Walker's age, mid-thirties. The white-suited passenger looked sixty or so, with wide shoulders and a bulging belly.

The suspect vehicle shot forward. The two canine teams darted to the safety of the curb, but the SUV clipped Lulu's leg.

"I've got her!" Agent Potter shouted, taking Lulu's leash as the suspect vehicle sped off. Walker leapt to his feet and sprinted across the first road, cutting across the parking lot, hoping to catch the suspects on the second road.

"K-9 six to dispatch!" he barked into his radio, still gripping his service weapon in the other hand.

"K-9 six go ahead."

"I'm in foot pursuit of a white Alpina fleeing westbound on Airport Terminal Road. Its occupants are wanted for vehicular assault of a peace officer and suspected for possession of narcotics."

"Ten-four."

Walker made it across the parking lot in time to take aim, but he didn't fire for fear of collateral damage. He lowered his Glock and inwardly recited the license plate number over and over again.

***

Martinez and Carli glared at each other while construction workers labored nearby. One might have expected the pair of human traffickers to be ecstatic at the prospect of occupying the entire top floor of the Castlefield Waterfront Hotel's tallest tower, but they were in no mood to be grateful. For hours they'd been arguing about the renovation project they were overseeing: a conversion of four penthouse suites into a sprawling office space. Martinez wore a perfectly pressed gray suit. Tattoos peeked out from under his cuffs, but his face and neck were unblemished, his hair gelled back and neatly trimmed.

Carli was an enormous man whose dark features and skin tone suggested no or very little ancestry other than African. He was decked out in white slacks, black dress shoes, and a black short-sleeved polo shirt. He turned his back on Martinez, snorting with disdain and peering through a floor-to-ceiling window. The sun glittered like diamonds on the surface of San Diego Bay, where white sailboats motored out of the marina and slowly circled North Island. To the south, the Coronado Bridge stretched from the island to Downtown, with the hills of Tijuana rising in the distance.

They heard a rapping at the door to the megasuite.

"*¿Quién es?*" Martinez demanded.

"*Soy yo, Beto.*" The visitor's voice was tinged with a lilting Caribbean accent. He, like Carli and everyone else in the organization except for Martinez, had been born and raised in Honduras.

"You're late," Martinez snapped as the young man came in.

"We had a problem," Beto replied. He went on to report Marcela's final act.

"Have you disposed of the body?" Martinez asked.

"Not yet."

"Do it today."

Beto gave a subtle, almost imperceptible nod as he looked down at the water. His frown and his dull eyes remained unchanged.

"Come here," Carli ordered him.

Beto strutted across the workspace and took his place at the window next to the sharply dressed giant. By comparison, his baggy jeans and oversized, untucked polo shirt made him look like a young thug in a street gang. Which wasn't far from what he was.

"Isn't this a wonderful view?" Carli asked, nodding at the Embarcadero Marina.

"Yes, sir," Beto replied gloomily.

"Did you know I keep two boats down there?"

"No, sir."

"Would you like to be in my shoes someday, Alberto?"

Beto simply nodded and winced, bracing himself.

Carli abruptly encircled the young man's neck with his massive arm, immobilizing him in a headlock. "Then stop beating up the girls, goddammit! Of course you have to scare them sometimes, but you must never put them out of commission."

"Yes, sir. I understand," Beto managed through his constricted airway.

On the other side of the room, Martinez lifted a large manila envelope from his desk and held it up for Beto to take. "Take this to Mr. Delgado. Right now."

Carli let the youngster go.

Rubbing his throat, Beto nodded, crossed the room with much less arrogance than before, took the envelope, and hurried out.

Then Martinez and Carli resumed their verbal dispute, which went on for the rest of the afternoon.

***

Beto was tough, but Carli and Martinez had scared him. To settle his nerves, he sucked down four cigarettes while driving out to East County. As he sped down the final hill, a massive casino resort came into view. He tossed his smoke out the window and started taking deep breaths.

He had to pass through several layers of security before being allowed into the farthest reaches of the casino. Finally, a guard let him in to a lavishly-furnished office, where he was offered a seat by a large, imposing man in a white suit at a desk. The crime lord's gaze crawled over his skin like a thousand tiny insects.

Beto never looked forward to any kind of contact with Mr. Delgado. If he was afraid of Martinez and Carli, he was terrified of their boss, one of the two heads of the human trafficking and money laundering organization sometimes referred to as "The Honduran Connection." Now in his early sixties, Delgado had outlived all his rivals. The same funnel of natural selection that had shaped his underlings into capable criminals had developed in him an even broader array of deadly skills. With thick arms and shoulders and a skilled shooting hand, he dominated every man under him, though he rarely kept female company. Flores, the other head of the Honduran Connection, was better known for that pursuit.

"How are you, my boy?" Delgado asked with a leering grin that made Beto squirm in his seat.

"I have something for you, sir." Beto handed over the envelope.

"I have something for you, too," Delgado said with a wink. "Martinez told me you'll be visiting the crematorium." He tugged out a fat wallet from his trousers, extracting three crisp hundreds and, after a moment's thought, a fourth for his favorite errand boy. "Here. Have some fun on me."

"*Gracias, Señor Delgado.*"

With warm wind blowing through his open window, Beto cruised back to town. He felt better now that the two meetings he'd dreaded were behind him, and he was looking forward to spending his hundred as soon as possible. Split among his friends, however, it wouldn't go far. The solution he came up with was to get his friends to help him sink the body. The corpse would still be gone, and four hundred would pay for a proper party. No one would ever know.

He changed lanes, took an earlier exit, and headed south to an oceanfront RV park. There he met up with four other street-smart young men and spent all of Delgado's money on drugs and alcohol, funding a rowdy celebration in a recreational vehicle. That night, concealed by darkness, he and his buddies hefted Marcela's corpse out of the trunk of his car. They carried it out onto a jetty and heaved it into the bay on the count of three.

***

The next day, Officer Walker was on his lunch break at Seaport Village, eating ridiculously expensive tacos with his best friend Tony Park. Park's massive frame stretched the seams of his slacks and sport coat. At six-three, two-thirty, he was taller and even wider than Walker. They'd worked together as beach lifeguards before joining the Harbor Police at the same time, yet Park's experience as a Navy SEAL had led to his rapid promotion to the investigations unit, while the extraordinary events in Walker's own past had evidently counted for nothing.

As usual, Detective Park's Asian features were friendly. He smiled as he soaked up the sun, his eyes shielded by dark shades. Apparently, he had no pressing commitments, while Walker, who had to be back at the airport in fifteen minutes, grumbled one-word answers between wolfish bites.

"Did you find anything when you ran the Alpina's license plates?" Park asked.

"Nothing useful," Walker replied. "They were stolen off a car in East County."

"What about in the mugshots?"

"*Nada.*"

"Vehicle records?"

"Good question," Walker replied, nodding as he wiped his mouth. Park was the smartest person he knew. "Vehicle records were actually our best hope since only two thousand XB7s are sold nationwide per year. But nothing's turned up so far."

"Here's hoping something does."

"Thanks, man," Walker said, upending his can of club soda to finish it and cleaning his hands with a napkin. "The bad news is that Lulu's leg is broken. The vet said he might have to disqualify her from service. In that case, I'd have to get a new canine partner."

Park frowned. "And the good news?"

"If she retires, I get to keep her." Walker raised a hand for the waitress. "Thank you, miss," he said, handing her a fifty. "Keep the change."

To Walker's surprise, she shook her head. "Your friend already paid, officer." She graced him with a smile and hustled off.

"Thanks, bro," Walker said as he got up to leave. "I gotta run."

"No you don't," Park retorted, an ear-to-ear grin spreading across his face. "You've got the afternoon off."

Puzzled, Walker sat back down.

"And you won't be getting a new dog no matter what happens," Park said, still smiling. "That's why I asked you to lunch, which was on Chief Downing, by the way. How did he put it?" Lowering his vocal register in a perfect imitation of their ultimate superior, Park recited, "'In the incident at the airport, Walker displayed superior physical and mental agility. With that and Sergeant Terry's recommendation, he's earned himself a promotion.'"

Walker could not hold back his grin.

"Dude," Park said, "I'm here to ask you to submit a memorandum of interest in joining the investigations section."

Walker held his chin high. "Detective Walker," he said. "Mom would have been proud."

"Your dad, too."

Encouraged for the first time in a while, Walker drew a calming breath. As always, the seaside air reminded him of his mother, with whom he'd spent every Sunday at the beach when he was a boy. This led to a series of more tragic memories, but Walker stopped to remind himself that his buddy had taken time out of his day to bring him the good news. "Superior physical and mental agility," Walker echoed in a second but very bad impression of the chief, chuckling. "You've got a great memory, man."

Park's photographic memory had proved useful on many occasions. "The mind is a muscle you can strengthen," he replied, as he always did. "Congratulations, bro. You deserve it. Cheers." He held up his own can of club soda for Walker to clink against. "We'll have to get a real drink after work."

"Confirmed," Walker replied.

Neither lawman spoke for a time as they watched the boats on the bay and the people strolling by. Walker considered asking about Carla, Park's wife, but he didn't, since their situation was even worse than his and Tina's, but it wasn't because they were fighting.

"Okay, man," Park said, as if he'd sensed the conversation might turn to his home life. "I'd better go. See you after my shift? I'll pick you up."

"Nah, let's meet at headquarters," Walker said. "I've got some paperwork to do."

They locked palms and thumbs in a powerful Hawaiian handshake and headed in separate directions, Walker to his house in Chula Vista to break the good news to Tina, his wife. He'd thought it would help to smooth things out between them, but instead they disagreed on some trivial point, disrespected each other, then shouted and screamed until she stormed out to visit her parents, while he took his daughter to the park.

Tina Michelle, his two-year-old curly-haired treasure, squealed with delight as he pushed her on the swings. Then he helped her on the slides. Then they got popsicles. Not a single cloud marred the light blue sky and a breeze cooled their backs while making their way back to the car holding hands. Once home, they played with a red and blue dodecahedron, pushing different yellow shapes through matching holes on each face of the twelve-sided toy. Father and daughter beamed at each other, each one reveling in the presence of their favorite person in the world.

5

DYING DREAMS

When Tina returned from her parents' house, Walker headed out, his Mustang roaring and growling all the way to Harbor Police headquarters. He made his way to an unoccupied workstation and logged in. As he filled out a report, many of his fellow patrol officers came by to clap him on the back or shake his hand, wishing him well in his new role.

"Ready, partner?" Park asked after a while. They hit the parking lot and hopped into Park's pickup. The blue Toyota 4x4 sported a jacked-up suspension, a heavy-duty grill guard, roll bars, and a custom V8. It was fifteen years old but in showroom condition.

A short drive up the coast took them to Sammy's Bar & Grill, a restaurant on the Pacific Beach boardwalk. They settled onto stools at the bar, where Park proposed a toast: "To you, bro. Congratulations and respect." He offered his double scotch for Walker to clink a cold beer against.

"Thanks, brother," Walker replied. "Couldn't have done it without you."

They savored their drinks in silence for a time. The boardwalk was crowded with joggers and rollerbladers squeezing in a workout before dinner. A smattering of clouds were lit orange, pink, and gold by the last warm beams the sun had to offer. Out on the sand, only a handful of beachgoers remained, a late-autumn chill having sent the rest of them home. Walker fixed his gaze on a nearby lifeguard tower. "You miss the old job?" he asked.

Park took a look at his former post, studied it for a second, and shook his head. "Nah." He downed his drink and signaled for the same again. "What about you?"

"Yes and no." Walker ran his fingers through his blond buzzcut, which still felt strange to him after living with a surfer's mane for so many years. "Those were good times, for sure, but compared to police work, the beach is for kids."

The bartender set down Park's second double. When Park turned back to Walker for another toast, his liquid eyes showed pain. *Kids* had been a poor choice of words.

"To you and Carla," Walker blurted out, raising his beer.

Park lowered his eyes and nodded thanks. Then he slammed his drink in a single gulp.

Another quiet moment ensued as the sun, by then a red-orange pinpoint on the horizon, disappeared with such slowness that for a moment it left Walker wondering whether it was really gone. "You know what we need?" he said. "A surf trip to Boca Negra."

"Yes! Just don't go out alone this time."

"I won't," Walker promised, motioning for a second beer. "That was the dumbest thing I ever did."

"Do you still have the old house in Tijuana?"

"No, I sold it. That's how we paid off our place. With that and the last of the inheritance money." Now it was Walker's turn to feel a surge of melancholy, brought on by the word *inheritance.* When his second Sierra Nevada arrived, he guzzled down half of it in a single pull.

Too soon it was time to go home. Walker retrieved a backpack he'd left in Park's truck, then changed into workout clothes and set off on a six-mile run back to headquarters. It was his second workout of the day, but he was serious about getting back in shape. Semi-serious, anyway; his beers sloshed around in his stomach as his sneakers pounded the road.

***

Tina Garcia and Carla Reyes were both Mexican American and could pass for sisters. They worked at Bella, a beauty salon and spa in Pacific Beach. Sammy's was located in the same quaint beach community. Carla and Tony lived in a cozy duplex unit in Pacific Beach, while Park and Walker often played pool at a place on the main drag, and their good friend Lynn Peters lived in a penthouse condo a few blocks away. Needless to say, PB was somewhere they all knew well.

After parting ways with Walker at the bar and grill, Park drove five blocks to Carla's cozy duplex. It was a short ride but also a sad one. Walker's innocent reference to children had triggered bitter emotions: five years earlier, Carla had been sitting on top of the world, surrounded by friends and family at the wedding of her dreams and pregnant with a baby girl. Then she'd miscarried and, with no luck in the intervening years, her dream of becoming a mother was dying. The clinic's diagnosis of "unexplained infertility" hadn't been helpful. To the contrary, it was a major factor in the couple's depression and chemical dependence.

"I'm home," Park announced gloomily, wearily, almost too softly to hear. He didn't expect a response. He locked the front door behind him, then plodded to the kitchen to make his own meal. By the time Carla emerged from their room, he was sitting on the couch cradling his fourth post-Sammy's drink. He wobbled to his feet to greet her and she stumbled into his arms. They held each other in an unsteady embrace for a full minute.

Carla's curly brown hair was all tangled up, her eyelids droopy, and her perfect skin had gone blotchy and dry. Park caressed her back and planted kisses on her cheek, wondering how many sleeping pills she'd swallowed that day after calling in sick.

"You're looking a little thin, babe," he told her, so as not to say *emaciated*.

"I'm fine. Just lonely," she said over her shoulder, shuffling in her slippers to the kitchen for a glass of juice, which Park had often reminded her did not count as a meal.

He scrubbed off his long day in a scalding-hot shower with a startlingly cold rinse. When he slid between the sheets beside her, he grabbed his phone off the nightstand and scrolled through social media, not sure what to say to her. It was she who broke the ice.

"I was looking forward to spending some time together today," Carla said with a theatrical frown. She was good at laying a guilt trip.

"Me too, hon, but it's tough to say no to time and a half." Park was saving for a down payment on a house, but that dream was dying as well. Without any kids, the purchase would be pointless. A bad move even, given the higher property taxes and increased maintenance it would mean, not to mention the initial cost. "I'm here now, though," he managed through the fog, slurring his words. "Sowhatveyoubeenthinkinbout?"

"Well," she said, with a surprising trace of enthusiasm, "I've decided to become a helicopter pilot."

"Sounds great," Park replied, but he didn't mean it. He knew how expensive flight training was. And after taking so many sick days, she was in danger of losing the one job she already had.

They turned out the lights, kissed goodnight, and sailed off into separate nightmares.

Park dreamt of his final mission as a Navy SEAL, in which he'd led a full platoon on a raid of a Taliban compound. They had made the drop at night, landing two klicks away. Then they launched a thermal imaging drone that detected only six bodies. That should have been his first clue. At five hundred yards out, the four-man overwatch team headed for high ground while the twelve-man infiltration element made its way into the camp, splitting up into three fire teams.

A rush of horror flooded Park's body when his squad came upon an enemy with a great number of explosives strapped to his torso and a detonator in his hand. "Abort. Abort!" he barked into his headset as they took off running, but they were too close to the trembling man. All three of Park's teammates were killed. The other fire teams were similarly decimated; only McDonald and Park made it home. Worse yet, when they failed to receive any reply from the overwatch team, they hurried to high ground and found all of them shot dead.

"Abort," he said, softer this time, whimpering in his sleep.

"You okay, babe?" Carla asked drowsily.

Park sat up, heaving for air, heart hammering, wishing he, too, had met his end in the Middle East along with his best friends. "Yeah. Fine," he whispered. "Love you, honey."

"Love you too," she mumbled, then rolled over and started snoring.

The alarm clock read 2:30 a.m. in blood red. Park slipped out of bed, threw on a sweatshirt, and made straight for the kitchen where he filled a tumbler with scotch. He knew it was a bad trade: if he was lucky, he'd get ten minutes of euphoria and an hour of oblivion in exchange for an entire day spoiled by pounding headaches, acid reflux, and a persistent foul mood.

I know every stone in this road, yet here I go again, he lamented inwardly, gulping down the scalding tumblerful as though it were as refreshing as chilled apple juice after a long run on a hot day. He spilled some on his sweatshirt in his hurry to choke it down.

***

Walker slowed his pace toward the end of the run, cooling down as he came to Harbor Police headquarters. He spotted his white Mustang in the rows of cars and his soul ached. A lump formed in his throat and gathering tears blurred his vision. When it was new, the street-legal race car had been a gift from his buddy David Goode. It was a Ford Mustang Shelby GT500 in Oxford White with hand-painted Guardsman Blue racing stripes. Now six years old, it would have been a joy to drive if it didn't remind Walker of his "brotha," a close friend who'd sacrificed his own life to save him.

Fifteen miles later, he took the exit for Chula Vista and eased off the gas, reluctant to face his wife again. He quelled an impulse to stop at El Papagayo for pool and more beer, which would only make things worse.

He trudged into his house, set his bags down, washed his hands, and joined the family at the dinner table where they were already seated. He kissed Tina Michelle on the head but not Tina. She would have moved her head to avoid it.

Tina's rounded belly hinted at the arrival of a fourth family member. Another daughter, whom they'd name Mia. And her scowl hinted at a major, ongoing conflict. They hadn't actually fought over some trivial point. Their mutual animosity ran deep. After a silent, uncomfortable meal, Tina took the toddler down from her high chair, cleaned her up, and met Walker in the kitchen, where he stood at the sink washing dishes.

She snatched her keys off the bar. "While I'm gone, why don't you have a look at those bills?" she spat out, eyeing a pile of past-due notices on the bar. "And don't even think about going out. I'm in enough trouble as it is."

"Where are you going?" Walker asked desperately, disinclined to be left alone, and especially averse to missing bedtime stories and night-night kisses.

"Where else?" she sneered as she scooped Tina Michelle up with one arm and strode out the door. Over her mother's shoulder, Tina Michelle looked at her daddy with confusion. *What happened to our perfect day at the park?*

6

— • —

NEW HOPE

Despite the turbulence of his home life, Walker was looking forward to his first day as a detective in the air-conditioned Intelligence and Investigations Section. He marched in to Harbor Police headquarters and headed for his new cubicle. Park had been assigned an office on his recent promotion to corporal, which had freed up a spot in the trenches for Walker. The first thing he did was seek out his new superior and render a stiff hand salute.

"Good morning, Detective Sergeant Cheatham! Detective Walker reporting for duty!" Walker bellowed, unaware that no Harbor Police detective ever verbally reported for duty.

Sergeant Cheatham, a stern and sharply dressed black man, didn't laugh at the rookie's blunder, but more than a few chuckles wafted up from the cubicles.

At the morning briefing, Sergeant Cheatham informed everyone about the new cases that had come in the night before, one of which was the discovery of a corpse floating in the bay.

"The body was in a standard white body bag, the disposable kind used by mortuaries and morgues," Cheatham said. "Park and Walker, you're on deck. See if you can get out to Kearny Mesa in time for the autopsy."

Park drove their unmarked squad car to the San Diego County Medical Examiner's Office in an unusually relaxed and careful fashion, so slow that Walker thought he might be drunk. But he knew Park would never cross that line.

The facility was only ten miles east, but it was far enough from the coast to make them sweat in their sport coats. They strode through the parking lot, entered through the main doors, and headed down the stairs. The autopsy room was windowless, white, and smelled like a Mexican butcher shop. At least it was cool down there.

"You got here just in time," said Dr. John Davis, the Deputy ME. He was probably in his early forties, but his gray hair and the bags under his eyes made him look ten years older. His white lab coat and those of his assistants were soiled with red-brown bloodstains. He nodded to a corpse lying on a stainless steel autopsy table. "We've just done the external examination, but you made it for internal." He led them closer. "As you can see, the cause of death was blunt trauma to the cranium. The decedent's cervical spine as well as the joints of her upper extremities were shattered and dislocated. You are looking at the result of a headfirst fall from height."

Walker's stomach gave a queasy twinge at the sight. "No bruising or lacerations to suggest a fight or struggle," he observed, choking back a dry heave. "Likely suicide."

"Very good," Dr. Davis said.

"I'm guessing the abdominal distension is from internal bleeding," Park noted, not to be outdone.

"It's possible," Dr. Davis conceded. "We'll know more after the internal examination, but my guess is that the bloating was caused by putrefaction gasses since the body was found floating. I wasn't able to identify the decedent," he went on. "No match occurred with the Sheriff's Department nor with State DOJ. And no domestic reports of a missing girl matching her description. My opinion is that she's foreign. Latin American, to be more precise, judging by her skin, dental work, and the smallpox vaccine scar on her shoulder. Should I send the prints to the FBI?"

"No thank you, doctor," Park replied, handing Dr. Davis his card. "I'll take care of that. Just send them to me, if you would." Park's eyes were bloodshot. He lowered his head and massaged his temples with his fingertips.

"Of course," Dr. Davis replied. Then he nodded to one of the autopsy technicians.

A hush fell over the room. The technician calmly inserted a scalpel into the corpse's left shoulder, splitting skin and muscle as she made a long incision all the way to the pubic bone. Then she made the same cut starting from the opposite shoulder, completing a Y-shape that spanned the entire torso.

This is why Tony was driving so slowly, Walker concluded, tasting black coffee mixed with stomach acid. He looked around for some basin or sink to puke in. The technician next peeled back the skin, exposing ribs and red muscle. She used an electric bone saw to cut free the chest plate, which she pulled out as a unit and set aside. After scooping out a half-gallon of thick, putrid fluid, she began to remove the organs and slice them into sections like soggy, multi-colored loaves of bread.

Walker dashed out of the semicircle of observers to vomit into a toilet mounted in the middle of a nearby wall. The stainless steel plumbing fixture had no seat and no surrounding partitions, so he reasoned it had been installed for that very purpose.

Seeing no need to watch the entire internal examination, Park and Walker climbed the stairs, both visibly grateful for the fresh air of the parking lot. Once downtown, they decided against breakfast, opting instead for coffee to go. They were on their way back to the sedan when their radios squawked to life.

"Dispatch to squad nine," came a female voice.

Park unclipped the handset from his belt. "Squad nine, go ahead."

"Nine, respond to the Edward J. Schwartz Federal Building for a possible PC 241 in progress."

"Ten-four, show us going."

They hopped in and zoomed off. The incident was only a few blocks away, which is why the dispatcher had radioed them first.

On arrival, Walker's anger switch was flipped into the "on" position when he saw a U.S. Immigration and Customs Enforcement officer exchanging blows with a smaller, younger man with bronze-hued skin. He flew out of the passenger seat, ran to the entrance of the large, modern building, separated the combatants, and snapped handcuffs on the smaller, younger man. The ICE officer was tall and strong but out of shape. He had several bloody cuts and bruises on his face, while the only visible damage on the younger man was to his knuckles. Park stayed with the officer at the entrance while Walker led the suspect to the car and spoke to him in what he correctly assumed was the young man's mother tongue.

"I'm Detective Jeff Walker of the Harbor Police. If you'd prefer to speak in English, that's fine, too. What's your name?"

The suspect's scowl softened. He said, "My name's Luciano Sanchez, but everyone calls me Murci. And I do speak English but not very well."

"No problem," Walker replied. "We'll stick with Spanish, then. Murci? Is that short for *Murciélago*?" Walker knew the word meant *bat,* as in the flying mammal, and judging by the young man's many tattoos, he guessed it was a street nickname given to him by his buddies.

"Yes, sir. *Murciélago*."

"So what happened?"

"I was up on the fourth floor asking a white lady about my missing sister, but she wouldn't help me, so I raised my voice and demanded she do her job. Then she called me an illegal and told me to go back to my own country."

Walker nodded knowingly. "Are you here illegally?"

"No sir," Murci said, producing his passport, his visa, and a picture. "And this is my sister."

Walker looked at the photo. The girl looked very much like her brother; both showed pure or nearly pure native Mesoamerican blood.

"Her name's Nayeli."

"Go on," Walker said, nodding encouragingly.

Murci gestured with his hands as he continued to describe his situation. "I'm desperate to find her," he said, "so I kept asking questions and arguing with the lady. She made a phone call and the officer came to take me outside. But by that time I was out of control, so I pushed him, insulted him, and it came to blows."

"That was stupid," Walker said with a frown. "You'll be lucky if he doesn't press charges. What happened to your sister?"

Murci told the story from when he found the flyer in the backpack to the confrontation with Mr. Beltran, to his long ride north and his visit to the Mexican consulate earlier that same day.

"What did they tell you there?" Walker asked.

"They suggested I try the massage parlors."

"Here, get in for a minute while I have a word with the ICE officer. Let's see what I can do." Walker left the suspect locked in the unmarked unit and headed back to the entrance. Park and the officer were still talking. Equipped with a passable explanation for Murci's actions, he managed to convince the officer not to seek criminal charges.

He let Murci out of the back seat, took down his number, gave him his, and said, "OK, you can go. We'll do what we can and let you know if we find anything."

Murci thanked him profusely, walked a block, and disappeared around the corner.

Later, Walker placed a call to Deputy District Attorney Lynn Peters, a good friend of Tina's, Carla's, and his.

"What's up, Jeff?" the prosecutor said. Her voice was friendly and polite, but rushed as usual.

"You're assigned to the San Diego Human Trafficking Task Force, right?"

"That's right."

Walker told Lynn about Murci and Nayeli, then asked her if she thought the task force could look into the matter.

"It's not much to go on, but I'll pass it along," she answered. "Wait a minute. You speak Spanish, right?"

"*Afirmativo.*"

"And I know Tony's got a ton of tactical experience. We're looking to reinforce our team and you guys would be perfect. Why don't you come to our meeting on Friday?"

***

Murci rode south from Downtown to his motel. He was glad Detective Walker hadn't patted him down since the eight-inch survival knife in his boot was the only weapon he had, and he'd just spent the last of his money on gas. So much for buying a pistol.

Back in his room, he used his phone to search for the keywords *massage, sex, Latina*, and *San Diego*. To his dismay and disgust, he obtained more results than he could handle. In the afternoon, he visited twenty so-called massage parlors, showing Nayeli's picture to everyone he met. He begged them for information, but no one had seen her, or so they said.

At the end of the day, Murci leaned on the railing outside his room, glumly munching on an apple as the sun went down. Below him, amid a haze of marijuana smoke, there was a gathering of mean-looking Latino youths. They weren't there for the sunset. Every few minutes, a shifty-eyed buyer would approach them and be smoothly passed a small plastic bag. From what Murci could see and overhear, theirs was a street gang funded by drug sales and various types of theft. He locked eyes with a few of them and exchanged wary nods. He thought about going down there and asking for a gun or money, but that kind of help would only be provided in return for involvement in a crime, assuming it was provided at all.

Murci hadn't always been the responsible, generally law-abiding young man who had kissed his mother, hugged his father, and roared north on his bike. At ten, he'd still been a timid boy who always let the older boys take his lunch. At twelve, he decided he'd had enough. In the school cafeteria, he snatched back his sandwich from a bully who'd taken it and immediately caught a fist to the face. That evening, his eye swollen and purple, young Murci went out to the stable to see his father.

His dad turned his attention from the horses to Murci's black eye. "What happened, son?"

"Enrique punched me." Murci gazed up at his hero with moist eyes and an undulating jaw. Eight hours of daily labor and fresh, natural food made his dad look like a god. To him, at least. On several occasions, he'd seen his father stand up for himself or others in fistfights he'd rarely lost.

"Don't be a wuss," Papá said, molding his boy's limbs into a fighting stance. "You can't let them treat you like that. Hold your arms up like this to protect your face. Now widen your legs but protect your balls. Hit my hand as hard as you can."

Over the following months, Murci squared off with Enrique and all the other boys who'd been pushing him around. By fourteen, he'd earned a reputation as someone who wasn't to be messed with. He regularly fought sixteen- and eighteen-year-olds. It was what he'd always remember his father for: teaching him to stand his ground.

Murci was from a small town so poor that the only thing given out less freely than money was respect. At eighteen, when he couldn't find a decent job to pay for the family's shrinking farm and his father's mounting doctors' bills, he joined a street gang. It was a local chapter of a larger organization that distributed crack cocaine, methamphetamine, and marijuana in central Mexico. He underwent the initiatory beat down, met his quota for home burglary, and acquired the requisite tattoos.

This early participation in small-time crime, though he wasn't proud of it, had taught him valuable skills, and it had also solved the family's financial problems for a time. One weekend, Murci took Nayeli, who was then thirteen, to a nearby city on a shopping trip for shoes, school supplies, and her first cell phone. On the way there, as the siblings sat at the back of the bus on a grimy bench seat that sent them flying at the slightest speed bump or pothole, three heavily tattooed, angry-looking youths stomped aboard and recognized Murci as a member of a rival gang.

"What've we got here?" the biggest one sneered.

Another thought he had a witty reply. "An easy beat down and a good lay!"

"We don't want any trouble, guys," Murci said.

"But we do," the first gangbanger stated, his fist suddenly wrapped in brass knuckles.

Murci dodged the guy's right cross, but all three toughs fell on him in a maelstrom of punches, one of which hit him just right and knocked him out.

When Murci raised his throbbing head, his sister was gone. With blurry vision and a nauseating headache, he peered through the back window. Growing smaller as the bus picked up speed, the gangbangers were shoving Nayeli down the road.

"Let me out!" Murci yelled, mashing a red button on the metal handrail. As soon as the rear doors folded open, he charged out of the bus like a racehorse out the gate, screaming so madly that the would-be rapists must have taken him for a death-heralding banshee flying their way. The smartest of the three dropped his knife and sprinted to safety, but the other two froze, so Murci picked up the blade and plunged it into their bellies with maniacal fury. Once they were down, he dropped to his knees and dispatched them one at a time, slicing upwards, ripping sideways, stabbing them with relish and turning the dirt into mud.

As a result, Murci boarded another bus with a new pair of brass knuckles and some extra cash, which he gave to his sister to spend on their trip. The incident also led to a bitter feud between the two gangs, which was why, with the last of his savings, his father had sent him to the United States to work: to prevent Murci's execution.

***

It was on that bloody shopping trip that Nayeli found out how far her brother would go to protect her, so she was sure he'd come for her—if only he knew where she was. But that was highly unlikely, so her next move had to be sending him a message. After being startled awake by a door slamming, she sat up from her massage table in near darkness; only a few beams of moonlight passed through the bent Persian blinds. Her digital clock read 3:00 a.m. in blood red. None of the other girls would dare make a noise at this hour, so it must have been Beto coming back from a late night out. She sat there for a minute marshaling her courage for a fight to the death. It would be her first. Then she tied a robe around her waist and stepped into the dimly lit hallway.

She crept through the corridor, counting ten doors, five on each side. Up ahead, at the end of the hall, there was a locked door that led to the roof. Tears stung in her eyes when she recalled what she'd said to Marcela the night they'd tried to escape from Martinez's mansion: *I'd rather die than keep on doing what we're doing.* Blaming herself for her friend's death, she put her hand on the roof access door. She hung her head and let the tears flow for a moment, but a moment was all she could spare.

The door to Beto's quarters was just to the right. With a speeding pulse, she checked the handle and found it unlocked. She cracked open the door and peered inside. Her captor was sprawled on a loveseat with his legs dangling from one end. Apparently, he'd just given himself an injection: the whites of his eyes were showing, his mouth was open wide, and several telltale pieces of drug paraphernalia lay on the floor within his reach.

Nayeli slipped inside and tiptoed toward him, praying he wouldn't come out of his stupor. "Beto," she whispered, with no response. His breathing was shallow and slow. "Beto," she said again, in a normal speaking voice, and she bumped his leg with her knee. Nothing. He was in outer space. As she stood over him, she was tempted to take the opportunity to end his life. She would encircle his tattooed throat with her hands and squeeze as hard as she could as he squirmed and flailed, watching impassively as his eyes bulged and his face turned purple and his eyes went dead. Just like Marcela's had.

No. Escape was the first priority. Nayeli fished Beto's phone out of his pocket and unlocked the screen with his finger. She checked her Facebook messages, seeing all the attempts Murci had made to contact her. Then she thumbed in a reply:

HELP, WESTERN NAIL SPA SAN DIEGO

Nayeli's heart raced as she deleted Beto's browsing history and slipped the phone back into his pocket. Then she hustled back down the hall and into her room, where she climbed onto her massage table and pulled a flimsy blanket over her shoulders. Still shaking from the cold and the adrenaline spike, she breathed out a heavy sigh and began to relax. Some hope was better than none.

7

ONE DOWN, TWO TO GO

Having teased and fluffed her hair until it could get no better, Tina Garcia examined her reflection in the mirror and decided she was still beautiful. She lifted her goblet-like glass from Lynn Peters' bathroom countertop and sucked in a mouthful of virgin margarita as she gazed through the window. Ten stories down, parallel rows of glassy waves rolled toward the beach, leaving broad brushstrokes of white against a perfect turquoise sea, but the sight did little to lessen her anxiety.

She was back home after staying with her parents for a few days, though the issues between her and Walker remained. Jeff's gambling had sunk them into a deep hole, and since his credit was bad, she'd had to take out a sizeable loan. It would take a long time for her to forgive him, if she ever did. And now she had another problem: recently, while on the phone with her cousin, Antonio, the head of a Mexican cartel, she'd mentioned that Jeff would be joining the San Diego Human Trafficking Task Force. Antonio had asked her to press Jeff for information and pass it along in return for more than enough to pay off her loan.

Tina took another gulp, reminding herself that the point of the evening was to let go of her stress, not dwell on it. She drew a breath for a count of four, held it, let it out for another four, and took a final glance at the coastal scene below. Then she reached into her cosmetics bag and started on her makeup.

***

Tina doesn't know how lucky she is, Lynn Peters thought as she stepped into a blue silk dress that came down to her knees. Lynn yearned for children, but she also knew she'd have to hire someone to take care of them, and she didn't want that. It was either her or no one, and since she'd been working fourteen-hour days since college, it was looking more and more like no one. She'd already had one abortion, and she didn't want to go through that again. Her current five-year plan was to make chief deputy and stay away from men. *Or at least use protection*, she joked inwardly while giggling out loud. Unlike Tina's, her margarita was made with tequila and triple sec, and it was starting to work its magic.

Lynn took another frozen mouthful. "Ready Freddy?" she called out from the bedroom. Tina emerged, joining Lynn at the mirrored closet door in the master bedroom. The view through the windows was the same as in the bathroom, but the view in the mirror was even nicer. Each woman was blessed with her own type of beauty: one was a curvy, Latin American knockout, the other a blond-haired, blue-eyed Scandinavian stunner. Tina's white dress showed off her flawless bronze skin, while the blue folds of Lynn's gown spilled attractively down the front and back of her body. Both took care of themselves and were proud of that fact.

"Our ride's on the way," said Lynn, meeting Tina's gaze in the mirror. Excited at the prospect of a rare girls' night out, they faced each other, clinked glasses, finished their icy drinks, and proceeded past sliding doors into Lynn's private elevator.

A stone's throw north of the Castlefield Waterfront, the new InterContinental Hotel stands two hundred and fifteen feet tall. Mayor Rick Rivera, a friend of Lynn's ultimate supervisor, the district attorney, was hosting a private party there. Mayor Rivera had even sent them a car, which now glided to a halt under the InterContinental's vast portico. Their chauffeur hurried around and held the door open for them as they stepped onto a red carpet in heels. Tina felt like a movie star, smiling for photographers asking her to look their way.

The two friends strode through the lobby, in awe of its polished, intricately designed floor and the high ceiling supported by thick, shiny columns. According to their invitations, they were to look for an antique copper diving helmet.

When they found it, Lynn whispered their names and a password into the face plate. Soon they were joined by a handsome young man in a tuxedo, who showed them to a hidden elevator. They rode up to a large outdoor patio. Many guests had already arrived, all dressed to impress.

While Lynn found them a place to sit, Tina headed for the bar. "Can I get two mojitos?" she asked the bartender. "One with rum and one without."

"Sure, if I can get your phone number," the young man replied with a flirty smile. Tina laughed it off. It was flattering, though from the shape of her belly and the hyper-healthy glow she gave off, he might have guessed she was already spoken for. She carried the drinks to where Lynn sat waiting: a bright orange sofa on the waterfront end of the massive terrace. The nighttime view of the bay and the sounds of tiny waves slapping against the embarcadero made it a special place to sit and catch up with an old friend. They clinked glasses.

"Have you talked to Carla lately?" Tina asked between sips.

Lynn studied her high-heeled shoes. "She's not answering my calls."

Tina also studied Lynn's shoes. They must have cost a fortune. But since Carla was Tina's closest friend, the topic was an important one. Tina brought her eyes back up to Lynn's and said, "She's not picking mine up, either. I haven't seen her in weeks, not even at work."

Their chat was put on pause when a man in a dark suit came their way. He grinned affably under a bushy but well-trimmed brownish-red mustache. He had dark brown hair, which he wore slicked back. *Definitely a policeman.*

"Good evening, DDA Peters," he said with exaggerated formality.

"Good evening DAI Rogers," Lynn said in the same dramatic manner. She rose to give him a cheek-to-cheek greeting, then looked to Tina. "Matt Rogers, Tina Garcia."

Rogers shook her hand gently. "Glad to meet you, ma'am."

"Tina, please. And the pleasure's all mine."

"Matt's the leader of the Human Trafficking Task Force," Lynn explained as they all sat down, Rogers on a matching orange armchair that sat perpendicular to their couch. "He used to be a lieutenant with the SDPD and now he works with us as a district attorney investigator."

"Lieutenant," Tina echoed with respect for the rank. "My husband just made detective with the Harbor Police, and if I'm not mistaken, he has a meeting with you tomorrow."

"Yes, he does," DAI Rogers replied, raising a hand to gain the attention of a waiter.

After a second round of drinks, Mayor Rick Rivera and Susan Whittleman, the district attorney, approached the group with the energy and joviality of a pair of VIPs.

"What do you all think of San Diego's newest speakeasy?" Mayor Rivera asked. Clad in a tailored silk suit that de-emphasized his girth, he looked like a million bucks. *At least a couple thousand,* Tina knew.

"I'm glad prohibition's over, that's for sure," Matt Rogers joked, drawing a group laugh.

DA Whittleman was dressed in a navy-blue skirt suit and three-inch heels. Her hair and makeup looked good, but in Tina's professional opinion, the city's senior prosecutor had been in too much of a hurry while getting ready.

The last person to join the standing circle was Chief Deputy District Attorney Pat O'Connell, Head of Investigation and Lynn's immediate supervisor. He arrived with a firm handshake for the men and a softer, longer one for the women. O'Connell ran his gaze around the circle, checking to make sure everyone had a drink, then lifted his glass. "To DAI Peña," he intoned.

Everyone brought their glasses together and took a silent drink.

After a pause of appropriate duration, Mayor Rivera shared a lighthearted anecdote, then sipped and nodded for a while, listening to the others. Before long, he and DA Whittleman excused themselves and continued to work the crowd. Chief Deputy O'Connell went to order another drink while Rogers and Lynn bid each other goodnight. Rogers apparently had somewhere else to be. The chemistry between them was palpable and this pleased Tina; Lynn hadn't been in a relationship with anyone since Dave Goode died. *Good thing he signed over his multimillion-dollar condo to her just before that happened,* Tina noted with a pang of envy that surprised her.

This left Tina and Lynn just as they'd started: sipping mojitos on the sofa with soft harbor sounds in the background. Tina set her drink down on a glass table and asked, "What happened to DAI Peña? I'm guessing he was a member of the task force."

"Good guess," Lynn replied. "He was hit head-on by a truck. Both he and the other driver were killed."

Tina frowned and shook her head. "Which is why you're looking to strengthen your team."

"Right again. We needed only one replacement, but I thought it'd be a good idea to bring Tony on, too."

Tina nodded knowingly. "He'd die to protect Jeff. I appreciate you looking out for my husband," she said.

"Of course," Lynn replied, squeezing Tina's shoulder. "You know you're like a sister to me, which makes him family too."

Just then, the handsome young man who'd shown them to the elevator stopped near where they were sitting. "Dinner will be served in a few minutes," he said with an affable smile. He showed them and the other invitees to a "secret" dining room, where they enjoyed southern Italian cheeses, traditional handmade pasta, grilled boar sausage, and strawberry gelato.

By the time Tina eased her front door shut and tiptoed to the back of her house, she was several pounds heavier and her family was out for the night. She kissed Tina Michelle on the forehead, then crossed the hall to her room and slipped between the sheets next to a snoring detective. She planted a soft kiss on his forehead, too, glad to be getting along better for the time being. Even so, she couldn't sleep. Her mind swirled with thoughts of her cousin. Antonio had promised that no harm would come to Jeff or Tony, but that didn't seem like enough. Her complicity would be a betrayal and a crime, and harm would probably come to other people she didn't know. On the other hand, a hundred grand would get rid of her debt and then some. And the money she owed was Jeff's fault, not hers. She could say it was a gift from her rich cousin, about whom Jeff knew almost nothing.

Antonio had also asked for Carla's number, which further worried Tina since she knew Carla wanted to be a helicopter pilot. Tina thought he might have sent Carla money for her flight training. She made a mental note to drive up to PB and knock on Carla's door. It would be a good excuse to check on her, since an unannounced visit explained by "I just wanted to see how you were doing, again, this time in person" might seem condescending and pushy to a person who wasn't picking up her phone.

That was as far as she got before slipping into sleep.

***

Downtown San Diego was so brightly lit that Martinez cruised the city in what almost seemed like day. Sporting one of the many gray suits in his wardrobe, he lightly tapped the accelerator of his brand-new Alpina XB7, an ultra-high performance "sport activity vehicle" with an electronically limited top speed of 180 mph.

Why the hell did I buy this car? he berated himself, rocketing forward, barely in control of the turbocharged vehicle. Just a month ago, he'd had enough money to last him a year, but now he'd blown it all. Worse yet, his old car, still a recent model, had been getting him from A to B just fine. Born in Mexico and now doing well in San Diego, Martinez was fully aware that his opinion of himself was too high. Sometimes. At other moments it was correspondingly low, especially after seasoning a new girl. His impulse buying was triggered by both extremes.

At the moment, he and Carli were heading east, traveling to their monthly meeting at Hernan Delgado's and Chrystian Flores' casino resort.

"I have a bad feeling about the new megasuite," said Carli, who was so large that his shaven black head skimmed the roof lining and his thick left shoulder encroached into Martinez's part of the cabin.

"You don't like your top-floor view of the bay," Martinez suggested dryly, keeping his eyes on the road.

Carli shook his head. "Of course I do."

"Eight thousand square feet is not enough space," Martinez ventured again, his voice dripping with sarcasm.

"It is much more than enough," Carli replied quickly and with irritation. "My problem is the North County Kings. Giving orders and stomping around like bosses. Matón is the rudest man I've ever met."

Unlike Carli, Martinez found it easy to relate to Chucky Matón, the leader of the local biker gang. His secret partnership with Matón was about to take his life to a new level. Martinez snapped his gaze down to the dashboard, pretending to notice a warning light. "Fuck!" he barked.

"What is it?" Carli asked.

"We must have run over a nail or something. The back tire's way too low. Let me take a look." Martinez pulled to a stop on the side of a dark, deserted stretch of highway. Feigning anger, he slammed the driver's door and walked to the rear of the vehicle while slipping his pistol out of his shoulder holster. "Hey, can you give me a hand out here?" he called out.

When Carli stepped out, Martinez shot him twice. The enormous black man dropped to his knees, new knowledge dawning in his eyes as two crimson patches spread across his shirt. Then he fell face-first onto the dirt.

Martinez checked to make sure his former confederate was dead. He took his rings, watch, and wallet, then unfolded a body bag and stuffed him in. *One down, two to go.*

Thirty minutes later, Martinez strode into a richly furnished dining room with a long, dark, polished-wood table, at the heads of which sat his bosses. Delgado's dark, bulky features revealed his native Mesoamerican bloodline, while Flores was trim, bald, bespectacled, and appeared to have descended from Western Europeans. Both wore tailored suits, which didn't cover up their third-class qualities in Martinez's view. Hondurans were lowly scoundrels in his experience. Foul-smelling and uncivilized. He took a seat next to Mama, whose chair was much closer to Flores' than to his.

"Where's Carli?" Delgado asked Martinez. "I thought he was coming with you."

Martinez calmly met his boss' gaze as he laid his napkin across his lap, which, he hadn't failed to notice, none of the Neanderthals had done. "He said he had an emergency and that he'd be here as soon as he could," he lied.

Facing Martinez and Mama were Carkas and Chasquas. The four of them—Carkas, Chasquas, Carli, and Martinez—held the second-highest rank in the organization, that of a lieutenant. Carkas wore his black hair short, sported a bushy goatee, and bore battle scars all over his hands and arms. Chasquas was taller and thinner, and like his younger cousin Beto, he was covered with what Martinez considered disgusting amateur tattoos. Martinez's own body art had been professionally drawn in places his suits could hide.

"Let's eat," Flores said. His valet brought out hundred-dollar steaks for everyone except Chasquas, who refused his plate and stuck with beer and cigarettes. Chasquas was thin and twitchy. Martinez figured the man hadn't eaten in at least a day.

Original oil paintings adorned the wood-paneled walls, a chandelier hung from the ceiling, and plush carpeting stretched from wall to wall. Martinez was incensed to see these dirty Central Americans living so well while he had to watch his spending and take their orders. *Not for long.*

Classical compositions played softly in the background. "Do you like the music?" Flores asked Mama, pushing his glasses up on his nose. "I chose it myself."

"Yes, honey. *Mucho*," said Mama, who in Martinez's opinion was too-heavily made up and wore an excessive amount of perfume.

While they ate, Flores rose to update them with the latest news, a sort of verbal newsletter he delivered every month. "As most of you know," the thin man announced, "we've entered into an alliance with the Cartel del Norte and the North County Kings. So in addition to our own earnings, we'll be processing theirs. As of Monday, the four of you will work exclusively in the megasuite, which they've set up for us out of gratitude for our cooperation."

Carkas scowled and muttered something inaudible that included the words *Chucky Matón*.

Flores eyed Carkas and nodded, implying understanding if not agreement with the angry sentiment. "It's true that Matón and a few of his men will be there as well, at least on occasion. But you all must make every effort to cooperate, and we'll make it worth your while. In fact, we have something for you," Flores said, pulling four white envelopes stuffed with cash from his jacket pocket. One for each man. When he found himself with an extra envelope, Carli's, and slid it back into his pocket, Mama looked up at him with what looked like resentment. Flores didn't notice or didn't care. And Martinez wouldn't have given it to her, either.

After dessert, Mama took the three lieutenants down to the first floor and across the grounds to the health spa. Each of them selected a masseuse to hang on their shoulders while gambling. Then the madam led the group back to the main building, where she left them on the casino floor.

Meanwhile, Delgado shook hands with Flores and lumbered down the second-floor hallway to a suite of rooms virtually identical to the one he'd just left. Once inside, he nodded to his security detail and whipped out his telephone. Most Southern Californians were already in bed at that hour, but for Delgado, it was the start of a new business day.

8

MEET THE TEAM

Having eaten the last of his apples the night before, Murci woke up hungry. He needed some kind of break today or else he'd have to ask the street gang for a favor. It was either that or sell his bike at a heavy loss. He dropped and gave himself forty, then drank four cups of tap water to fool his grumbling stomach. Resignedly, he picked up his phone and checked his messages for the thousandth time, expecting nothing. But there it was, sent only a few hours earlier. He scrolled through his contacts and made a call.

"Walker."

"*Buenos días señor*. This is Murci Sanchez. I know where Nayeli is and I'm on my way there now."

"*¡Excelente!*" Walker replied. Wind blew into his phone, distorting the reception. "But don't do anything yet. Park and I are on our way to a meeting, and after that we'll check it out. I'll call you back in the afternoon."

***

Walker clicked off and put the phone away. "We've got a lead on the missing girl," he said. Park sat beside him driving. Cold wind rushed in through the driver's side window.

"Excellent," Park replied with feigned excitement, but he wasn't fooling anyone. He was hung over again, and his smile faded quickly to a frown.

Walker knew his partner wasn't in a talking mood, so he let his own mind wander. He was glad Murci had located his sister, happy to have helped the young man in some small way. But it wasn't just Walker's perfect Spanish that had allowed it to happen. Walker had been born and raised in Mexico, growing up with plenty of guys like Murci, who would certainly identify with a few of his tattoos if he saw them.

Walker's father, a fighter pilot stationed in San Diego, had been murdered just before Walker was born, so Walker's mother had fled the United States and raised him in Tijuana. She'd died of cancer when he was sixteen. Two years later, he moved to San Diego and eventually found work as a beach lifeguard. That's where he met Tony Park, with whose help and that of many others he'd tracked down his father's killer, and it was that experience that had inspired him to go into law enforcement.

"I don't suppose Lynn told the task force about my psycho discharge?" Park asked, snapping Walker back to the present as he steered into a paid parking lot.

Walker shook his head. "I doubt it. But you've got nothing to be ashamed of, man. Look how far you've come." Walker wasn't just trying to make his friend feel better. Park had indeed made an incredible comeback. After returning from the Middle East with crippling PTSD, he'd applied for a job as a beach lifeguard, figuring it would soothe his soul. He'd figured right: watching the waves roll in for years had dramatically improved Park's mental health. He was later promoted to leader of the dive rescue team. Now, as a Harbor Police detective, Park was back on the front line, taking on positions of increasing responsibility.

After a four-block walk to the Hall of Justice, they stepped into the lobby and passed through security. When the elevator doors slid open on the thirteenth floor, Chief Deputy DA Pat O'Connell and Deputy DA Lynn Peters were waiting for them in the hallway. Lynn's golden hair contrasted attractively with her royal blue pant suit, while O'Connell's big arms stretched the seams of a navy-blue blazer over khakis. The man was definitely in his fifties. Maybe sixties. Either way, he was at an age when one would expect muscle mass to decline, but O'Connell's biceps seemed to grow even larger even as Walker looked at them.

Lynn offered cheek-to-cheek greetings and O'Connell gave them a hearty handshake. They led the detectives to a spacious meeting room, where four grim-faced people wearing business casual sat gathered around a long, golden oak conference table.

"Thanks for coming in, guys," Lynn said after she and O'Connell followed them in. "It's always a pleasure to see you. Meet the San Diego Human Trafficking Task Force."

Handshakes were given and names exchanged. Then everyone settled into chairs at the table except for Lynn, O'Connell, and DAI Matt Rogers. "Do you know what the HTTF does?" Lynn asked.

Park rolled his eyes upwards and slightly to the right, something he always did while searching his hard drive. Then he met Lynn's gaze again and smiled winningly. "It's a multi-agency organization that seeks to disrupt and dismantle human trafficking in San Diego through a comprehensive, collaborative, and regional response," he quoted. "There's one deputy district attorney assigned full-time—I'm guessing that's you—along with two district attorney investigators and other members from local, state, and federal agencies."

Lynn and O'Connell raised their eyebrows at each other. "That's incredible," said Lynn. The rest of the room also looked impressed, except for Walker, who had seen the party trick performed many times.

"The mind is a muscle you can strengthen," Park replied.

"I agree, but you have to admit you have a gift," Lynn countered. "As you know," she went on, "my role on the task force is like that of an administrator. At least until arrests are made. So we'll let y'all get to work." With that, she waved, smiled and spun on her heels. O'Connell moved to hold the door for her, then nodded to Rogers and followed her out.

Rogers' shoulder rig peeked out from under his open blazer. His hair was gelled back and his bushy mustache was neatly trimmed. Speaking directly to Park and Walker, he said, "Morning, gentlemen. Thanks for coming in so early. Before we get started and in the spirit of full disclosure, I should tell you why we need a Spanish-speaking investigator. One of our members, DAI Oscar Peña, recently passed away."

Walker knew the story, but Park raised an eyebrow.

"It was an automobile accident," Rogers continued. "Peña was hit head-on by a drunk driver, who also met his end in the crash. I just felt you ought to know."

"We appreciate that," Park said.

"Thank you, Detective," Rogers replied. "Why don't you tell us about yourselves."

Walker looked to his higher-ranking partner but Park muttered, "You're the Spanish speaker."

Walker stood. "Good morning, everyone. Corporal Park and I are with the Harbor Police. We've both got five years on. Park's too modest to tell you that he's a retired Navy SEAL team leader, and I'm a native speaker of Spanish, which means I speak it as fluently as I'm speaking to you now in English."

"Thank you, Detective Walker," Rogers said. "Now I'd like you to meet the team." He glanced warmly down at the person next to him, the only woman in the room. "Ayla Sami is a level four district attorney investigator. She's as smart and tough as anyone else here." Sami was trim but curvy, with dark features and long, frizzy hair, seemingly of Middle Eastern descent.

Rogers next motioned toward a large, square-jawed white man. "Agent John Seley, BORTAC operator." Seley's hair was buzzed military-style and his rolled-up shirt exposed one brawny forearm covered in a sleeve of tattoos. He was just as big as Park.

"BORTAC?" Park asked.

Seley's gaze locked onto Park's. "It's the U.S. Customs and Border Protection's tactical team, like the Harbor Police's MARTAC." He'd done his homework.

Rogers gestured in the direction of the fourth member: a thin man with sharp black eyes, a hooked nose, and a closely trimmed beard. Like DAI Sami, he appeared to hail from somewhere near the Arabian Peninsula. "And this is Mr. Ali Hassan, our technology and intelligence analyst, on loan from the San Diego County Sheriff's Department."

"Welcome, guys," said Hassan. "Since Matt is also a modest guy, it falls on me to tell you that our fearless leader is a decorated law enforcement officer. A former lieutenant and SWAT team commander with the SDPD, he'll be up for DAI level five in the spring."

"I appreciate that, Ali," Rogers said, lowering himself into his chair. "Ayla?"

DAI Sami rose and moved to one side of a projection screen, which Hassan controlled from a laptop.

"First a little about our methods," she said. "The good news is that the IMBs, or illicit massage businesses, are easy to find. For instance, yesterday I had the displeasure of visiting this website." She gestured toward the internet browser shown on the screen. "I had to slog through pages and pages of reviews posted by men who frequent these places. They leave starred reviews, sharing details such as breast size, presence or absence of pubic hair, and reasons for their satisfaction or dissatisfaction with services rendered."

Park and Walker exchanged disgusted looks as Hassan brought up another slide.

"As I'm sure you're aware," DAI Sami went on, "law enforcement has traditionally focused on arresting sex workers, but that's not our focus since they aren't the real problem. It's a huge industry, the third most lucrative illegal business in San Diego after drugs and guns. Worldwide, human trafficking generates a hundred and fifty billion dollars per year, but these forced laborers never see that money. So one priority is to hold the real criminals accountable under the law, but it's not easy—they hide behind a tangled web of registered agents, beneficial owners, and shell companies. It's almost as if the laws were designed to protect them."

"I wouldn't say almost," Rogers corrected her. "The laws are actually designed to facilitate anonymity in business. Remember the golden rule—he who has the gold makes the rules."

"She or he," said DAI Sami. Rogers nodded deferentially and she went on: "Finally, there are many federally funded benefits available to survivors of human trafficking, regardless of immigration status. So in addition to putting away the actual culprits, we also aim to recover the victims and refer them to these support services. Thank you."

"Thank *you*, Ayla," Rogers said. "That's it for us, guys. What about on your end? DDA Peters said you're already working an HT case."

"We are," Park replied. "About a week ago, the corpse of a fourteen-year-old girl was found floating in the bay. The FBI identified the body as that of Marcela Gonzalez, reported missing from Mexico. At the same time, another girl named Nayeli Sanchez disappeared from a nearby Mexican town. Nayeli's brother is here in San Diego looking for her, and just this morning he told us he knows where she is. Western Nail Spa."

"I know that place," Rogers said. "Let's check it out."

9

HASSAN SMELLS A RAT

After a month-long losing streak, Martinez had finally won big at blackjack. He cashed out his chips, handing three hundreds to the hard-eyed health spa employee who had stood by his side all night. She pecked him on the cheek and sashayed off without a word. Fitting the rest of the money into his billfold, he headed outside to the executive parking area, his wallet so overstuffed that it wouldn't fold shut, so after sliding behind the wheel of his Alpina, he put it in the glove box.

As he sped back to San Diego, his phone vibrated in his pocket and a ringtone blared through the sound system. He punched a button on the dashboard.

"Get over here now, *cabrón*!" Mama shouted. "We're going to be raided in thirty minutes, so I need you to take the girls to King for a Day."

A few minutes later, Martinez burst through the front door of the massage parlor that had been giving him and his bosses so much trouble. For some reason it was always Western Nail Spa that presented problems, like when Marcela leapt to her death because some idiot Honduran forgot to lock the roof access door. Or when that same Neanderthal beat one of the girls half to death. Maybe the nail spa wasn't the problem.

He rushed into the office and saw Mama at her desk and the idiot Honduran slouching on a stool. "Rooms clean?" he asked.

"Of course they are," Mama retorted.

"Good. Get the girls outside. I'll wait by the car and get them in. Beto, cover me."

"Yes, sir," Beto muttered, then followed Martinez out front and stood guard by the door. Martinez opened the SUV's rear tailgate. Carli's corpse lay zipped up in a white body bag on the folded-down rear seats.

"Hurry up!" Martinez barked at the girls as they came out in single file. If that command made them walk any faster, the increase was imperceptible. They all trudged along like animals to the slaughter, being led against their will. Scowling and cursing under his breath, Martinez brusquely helped them aboard, where they crowded around the body, three girls along each side. No one asked about the covered corpse.

Martinez hadn't slept at all. He slammed the tailgate, hurried into his seat, banged his own door shut, and stomped on the gas, driving recklessly to King for a Day, another establishment in the chain owned by Delgado and Flores. Soon the Alpina bounced into a strip mall parking lot, which Martinez cut across at speed, screeching to a halt at the curb. Chasquas popped out of the front door to receive the girls. Martinez nodded a curt greeting to his fellow lieutenant as he stepped out, lifted the tailgate, and watched the girls go inside.

Martinez cut back across the lot and headed for the crematorium, frowning as he sped away. He'd grown tired of seasoning the new girls, and he was insulted that at this point in his career he still had to transport them like a lowly taxi driver. He was anxious to take Delgado's and Flores' place, though he'd still be reporting to someone: Toño del Real of the Cartel del Norte. At least he'd be number one on the north side of the border, commanding Chucky Matón and the North County Kings.

He eased off the gas a bit since he felt home free, confident that he'd gotten away with killing Carli. The cremation technician wouldn't dare unzip the cadaver bag, not while Martinez was watching, and in the unlikely event that he reported the unscheduled visit to Delgado and Flores, Martinez would say someone had seen him win at blackjack and tried to relieve him of his winnings. He then shot the would-be robber and took the body with him to dispose of the evidence.

Martinez couldn't hold back a self-satisfied grin. He figured he was the only Alpina owner in the world who kept a supply of body bags in his car.

***

Of course Murci wasn't going to wait for the detectives to check out the nail spa. By the time they showed up, Nayeli might be gone. Or dead. Any number of things could have happened. So as soon as he hung up with Walker, he straddled his black bike, started her up, and headed east.

The trip was a quick one. Murci's mind was so full of worry for his sister and about what he might find on arrival that he came to his destination before he knew he was there. He continued on for a block, leaned the bike on its kickstand, and ran to the so-called beauty center.

There was no one outside the establishment. It looked like a house that had been renovated for business purposes. A large wooden sign over the porch gave its name and listed the services offered. *Supposedly offered.* An expensive-looking white SUV was parked at the curb. Murci stooped low and hurried toward it, staying on the far side of the vehicle so no one in the nail spa would see him try the door. It was unlocked. "Big mistake," he said out loud, opening the driver's side door and running his hand under the seat. He found nothing, but when he popped open the glove box, his eyes widened at the sight of a fat wallet, which he deftly removed.

As he slipped back out, the front door to the nail spa began to swing open, so he flew back across the street in a crouch, then straightened and strolled casually back to his motorcycle as if he were out for a walk. When he reached his bike, he hid behind it, still with a decent view of the nail spa. A Latino in a gray suit stood next to the SUV while a younger guy near the front door covered him, his pistol drawn but pointed down.

That's when he saw her. Murci's heart leapt as several girls filed out the door. Nayeli trudged slowly to the SUV with her head down. When Gray Suit screamed at them to hurry, Murci had to force himself not to run across the street and slit his throat. His pulse raced as Nayeli and the others climbed into the back of the utility vehicle.

When the SUV started up and raced past his hiding spot, Murci threw his leg over the bike and followed it at a distance. While speeding through side streets, he figured now was the best time to catch up to the car, skid across its forward path, and force it to stop. Then take out the driver. Gray Suit would definitely be armed, but Murci was pretty sure that at whatever his destination was, there'd be more guys and more guns. He rolled the throttle toward him to accelerate, but the bike failed to respond. It lost power, slowed, and sputtered to a stop. Murci's stomach turned in on itself. He was out of gas. He'd known he was low, but with no money it had been a non-issue.

A primal growl escaped his lips and tears plunged down his face as he watched the SUV disappear from view. He stepped away from the bike and let it fall, kicking it until pain took the place of rage.

He pushed the motorbike to a gas station, wishing he'd had the guts to attack Nayeli's handlers, but deep down he knew he'd made the right call. When he was almost there, he had to run with the bike to gain momentum and strain his legs to push the heavy machine up an incline into the filling station. He filled it up and bought two sandwiches, his thoughts racing wildly as he wolfed down his meal. In the end, he decided his best bet was to stake out the nail spa and wait for the SUV to turn up again. If it didn't show, he'd barge inside and torture someone until they gave him his sister's location.

***

Nayeli hated taking orders but she'd kept her eyes down as she and the others trudged grudgingly toward the SUV. The sight of Martinez standing there in his fancy suit made her features curl with hate. She couldn't even look at him, and she jerked her arm away when he tried to help her into the back of the car. While the six of them were still scooting around a stinking body bag, Martinez banged the tailgate shut, slid behind the wheel, slammed his own door, and stomped on the gas.

Since she was facing the rear window, she could have sworn someone was following them on a bike. It looked like Murci and his Kawasaki, but the rider pulled to the side of the road and faded away in the distance. Even if it had been him, she realized, now he'd have no way of finding her at the new location. She hugged her knees. Looking around at her fellow captives, she knew by the desperate looks on their faces that no one was far from losing hope. Including her.

***

Walker and Hassan rode with Park in the unmarked sedan, following a blacked-out Suburban driven by Rogers and carrying Sami and Seley. The two vehicles stopped at the curb outside the suspected IMB and the group strode to the entrance, each with a sidearm in a hip or shoulder holster. They were met at the door by one Mary Baretta, who identified herself with a California driver's license and smelled strongly of perfume. She wore a colorful dress two sizes too small for her. Ms. Baretta showed them to a tidy office ventilated by open windows. The fresh air hadn't rid the workspace of the stale odor of indoor smoking, the only clear evidence of illegal activity they would find. The woman appeared nervous as she planted herself into a chair behind a desk. Rogers took a seat facing her, while everyone else stayed standing.

"I'm afraid this is going to be a short visit, sir," she told Rogers in Spanish. "I don't speak English well at all. Just a few words."

Walker addressed the woman in her native language. "That's all right, ma'am," he said. "I'll interpret for you. You can speak Spanish and I'll tell him what you said."

"No, you go ahead and interview her," Rogers said, rising to leave the room. "I'll run her ID."

When Rogers came back, his reluctant nod told everyone that her ID had checked out. Walker summed up what he'd learned in the interview. "She says she's the manager here, and that they don't offer any services other than what the sign says. She claims she's never heard of Marcela Gonzalez or Nayeli Sanchez but if we'd like to meet some of the girls who do work here and take a tour, we'd be more than welcome."

"Perfect," Rogers answered. "Let's have a look around."

Ms. Baretta showed them the ground floor first, introducing them to three nail technicians dressed in matching white spa tunics, loose-fitting scrub pants, and slip-resistant footwear. They had bright smiles plastered on their faces, but their eyes were shifty. Rogers and Walker asked them a few questions and received satisfactory answers. No inquiry was made as to their immigration status. Upstairs, the facility was equally clean. Too clean. Most of the massage rooms were unoccupied and smelled like they'd just been mopped. In one of them, a bent set of Persian blinds clattered against a cracked-open window.

"What do you guys think?" Walker asked Park and Hassan as they headed back to the sedan. He got in on the passenger side while Park slid into the driver's seat and Hassan had the back seat to himself.

"They were ready for us," Park said as he turned the key in the ignition and set off for the Hall of Justice.

Hassan fastened his seat belt. "I agree," he said. "But how did they know? Who told them we were coming?"

10

ROASTED PIGLETS

Feeling home free as he drove to the crematorium, Martinez popped open the glove box to feast his eyes on his fat wallet, but it wasn't there. Thinking it might have fallen between the seats, he pulled to the side of the road and performed an exhaustive search. After a solid minute of speculation, recollection, and ruling out possibilities, he came to the realization that he'd been robbed.

None of the girls had done it, since they'd been sitting in the back with Carli's corpse. Speaking of which, the dead body was beginning to emit a sharp, putrid odor like what wafts out from a garbage dumpster in the sun. Martinez had read somewhere that when you smell it, the bacteria stay in your nostrils and multiply. He forced back the scalding vomit in his throat, fearing it would take a year or more for the smell of the dead Honduran to fade from his hundred-and-fifty-thousand-dollar car.

For all his faults, Martinez was neither unintelligent nor uneducated. He was able to perceive the irony of his having considered Beto an idiot for not locking the roof access door, while his own failure to press a single button on his key fob had cost him five grand, as well as the time and trouble it would take to replace his cards and IDs. Both fake and authentic.

He gave a shout and punched the wood paneling on his door, then whipped the turbocharged SUV into a U-turn, speeding back to the nail spa. He was sure the trip would be in vain, but at least it gave him time to mull over a nagging question in his mind. He'd been puzzled as to how the police had come so close to catching them at the nail spa, but as he drove he had an idea. He pressed the button on the dashboard.

"Hello?" came Mama's raspy voice through sixteen high-end speakers.

"Did the police tell you how they found out about Western?" he asked.

"No, but they did say Marcela's body was found floating in the bay," she replied. "That's a connection to us."

Martinez slammed his fist into the door again, three times. "Where's Beto?" he hissed.

"He said he was going to the RV park."

"Right. You're closed for business. You didn't find my wallet out on the street, did you?"

"No, but I'll go look—" she started to say, but Martinez ended the call. Sensing an opportunity to kill two dumb-ass birds with one stone, he mashed the button once more.

"What's up?" answered Carkas.

"Can I come and pick you up? We have a leak that needs plugging."

***

Beto's mind clicked and whirred, estimating the purchasing power of the crumpled hundred his cousin Chasquas had loaned him, in theory only since neither expected Beto to pay it back. With his eyes on the freeway, he blindly fished out a pack of cigarettes from the armrest box. Then he lit a smoke and turned the stereo up to blasting.

As usual, his friends were thrilled to see him when he knocked on the door of their RV. With very little delay, they headed all down to another trailer, bought drugs, and came back up to consume the illicit powders and pills. Soon they were in their comfort zone, arguing loudly, wrestling, and drinking like there was no tomorrow, which was, in fact, the case—for them there would actually be no tomorrow.

"Like little pigs in a pigsty," said Carkas to Martinez, peeking into the window through a crack in the curtains, the music blasting inside.

"Little pigs about to be roasted," Martinez said.

"Now you're making me hungry," Carkas said, licking his lips eagerly. "Have you ever eaten roasted suckling piglet? Next time we go to Honduras, it's on me."

"Deal. I'll get the beers," Martinez promised falsely. Carkas was about to be roasted, too. "Ready?"

Carkas nodded and stepped around to the other side of the RV, where he couldn't be seen. Martinez rapped his knuckles on the thin aluminum door. The shouting ceased and the blaring music was cut off.

"Who's there?" came Beto's voice.

"Martinez."

"Why didn't you say so, boss?" Beto said, pushing open the door with a goofy, mindless perma-grin. "You freaked us all out. Come in and snort a fat rail. It's on Chasquas!"

The three young thugs beside him erupted into a cacophony of guffaws.

"I need some help," Martinez said. "Some guy tried to rob me outside the casino. I smoked the motherfucker, but now I need to get rid of the body. Delgado gave me the three hundred but I'm short on cash. I'll give you guys a hundred to help me carry it down to the bay and toss it in."

Under other circumstances, Beto might have been suspicious. Why hadn't Martinez called ahead to ask for help? Why didn't he just drop the body off a bridge? But the young man's neurons weren't firing properly, so he agreed without hesitation.

"You got it, Marty," Beto blurted out. The drugs must have made him think he'd been blessed by the gift of comedy. They'd also loosened his tongue. "I thought I was the only one who was keeping money."

Martinez was going to kill them all anyway, but he was gratified to know he'd been right. As the kids carried the body bag down to the water, he screwed in a silencer, strode forward, and shot them all in the head at close range and in rapid succession. The gunfire was suppressed, but it could still be heard all over the grounds, so now he had to be quick. Carkas came running to help him drag the bodies back up the hill, stuff them into body bags, and heave them into the Alpina.

"Thanks, bro," Martinez said, after all but one of the body bags had been loaded.

Carkas leaned over to pick up the last one, using both hands to lift his end, but instead of helping, Martinez shot him three times in the chest.

As he peeled out of the RV park, Martinez felt like he'd found his wallet with more cash in it than he'd lost. Now that Carkas and Carli were out of the way, his mission status was sixty-six percent complete. Two down, one to go. Soon he'd have more money than he could spend. Exhausted by a long night of gambling followed by a full day of herding dirty girls and plugging leaks, he was finally on his way to the crematorium. He'd have to ask for more body bags since he was fresh out.

***

Murci took a seat in the shade at a bus stop with a good view of Western Nail Spa. He'd given himself a long, boring stakeout limit of five hours before he'd charge inside and beat the truth out of someone, so he was shocked when almost immediately the white SUV skidded to a stop exactly where it had been before. The same guy got out, his sister's handler, the one in the gray suit. The man scoured the street and the front yard for the missing wallet, which made Murci smile for the first time since Nayeli left home. Then Gray Suit set off again and Murci followed him to the RV park, where he watched in horror as the human trafficker executed everyone around him.

In the fading light of dusk, Murci trailed the SUV to an older district east of Downtown. There he watched as Gray Suit and a greasy-haired man in a white coat began to secure the bodies to a stretcher and wheel them into a crematorium one by one. With no need to see that process through to completion, he stole around to the rear of the building, where he found the back door locked. There was a small window above his head. With his fingers on the windowsill and his shoes on the wall, he pulled himself up and slid the portal sideways with one hand before dropping back down. Then he repeated the tricky move, this time squeezing himself through the narrow opening. Hitting the floor in a crouch, he sneaked down a dark hallway until he came to an open door on his left. He chanced a peek. The body bags were stacked in a pile. Gray Suit and Greasy were lifting them onto a pair of moving conveyor belts that fed into twin cremation chambers. Gray Suit was armed, Murci knew by the bulge in the man's jacket. Greasy, probably not, but it was impossible to know for sure.

Dying to learn where they'd taken his sister but hesitant to fight the men without a gun, Murci figured his best course of action was to report his observations to Detective Walker and arm himself that same night. He waited until the crooks were distracted, then dashed past the doorway, through the reception area, and out the front doors. With new information and a fat wad of hundreds in his pocket, he breathed a little easier on the way back to the motel. Once there, he called Walker and gave his report. Then he went downstairs and bought a Sig Sauer pistol and a pair of extra magazines from the local gang.

Now he was ready for his sister's handler.

***

The Hall of Justice was a one-hundred-and-seventy-foot modern architectural feat, but it had been built with government funds, so the main conference room in the DA's Office had plain industrial carpeting and run-of-the-mill office chairs. It did, however, boast a wall's length of windows offering an aerial view of the bay, with Coronado Island in the center and Point Loma jutting out along the horizon.

As the HTTF waited for the early morning meeting to begin, they eyed each other warily.

"Anyone know where Seley is?" District Attorney Investigator Ayla Sami asked morosely. She appeared to be in urgent need of caffeine.

"You know how those military types are," Park joked.

"Totally unreliable," Walker added with a grin.

Clad in a black skirt suit, DAI Sami had gathered her long, curly black hair with a claw clip at the back. She rewarded their efforts to cheer her up with a hint of a smile before her features fell back into stony resignation.

"Let's get started without him," DAI Rogers said. "Ms. Baretta at the so-called nail spa obviously knew we were coming. I think we can all agree on that." All heads nodded. "More importantly, for those of you who didn't know, the upstairs rooms were identical to what we've seen at other IMBs."

Ali Hassan turned to Park and Walker and said, "A locked stairway door, too many massage rooms for a tiny nail spa, and bars on every window."

"So who could have warned them?" Walker asked. "Besides us, of course."

"Who else knew about our visit?" inquired Hassan.

"It's a short list," Rogers said. "Lynn Peters and Chief Deputy Pat O'Connell."

"When was the last time this room was screened for surveillance equipment?" Park asked. His face was the freshest at the table, his cheeks still rosy from a ten-mile run.

"Good question," Sami replied. "This morning, actually, but it's only done once a week."

"Let's make it once a day," Rogers said. "Ayla, will you take care of that?"

"Sure."

Silence settled over the group as they considered what had been said. Someone was guilty of something, either the disclosure of secret information or the placement of surveillance equipment. Walker knew Lynn Peters very well; it couldn't have been her. And Chief Deputy O'Connell's reputation was solid. So, assuming O'Connell was in the clear, who else could it be?

Heavy boots clomped in the hallway, preceding John Seley's entrance. He dropped his heavy frame into a chair. "Sorry I'm late," he said with a boyish grin. "Bad traffic."

Sami, Rogers, and Hassan chuckled softly, but Park and Walker laughed out loud. Walker figured it was a running joke.

"So there's a leak and we're not sure who to trust," Sami summed up for Seley's benefit. "What's our next move?"

Rogers rested his elbow on the table, supporting his chin with his fist. His only reply was lowered eyes and a discouraged shake of the head.

"Let's raid all the IMBs," Park suggested half-seriously. "We could deploy MARTAC."

"BORTAC would be better," Seley countered with a smile spreading across his face.

"MARTAC!" Park and Walker exclaimed in near unison, producing a badly needed bout of laughter.

"We don't have enough evidence for a warrant on any of them," Rogers said as the noise died down.

"We've got something to go on," Walker announced. He relayed Murci's account of what had happened at the RV park and the crematorium, then said, "Murci's description of the gray-suited killer and his vehicle matches my observations at the airport: a man referred to as "Martinez" in a gray suit and a white Alpina. So another person of interest may be a stocky, sixty-something Latin-American man. The one who climbed into the passenger seat and yelled at Martinez before the bastards broke my dog's leg."

"We think he's Martinez's boss," Park added.

"Nice work, guys," Rogers said, quickly and with excitement. "Finally a bit of luck. Ayla and I have meetings all day for another case, so you are on your own. Walker, I want you and Murci to meet with a forensic sketch artist to get drawings of Martinez and all other unknown actors. Park and Seley, go down to the crematorium and check it out. Ali, look into the business records for Western Nail Spa, the crematorium, and the rest of the suspected IMBs to see if you can find any connections. Be careful out there."

***

East of Downtown, near San Diego State University, Seley rode with Park in the unmarked sedan since he didn't have a car; the BORTAC operator had ridden a motorcycle all the way from Texas.

Park's anxiety heightened with every passing mile. If the short list of people who could have warned the nail spa were complete, then there was a good chance whoever they'd meet at the crematorium would be ready for them. *Unless the rat is sitting right next to me*, Park thought, eyeing his wingman with distrust.

As Park brought the car to a halt, Seley said, "I'll go in first, and if it's all clear, I'll let you know. No sense in both of us getting killed."

Absolutely not. If Seley was the culprit, that would give him time to set something up inside. "What if it's not all clear?" Park returned, unbuckling his safety belt and hopping out. "Then you're dead. I couldn't handle that. I'll give the go-ahead and you stay outside."

"Negative," Seley barked over the roof of the vehicle as they checked their gear. "We'll go together. Let's take a recon walk around the perimeter."

At the rear of the building, they found a locked door and an unlocked window, but they were too big to squeeze themselves through the narrow aperture. Not only that, but without a warrant, their only option was to enter through the front door and flash their credentials right away.

A greasy-haired man in a white lab coat received them from behind a counter. Instead of focusing on that man, Park scanned for signs of trouble. Seeing nothing unordinary, he said, "Good morning, sir. I'm Detective Tony Park with the Harbor Police."

"And I'm Agent John Seley from U.S. Customs and Border Protection."

"Good morning, officers. How may I help you?" the cremation technician said, his brief smile as devoid of cheer as the facility itself.

Seley took a few steps toward a dark hallway, apparently straining his eyes for any danger. Park answered the tech. "We'd like to ask you a few questions," he said.

"Yes, of course, Detective Park. Please follow me," the white-coated tech replied, leading them down the hallway into an office with a desk and two visitor's chairs.

The tech sat across from them, and as the conversation progressed, he denied any knowledge of illegal cremation taking place on the premises. He also said he hadn't been on duty the night before. His anxious bouncing leg and the sweat on his brow belied his words, but they weren't evidence of any crime.

There was a faint click and a hissing sound, like an air-conditioning system switching on.

"We'd like to take a look around," Seley said.

"You bet, officer. I'd be happy to show you around." The tech gave an embarrassed half-smile. "First let me hit the head. Can I get you guys a cup of coffee or some water?"

The lawmen shook their heads impatiently.

As Park watched the tech hustle out of the room, he gave him the benefit of the doubt, figuring the man might have some sort of gastrointestinal infection. But when he locked the door behind him, both Park and Seley leapt to their feet. With shoulder smashes, back kicks, and bullets, they did their best to break it down. They almost succeeded before their eyelids grew irresistibly heavy and they crumpled to the floor.

11

BOILING EYES

When Park came to his senses, he was in motion, trapped inside a rough wooden casket being carried by some kind of conveyor. In a crematorium.

He was about to be burned alive.

The adrenaline dump ripped him out of semi-consciousness into a state of panic. He punched and kicked the lid, but it was too tightly sealed. Then the casket jolted to a stop and the sound of a door sliding shut made Park's heart pound even harder. Next came the unmistakable whooshing of flames and a sudden rise in temperature. Within seconds, the casket began to pop and crackle and fill with thick smoke. He screamed for help but no one came.

***

After the morning meeting at the DA's Office, Walker had driven a different unmarked unit down to San Ysidro, where he picked up Murci at his motel. He headed for their meeting with the sketch artist, but there'd been something nagging at him all morning that finally changed his mind: given a past or present leak in the conference room, Park and Seley could be marching into a trap. Or Seley could be the rat, which might be even worse.

Walker cranked the steering wheel to its limit of travel, then let it spin back freely as he flipped a U-turn, neatly catching the wheel as he stomped on the gas.

The sedan's big six-cylinder engine did its job as the rear end fishtailed slightly before the car gained traction and reached high speed.

"Change of plans," Walker said, his gaze locked on the road.

Soon they skidded to a stop close to Park's unmarked unit at the rear of the crematorium. Murci took Walker to the unlocked window, disappeared into it, and after an excruciatingly long minute, he pushed the back door open.

"It pays to be a shrimpy Mexican sometimes," Murci said, but Walker knew modesty when he heard it. The younger man's muscles were as hard as rocks and Walker had already seen what Murci could do in a fistfight against a larger, well-trained opponent.

Walker peered down the dark hallway and flicked his chin toward the far end. He pulled his Glock. Murci drew a survival knife from his boot and they advanced, slowly, until Park and Seley started screaming. Then they raced toward the noise, which was coming from behind a closed door marked "Cremation Room."

They exchanged a single nod. Walker threw the door open, his weapon at the ready, spotting a lanky Latino covered in tattoos and a greasy-haired man in a white coat standing next to a pair of conveyor belts, each belt leading to a cremation chamber, the source of the screams.

"Harbor Police!" Walker shouted, leveling his weapon in a two-handed stance with his finger on the trigger. "Hands up!"

As Murci and Walker entered, the inked-up Latino charged Murci, whose thick, serrated blade was sharp, but not as deadly as Walker's Glock. He stayed on Murci's far side so Walker couldn't shoot him.

The Latino protected his face with his forearms, which Murci sliced to the bone. Blood shot out like water through a crack in a dam.

"Get those furnaces off!" Walker shouted.

Murci raced to the cremation chambers and slammed his palm on a red button beside each stainless steel door. This exposed the pair of flaming caskets, which he dragged out onto the conveyor belts with his bare hands.

To protect Murci, Walker sprinted away from the bleeding Latino and dropped the cremation tech with a left hook to the temple. Then he wheeled around and took one-handed aim but the Latino was too quick: he struck Walker's shooting hand with a hammer. Walker hollered and dropped his weapon, but still held the man off with one fist and both feet. The hammer skittered away as the brawl moved into the hallway.

As blood continued to sluice out of his forearms, the inked-up Latino ran out of gas, so Walker managed to gain the advantage despite his injury. Assuming a full mount position, the detective threw vicious elbows and forearm smashes into the man's eyes, nose, mouth, and throat, delivering further decoration to the criminal's illustrated features. When the criminal went limp, Walker glanced into the cremation room. Park and Seley stood there in a daze, wide-eyed and ashen, while Murci grabbed the woozy tech by the lapels of his white coat, lifted him off the floor, and stuffed him into one of the caskets. The soft gringo fought back, but he was no match for the livid Native American, whose wiry strength had been forged over years of hard work and training.

Murci hammered the lid shut, ignoring the tech's muffled cries. Then he pushed the half-charred casket back into the chamber and punched the red button. The door slid down and the column of flames hissed and spit while the tech screamed for help.

With the bloody Latino still apparently out cold, Walker had to decide whether he should try to save the cremation tech or snap a pair of cuffs on the slippery character he'd just pummeled. But the Latino was a slick fellow, indeed. He must have been feigning unconsciousness, since he instantly came to life, squirming out from under Walker and scrambling to his feet. Walker also heaved himself up, but his hands found no purchase on the slippery floor. He failed to catch the crook, who tore through the reception room and out the front door.

Walker hustled back into the cremation room. No sounds were coming from behind the sliding door, but he punched the red button anyway. The heat hit him in the face like a shovel, forcing him to take two steps back. The wooden casket had crumbled away to reveal a blazing red body with steaming, boiling eyes.

***

Park and Seley secured the premises, Walker called the incident in, and Murci found water for everyone. "We've got a cell phone over here," Park called out from the hallway outside the cremation room. He left the device where it was so that he wouldn't contaminate the crime scene. The four of them settled into couches in the reception area, drinking from large, red plastic cups as they waited for the evidence technicians and supervisors to arrive.

Walker caught Agent Seley's eye. "You know Chief Deputy O'Connell, right?"

"Yeah. We go way back," Seley replied. "He was the one who invited me to join the task force. A good friend of my father's."

"Tony and I know DDA Peters just as well," Walker said. "I'm guessing there's a traitor on the task force, and now we know it's none of us."

Seley ran his hand over his close-cut hair. "We talked about the possibility of bugs being placed in the meeting room," he said. "Maybe some outside person snuck them in, like a cleaning lady."

Park shook his head. "It'd be a risky gamble to sneak listening devices past the lobby screening station every week."

"What about someone else who works in the DA's Office, then?" Seley persisted, setting his empty cup on the table. "Someone who's not on the task force. Maybe they overheard us or set their phone out to record us."

"That's a good point," Park said. "We can't say for sure how Ms. Baretta knew about our visit, but I really don't think the conference room was bugged. And since it's being screened every day now, it'll be that much harder for someone to listen in, so if anything like that happens again, we'll know it's either Rogers, Hassan, or Sami."

Seley shook his head vigorously. "I know them," he said. "Very well after working together for years. We've saved each other's lives."

"Let's keep our suspicions to ourselves for now," Walker said. "If I'm right, the less those three know, the better. If Seley's right, no harm done."

The four brothers-in-arms held each other's gazes and nodded in agreement as various official vehicles pulled to the curb.

***

Twenty miles east of the coast, as the Laguna Mountains began their ascent, the five-star Cumbres Casino Resort loomed over every other structure nearby. For practical purposes, the project was owned and operated by Flores and Delgado, yet a convoluted trail of beneficial owners and registered agents concealed that fact. For twenty years, the two Hondurans had laundered the proceeds of their human trafficking business through Cumbres, but now that it had grown into a sprawling entertainment destination, they were able to process an even greater amount of money, hence their cooperation with the Cartel del Norte.

Flores and Delgado were nervous about an upcoming trip to meet with the Mexican cartel, so they had risen earlier than usual to walk to the resort's state-of-the-art indoor shooting range to refine their marksmanship and blow off some steam. The facility included a cigar lounge, a business room, a souvenir shop, and, of course, a so-called health spa.

As they crossed the lush, manicured grounds, Delgado and Flores nodded to their employees. They let themselves in to the shooting range, grabbed what they needed from the gun closets, and took adjacent positions at the firing line. The scenario-based retrieval system made it possible to develop accuracy as well as decision-making, since the targets were programmed to edge and turn, showing either innocent civilians or violent-looking men.

The deafening blasts echoed throughout the facility as they took aim and emptied their mags.

"We should shoot at the good guys, not the bad guys," jested Delgado, chuckling as he slid his target toward himself. When it came to a stop, he frowned at his shot grouping.

"Yes," Flores muttered absently as he, too, evaluated the cluster tightness of his bullet holes. Then he remembered Delgado owed him an explanation. "Hey, you told me you took care of that investigator but you never said how. Are we exposed?"

"No, we're not," the big man answered, replacing his target with a fresh one and pressing a button to slide it back fifty yards. "You'll like this one: I found a terminally ill cancer patient willing to kamikaze Peña for three hundred grand paid to his surviving family. So when Peña came out to talk with me, my man got good and drunk, waited by the side of the highway, and hit him head-on."

"Did you pay the family?"

"Yes, I did."

As they moved from pistols to semi-automatic rifles to full auto, their conversation became increasingly sporadic. The men's normal day-to-day was so confrontational that they needed this peaceful, relaxing moment to let their minds wander. So, as the trim, balding, bespectacled Flores raked his targets with hot lead, his thoughts drifted back to how he, Delgado, and Mayor Rivera had grown up together in Honduras.

Ricardo Rivera had come from one of the richest families in the city, attending bilingual private schools paid for by a father who traded in dollars, not lempiras. For some reason, he never fit in with his wealthy peers, preferring the company of streetwise boys from a neighboring shantytown, two of whom were Flores and Delgado. When they were younger, the lads' misdeeds were limited to fistfights and petty theft, but later there was murder, extortion, and all kinds of smuggling. So it was for his protection that fifteen-year-old Rivera was sent to live with his father's relatives in the United States, while Delgado and Flores stayed in Honduras, working in a human trafficking network that spanned from Nicaragua to Northern California. The three friends never lost touch, so by the time Flores and Delgado had learned enough about the trafficking network and out-fought, out-lasted, and out-not-given-a-fuck about their peers and moved to San Diego, Rivera was well established there as an attorney able to facilitate paperwork and invest in his friends' casino project.

A smile played across Flores' lips as his FN SCAR blasted his paper target to confetti. Shooting was his second-favorite activity. Beside him, Delgado, who had recently given Martinez a fat wad of corpse disposal money, fired his own rifle while recalling how he met the Martinez family, the current source of his sex workers.

In the 1980s, one of Delgado's early responsibilities in organized crime had been to transport truckloads and boatloads of vulnerable people from Honduras into Guatemala, Belize, and sometimes Mexico, which is where he met Martinez's father. Alonso Martinez Sr. was instrumental in the development of a small town called Tenancingo. The proceeds from his prostitution ring paid for more parks, schools, and community events than the government, which is how sexual exploitation came to be tolerated by a large part of the community.

One of the girls who was separated from her family and sold as property within this network, like Nayeli would be forty years in the future, was Ana Maria Baretta. She lived and worked in Honduras, and was Flores' favorite prostitute. He preferred her to such an extent that he took her with him to San Diego. By then, she was a bit old for sex work, but he thought she'd make an excellent brothel manager. In that capacity, she came to be called "Mama," and since she had a gift for numbers, she kept the books for her brothel and, later, for all of them.

The shiny floor of the shooting range now littered with spent shell casings, Delgado and Flores let in the staff, who cleaned up their bosses' mess and opened the building to the public. Under the bright morning sun, the crime lords ambled back to their respective suites, where they were served their usual breakfasts. As they chewed and sipped, they felt no guilt about the number of servants in their employ; after all, they'd started out even worse. Dirt-floor poor. And look how far they'd come. Theirs was a real success story.

12

— . —

INITIAL APPROACH

The marine layer shrouded most of the bay, but Walker could see the cold, choppy water through the thinner patches. He felt glad he wasn't a fisherman headed out to sea. Then his team leader spoke and he shifted his gaze away from the window.

"Good morning," Rogers said from the head of the golden oak conference table. "We've got lots of good news today." He nodded to Ali Hassan, who slid his laptop over to DAI Sami and rose, making his way toward the front of the room and the overhead screen.

"Hi everyone," Hassan said with a pleasant smile. He wore a navy blue suit and a white shirt, no tie, and his beard was trimmed short as always. "My team and I have had a couple of big breaks. The first is that Western Nail Spa, the crematorium, and twenty other beauty centers are all registered to the same group of shell companies." He nodded to Ayla Sami, who called up a map of San Diego County showing the establishments he'd listed. Then he said, "So now we have a better idea of the scope of the sex trafficking operation as well as a vetted list of illicit massage businesses." This prompted a round of positive murmurings from the group. "And the second finding is even more significant," Hassan proceeded excitedly. "Several matches occurred when we referenced the photos on the phone we found at the crematorium with our forensic sketches and the FBI's facial recognition database. Meet Hernan Delgado and Chrystian Flores." Two labeled photos appeared in place of the map. "They're Honduran nationals with permanent residence in the U.S., and they manage a casino resort out in Blossom Valley. We're fairly sure that what they're actually doing is running the IMBs and laundering the profits through the casino, but we can't prove it yet."

Seley raised a massive hand. "What evidence do we have that they're running the IMBs?"

"Good question, John," said Hassan. "First, we have the phone. Its call history had been erased, but we obtained the records from the cell phone carrier. There were many long calls made to and received from the Cumbres Casino."

"I know that place," Walker said. "Maybe whoever owned the phone was a gambler." He felt his face flush.

"Could be," Hassan replied. "But remember, you saw Delgado and Martinez together at the airport. And we know Martinez is a human trafficker."

Sami brought up a different image: a CCTV screenshot of a gray-suited Latino with slicked-back hair and a cruel mouth. "And here he is. Alonso Martinez," Hassan said. "Of the notorious Martinez family in Tenancingo, Mexico. On the surface, their business also appears legitimate, mainly motels and strip clubs, but according to the feds, they're a major provider in a human trafficking ring that runs from Nicaragua to Northern California. So we think Martinez is Flores' and Delgado's supplier of human resources, so to speak."

"*Forced laborers* or even *sex slaves* would be more correct," Sami said, holding everyone's gaze for a microsecond before bringing up the last image: that of a shaven-headed Latino whose steely face was covered in grisly tattoos.

"This is the owner of the phone," Hassan said smoothly as the picture changed. He and Sami were in sync. "We know him only as 'Chasquas.' He was arrested for narcotics in L.A., but escaped from a holding cell with handcuffs on. His tattoos are typical of the Mara Salvatrucha, or MS-13. The Maras are a worldwide criminal group that originated on the streets of L.A. Founded by Salvadoran immigrants, the gang is estimated at thirty thousand members living in many countries around the globe, most notably in the United States and Central America."

Rogers looked up from his notes. "How do we know Chasquas is the owner of the phone?"

"First, from the content of the text messages," Hassan replied. "Ayla's going to talk about that in a minute. But also because the device was found in the hallway, where Walker fought Chasquas after circling back to save Park and Seley."

At that, Park and Seley stood to shake Walker's hand amid a round of cheers and applause. Moments like this make it all worthwhile.

Then Hassan walked back to his seat and Sami replaced him at the front of the room. They exchanged smiles as they passed.

"Now, from what I could gather from the texts," Sami said, "Delgado, Flores, and Martinez are traveling to Mexico this week to meet with a group referred to as 'the cartel.' Someone named 'Matón' will be traveling with them, which leads to the conclusion that we're up against the North County Kings and the Cartel del Norte."

Park and Walker raised their eyebrows at each other at the mention of the two gangs.

When Hassan called another image to the screen, Sami said, "This is Chucky Matón." Filling the screen was the face of a man with shoulder-length black hair. He had a long goatee and light but not white skin. "He's the head of the North County Kings, a biker gang that works for the Cartel del Norte on this side of the border. The meeting will be held in Mazatlan at some point this week. That's all I've got."

"If I may," Park said. "Walker and I had a run-in with the Cartel and the Kings five years ago. The cartel smuggles drugs and guns into the U.S., and the Kings distribute them throughout the Southwest." He turned to Rogers and said, "You should get in touch with Dom Taylor from Oceanside PD. He's working that case with DEA."

"Will do," Rogers replied. "Maybe he's free for lunch."

***

Duke's Bar and Grill was a tradition in the San Diego law enforcement community. Located across the road from the Embarcadero Marina, the crowded restaurant was furnished with heavily varnished solid-wood tables and chairs.

Hung on the walls were framed articles describing heroic police action and official photographs of officers lost in the line of duty. The bar was lined with day drinkers facing a long window with a view of the marina.

They sat at two square tables pushed together: Lynn Peters' long blond locks flowed past her shoulders onto a bright red sleeveless blouse. Rogers settled in next to her, and Park and Walker across from them, all three men in slacks and sport coats. Lieutenant Dominick Taylor, head of the Oceanside PD Special Enforcement Section and still commander of the narcotics unit, was dressed more casually, in khakis and a short-sleeved polo shirt. He was at the head of the table, completing a U-shape of public servants. Weighing in at two hundred and thirty pounds, Taylor was as big as Park, while Rogers and Walker were the same width and only an inch or two shorter, possibly explaining why the waiter was so polite and attentive.

"The North County Kings are raking it in," Lieutenant Taylor said. "After Jack Cage fell off his pool terrace"—he shot Walker a pointed glance—"the Cartel del Norte assigned them all of Cage's territory, from San Diego to Sacramento and east to the Louisiana state line."

Rogers nodded and sipped from a thick glass of ice water as he listened. Lynn plucked a French fry from his plate.

"DEA has a semi-permanent field office set up near Mazatlan," Taylor went on. "And we've been working with them for years. That's how we know that for the last twenty-four hours, one of the two cartel mansions has seen a steady stream of visitors."

"The meeting," said Park.

Taylor nodded. "Our goal is to take down the Kings and that damn cartel while we're at it, if we can. In other words, we can scratch each other's backs. If y'all want to monitor that meeting, I can offer four men, myself, two DEA agents, and a jet to take us there."

Before anyone could reply, the thundering sputter of a pack of chopper bikes drowned out the background music and the chatter of customers trying to enjoy their lunch. All four lawmen scooted back their chairs and strode through the front door out onto the sidewalk. A long train of bearded bikers grumbled by, each with the same patch on the back of his black jacket: a grinning skull wearing a crown. The North County Kings circled the block, revving their engines menacingly and glaring at Lieutenant Taylor as they passed. "We go way back," Taylor explained.

After a few minutes, the so-called motorcycle club sputtered off. Their presence had been intimidating, but it left Walker wondering. How did the bikers know they were there? Someone had made a mistake. Now it was obvious that the bad guys were being fed real-time information.

"Let's do it, Lieutenant," Rogers said once they were back at the table.

Lynn Peters held up a hand. "I need to make a phone call first. I'm sure we'll get approval, but we won't know until later today."

As anticipated, the HTTF was given the green light to fly down to Mexico, although Chief Deputy O'Connell made it clear that no weapons were to be brought over the border. And some of the Human Trafficking Task Force would not make the trip; Sami, Hassan, and Seley were assigned to other avenues of investigation.

The next morning, Rogers drove Walker and Park in his blacked-out Suburban up the coast to Oceanside PD headquarters. The massive vehicle lumbered into the strip-mall parking lot and its occupants marched into the police station at six a.m. sharp.

Over donuts and coffee, Lieutenant Taylor introduced Rogers, Park, and Walker to the four members of his narcotics unit who would be taking part in the cross-border operation. He gestured toward two veteran lawmen and a pair of younger guys. "I'd like you to meet Sergeants Moore and Erikson, and Detectives Bernstein and Eggert." All four men gave solid eye contact and strong handshakes. "Park and Walker, I'm sure you remember Special Agents Andy Stare and Lee Cowgill." For Rogers' benefit, Taylor added, "These gentlemen are with DEA's Aviation Division out of Fort Worth. Their official job title is special agent/pilot. They'll be flying us to Mazatlan, where they run a semi-permanent field office."

Stare was fair-haired and square-shouldered with a friendly smile. Cowgill was darker, with rough hands and a bushy beard. They shook hands and clapped

backs in a cheerful reunion with Park and Walker. Five years earlier, Cowgill and
Stare had flown Taylor and his team to Mazatlan, helping Park save Walker from
Jack Cage, the man who'd murdered Walker's father. In the midst of a bloody
showdown, Walker threw Cage off a cliff, which is why Taylor had shot Walker
a pointed glance when describing Cage's "fall."

***

The sixty-six-foot Dassault Falcon raced down the runway, lifted its nose, and
took flight. Once it reached cruising speed, Matt Rogers let out an anxious sigh
and reclined his brown leather armchair, glancing at Lieutenant Taylor, who sat
beside him in an identical recliner in the forward section of the main cabin. "So
you made this same trip five years ago?" Rogers asked.

"Affirmative," Taylor replied, clicking off his phone and tucking it into a
pouch on the side of his seat. "Same two pilots, same Dassault Falcon, same
short landing strip at the DEA camp. Gotta hit it just right."

That was bad news. Rogers didn't like flying under normal circumstances,
but this piece of information made him even more uncomfortable.

"I'm told you were a SWAT team commander," Taylor said.

Rogers nodded. "That's right. For a couple of years I was. But I mostly
worked vice ops, which is how I got involved with the HTTF. How about you?"

"Criminal intelligence. Lots of back-and-forth with Mexican authorities."

"So you speak Spanish."

"I do."

"I don't, unfortunately," Rogers said. "I always have to use interpreters."

With the small talk out of the way, they moved on to the mission at hand.
Taylor pulled out his phone again and showed Rogers two photographs. "This
is Toño Del Real and Armando Jimenez Sr.," he said. "The leaders of the Cartel
del Norte." He went on to relate some of the history pertaining to the Mexican criminal organization. Then Rogers paid him back in kind, sharing what
he knew about Delgado, Flores, Martinez, Chasquas, and Ana Maria Baretta.
For the rest of the flight, they discussed their overlapping investigations and

went through the tactical plan for later that day. As Cowgill initiated the final approach, Rogers tightly gripped his armrests and held his breath, hoping for a safe landing and that everything would go as planned.

***

Walker and Park sat at the aft end of the cabin, sharing a plush six-seat cluster with Taylor's men. Park was telling a story about a group of Navy SEALs on shore leave. "So I said, 'Leave it to me' and drove off!" Park howled. Walker and the narcotics officers exploded into laughter.

Park was back in his element. It was just like the old days. Which reminded him of one person who might not be in her element at the moment. He checked his phone for the time and confirmed that Carla should presently be at the controls of a helicopter, far out of her comfort zone in her first hour of flight training. He sent her a loving text that wasn't delivered just then, but the time stamp would show he'd cared at the right time. And he had.

When they came to the foothills east of Mazatlan, Cowgill began his approach to the alarmingly short landing strip. Park experienced a surge of cold dread as the pilot steeply lowered the aircraft's nose, landed hard, applied maximum braking, and came to a neat stop. After disembarking down the airstairs, he stopped to take in some familiar sights: parked nearby was a navy blue van, a red Cessna 182, and three other dusty vehicles. Half a klick away, there was a cluster of five tan-colored shelter systems, like tents but much larger, all with metal frames. The biggest one might have measured forty feet wide by eighty feet long. It was the DEA command post. That's where they geared up, studied satellite images, and went through their objectives and tactics, just as they had five years before.

It was meant to be a simple surveillance mission, yet Park was shaking from nerves. Last time, when it was over, they'd flown home in that jet with their best friend in a body bag.

13

K.I.A.

Hidden in a cluster of trees and bushes across the street from a strip mall, Murci watched Chasquas hand-roll a cigarette, smoke half of it, and flick the remainder into the parking lot. Both of the man's inked-up forearms were bandaged, Murci didn't fail to note.

"Murci Sanchez?"

In a single motion, Murci drew his gun and whipped his head around to see an enormous shaven-headed man with a sleeve of tattoos on one brawny arm. The big newcomer dropped to a crouch with his hands up, gave a disarming grin, pulled his credentials, and said, "John Seley. Sorry, I don't speak Spanish. I work with Jeff Walker. Been watching the IMBs all week. Glad to run into you, but you need to move out." Murci didn't understand very much except "Jeff Walker," but the gesture that Seley used to illustrate "move out" made his message clear.

"I am police Mexican," Murci said haltingly. It wasn't completely true, but he'd say anything to stay where he was. "My sister." He pointed across the street, unsure whether Nayeli would really be inside, but Murci had looked in all the windows at Western Nail Spa, seen that the place was empty, and followed Chasquas from there to King from a Day, so it was definitely something Murci wanted to investigate before he "moved out."

Seley frowned, grunted, and lifted a pair of binoculars to his eyes. "I like your bike," he said.

Murci looked back toward the convenience store where he'd parked. His ride looked like a miniature model alongside a speed machine he'd only seen in pictures: an 1800cc Suzuki Boulevard M109R B.O.S.S. in Glass Sparkle Black with a dash of Marble Daytona Yellow. As powerful as a car but six times lighter.

Just then, at the front of the so-called massage parlor, four heavy-set motor-cyclists barreled through the door and hopped on their choppers. They brought their bikes to life, some of them staring at Murci and Seley. One even pointed.

Murci and Seley sprinted back to their bikes. "Follow me!" Seley shouted. With a lurch they raced out of the gas station at full throttle, Murci trailing Seley by three meters and slightly to the right, matching his sharp turns as they hurtled through alleyways and cut across empty lots. Bullets snapped past and pinged into nearby obstacles. Unfortunately, the bikers seemed to know these roads as well as Seley did.

Seley and Murci rode up a ramp, crossed a short bridge, and came back down, now traveling on the same freeway but in the opposite direction. Fifty yards behind them, the four bikers followed suit, but now Murci and Seley had a decent shot. At 100 kph, Murci took his eyes off the road, rotating his torso. Both he and Seley took aim at the bikers, squeezing off several rounds as their pursuers crossed the bridge. One chopper swerved, wobbled, and bucked like a bull, throwing its rider off the overpass into heavy freeway traffic. A second biker lost control and had to lay down his bike, which was destroyed by a passing pickup.

The two remaining bikers zoomed down the ramp while returning fire, hitting Murci's bike but not his body. Murci tucked his gun back into his waistband and twisted the throttle, launching his black two-wheeler back up to its top speed of 160 kph. Seley did the same, but his bike was much faster so he pulled away. Then Murci's power started to cut in and out, forcing him to pull to the side of the freeway. The cause of the power loss was easy to spot: one of his carburetors was destroyed and leaking gas. Far ahead, Seley executed an emergency one-eighty, while Murci reached for his gun again.

"Don't even think about it," came a harsh voice behind him.

A biker, presumably the one who'd spoken, pressed the warm muzzle of a recently fired pistol into Murci's neck behind his ear. A second one relieved Murci of his pistol, then pushed Murci off his bike.

"Get up," commanded the first biker.

Murci slowly complied, hoping one of them would make a tactical mistake and leave him an opening, but the bikers knew what they were doing. While the second one covered his partner with Murci's own pistol, the first slipped an arm around Murci's neck, nearly choking him, and with his other hand he held his gun to Murci's temple.

Seley skidded to a stop and jumped off his ride, stepping slowly closer, training his pistol on the crooks, one at a time, panning between them.

The bikers didn't look worried. "Take another step and the beaner's dead!" shouted the first biker over the wind and the cars whooshing past. "Drop your gun right now!"

Seley locked eyes with Murci as he complied. Dangling his Glock with two fingers, he dropped slowly into a crouch. "Take my bike. It's yours," he told Murci in a low voice, suddenly whipping his pistol back into firing position like a gunfighter in a duel, firing twice in quick succession, first into the head of the biker holding Murci hostage and then into the throat of the other. But the other one had time to fire. He shot Seley right between the eyes at close range.

Murci watched with wide eyes as Seley crumpled to the gravel with a bleeding hole in his head.

The first biker was dead. The second was turning blue as he drowned in his own blood. Another one had been turned into several piles of bloody hamburger strewn across a six-lane highway, leaving a fourth unaccounted for. Murci glanced back and up. The last biker was standing in the middle of the bridge looking down at him through the chain link guardrail. The man was too far away to shoot accurately with a pistol, Murci knew, but he wasn't taking any chances. He strode quickly forward and pried his Sig Sauer out of the drowning man's hand. Then, after a gut-wrenching last look at the hero who'd saved his life, he ran to Seley's bike and raced back to the safety of his motel.

***

For Ayla Sami, the trip to Cumbres Casino Resort was unexpectedly pleasant. She rode shotgun as Hassan drove her away from the coast through gently rising green hills and low-lying clouds, appraising his profile out of the corner of her eye. He wasn't blessed with large muscles, but he was handsome, with great hair, intelligent eyes, and, most importantly, a kind heart.

"I bet an employee would loan me her uniform for fifty bucks," she said.

"Not a good idea," Hassan replied, driving past the portico and declining the offered valet service with a hand gesture. He headed for the self-parking lot at the rear of the premises. "Not today, anyway."

"Why not?" Sami asked.

"Let's just stick to the plan," Hassan said as he steered into an open spot. "We don't want to get anyone fired, hurt, or killed. Especially not you."

They strode back to the main casino building through midday air that was unusually cool and crisp. Once inside, they marveled at the massive lobby, which rivaled those of the best hotels in Las Vegas.

The casino had been designed to make its patrons feel as though they'd already hit the jackpot. White marble walkways cut through soft blue and burgundy carpeting, and sparkling chandeliers hung from high, ornately carved ceilings. Sami and Hassan played the slots, moving from machine to machine as they scoped out the ground floor. There were two restaurants, several high-end shops, and a theatre featuring nightly entertainment.

Sami hadn't been to a casino since she was a little girl. Gone were the buckets of quarters or nickels. Now the machines accepted bills or paper vouchers and they only paid out with vouchers. Even so, the modern game play was entertaining. With stunning HD graphics, it bore a remarkable similarity to those free telephone games that feature falling rows of icons, giving points and multipliers when rows of icons link up and explode. After dropping thirty dollars in fifteen minutes, however, Sami felt it was time to move on. "Health spa?" she suggested.

They grabbed their bags and followed the marble walkway to the rear doors. While crossing the grounds, they passed the pool area. Two guests were swimming laps and ten or so were sipping drinks in an oversized jacuzzi.

"We no have massages for one hour," a dull-eyed health spa employee told them. "Want to sit in the steam room? No charge."

Sami and Hassan eyed each other.

"That sounds lovely," Sami replied.

"Enjoy," the attendant said, handing them towels and locker keys. She picked up the phone as they headed to their respective locker rooms.

Sami had bought a black bikini just for this outing. She stepped into it and turned left and right, studying her reflection in a full-length mirror. She liked the way she looked in it, and she hoped Ali would, too.

***

Hassan's arms and legs trembled as he stepped into his swim trunks. Exhaling nervously, he tied the strings, stuffed his bag into a locker, and snapped on a combination lock, then strode determinedly to the unisex steam room adjoining the men's and women's locker rooms. When he popped open the door, an oppressive heat blasted him in the face. He stepped in and pulled the heavy door closed. He was alone. Large, stepped wooden benches were built out from wood-paneled walls. Sweating already, he climbed up to the first bench, took a seat, and went over his plan.

Sami made her entrance with a stunning smile. He could not believe his eyes. Her perfect body was completely exposed but for a few strips of black fabric. She smiled tenderly as she took a seat beside him.

Awkwardly skipping the part of the plan that included a confession of his feelings for her, he inched closer and looked into her dark eyes. They leaned in at the same time and their lips met in slow, tentative kisses until they gave in to their instincts and the steam room got much hotter. "Do you want to get out of here?" she asked between hungry kisses.

Scalding water vapor continued to billow out of a hole in the wall at an alarming rate. The actual temperature in the room had risen so high that the new couple actually had no choice but to take it somewhere else. Hassan took her hand and led her through the boiling clouds to the heavy door. He pushed on it, but it didn't swing open. Then he used both hands and shoved twice as hard. It didn't budge.

"Help!" they screamed, pounding on the door with their fists and smashing it with their shoulders, but no one came. Hassan's racing heart felt like it was being crushed in a vice. He couldn't catch a breath. Too dizzy to remain on their feet, they lay down beside each other on the scorching tile floor and held hands, locking eyes as their bodies boiled like lobsters in a pot.

***

Chasquas had given the health spa attendant clear and stern instructions not to let anyone pass, both before and after the investigators showed up, but he still kept a wary eye out as he took off the chain he'd locked around the handles on the steam room door.

He dragged the red, steaming bodies out, heaved them into a laundry cart, covered them with towels, and wiped his fingerprints off the control knobs. Then, having forgotten to do so, he uncovered the dead lovers' faces and snapped a picture for Martinez.

"We need them out of the way before we get back from Mazatlan," Martinez had told him. "I'll only pay you if you can prove that it's done."

"Fucking racist," Chasquas muttered as pushed the heavy cart through the reception area, nodding conspiratorially to the health spa employee. And that wasn't all he was feeling about his fellow lieutenant at the moment; with Carkas, Carli, and Beto missing—all three of them Honduran like he was—and the North County Kings working ever more closely with the gray-suited Mexican, Chasquas was afraid for his life.

14

— : —

THE CARTEL DEL NORTE

"Quiet," Lieutenant Taylor said. "The call's coming in."

"*Buenas tardes* and thank you for calling Neximax," Walker said into his headset in perfect Mexican Spanish. "How may I be of assistance?"

"*Buenas tardes,*" came a deep, solemn male voice on the line. "We need someone to come out and fix our internet immediately."

"*Sí señor*, we'll have a technician out there in under an hour," said Walker.

The plan was for Walker to infiltrate the Del Real mansion posing as a Neximax technician. Once inside, he'd install hidden cameras and microphones all over the estate. The Mexican Federal Police had ordered Neximax to disable the cartel's internet, prompting the crooks to make that call to report the issue. In addition, the telephone company was ordered to reroute the call so Walker could answer it, making use of his language skills while Rogers steered the DEA van toward the Mazatlan coast.

After renting two connecting rooms at a local hotel, they were met by a federal police officer who gave them three Neximax uniforms to change into. Taylor's men and Tony Park stayed behind to set up the surveillance equipment while Walker, Taylor, and Rogers climbed back into the vehicle and headed for the cartel's home base.

Rogers eased to a stop outside a massive gate, past which the van would not be permitted. He and Taylor offered Walker knuckle smacks and direct eye contact. They didn't need to tell him that if something went wrong in there, he was on his own.

When the armed guards at the gate looked in his toolbox, they failed to discover the hidden compartment containing the surveillance equipment and a pistol. They waved a detection wand over his body, confiscated his cell phone for the duration of the visit, and allowed him to pass.

"*Con permiso, señores,*" Walker said, turning to hike up the long driveway. At the top of the hill, he had a panoramic view of the fifty-acre property, which boasted a lake, an airstrip, a golf course, the main mansion, guest houses, and other outbuildings. Instead of inspiring awe, it made him sick.

Walker's pulse pounded as the enormous front door swung open. "Come in," said a large man with cold eyes and a bulge under his blazer. He showed Walker where the access points were and followed him as he worked, but, thankfully, his attention was often diverted; the house was as busy as a bus terminal, with its own staff running around as well as hired servers and suppliers making last-minute preparations, all while the hosts mingled with guests who'd already arrived. When Walker's minder had to step out of earshot to take a call, or speak to other men in bulging blazers, or deal with other issues that kept cropping up, Walker would place a tiny microphone or camera in an inconspicuous location. He feigned an inordinate amount of difficulty finding the faulty connection, giving himself an excuse to access most of the main house. When his minder's expressions of impatience and anger grew dangerously frequent, Walker asked to use the phone and had the signal restored in seconds. This earned him a thick wad of pesos, the equivalent of a two-hundred-dollar tip.

"Well?" Taylor asked as a monumentally relieved Walker climbed back into the van.

"Mission accomplished," Walker reported as Rogers drove them back to the hotel. "And lunch is on me."

As promised, Walker paid for lunch, handing the restaurant manager all the cash he'd been tipped; he didn't want to keep one peso of it. Then they settled in at the monitors, watching the guests convene at three main locations: the first hole of the golf course, where a firing range had been set up, a dining room where a buffet was laid out, and a billiards room complete with a smartly dressed bartender pouring drinks.

***

At forty years of age, Toño Del Real was the youngest cartel boss in Mexico. He was six-foot-one and weighed in at two hundred and thirty pounds. His street fight record, amassed in younger years, was thirty-one and two with eleven knockouts and twenty kills. Later, as a cartel hitman, he'd executed well over a hundred men and some women by the time he lost count. Now that his professional activities were more administrative and sedentary in nature, Del Real missed that violence and often wished for more of it in his life. Nothing else came close to the excitement of spilling blood. Del Real's right-hand man was Armando Jimenez Senior, who was older than Del Real, closer to the Hondurans' age, and his jet-black hair was obviously dyed. Jimenez Sr. had been a member of the organization since Del Real was a boy.

"How's Martinez doing?" Jimenez Sr. asked as he strolled with Del Real along a path that led from the main house to the golf course.

"Two lieutenants down, one to go. Then, of course, there's Flores and Delgado."

"Remind me why we shouldn't shoot them today."

"Plenty of reasons," Del Real replied. "But mostly because they've still got our two mil and the sale of the Castlefield Waterfront isn't final." When they came to the first hole, Jimenez Sr. set his empty glass on a roving waiter's tray and picked up a full one. "Plus, if we were to kill them today," Del Real went on, "I could be held responsible. What if we're being watched? No, I'd rather everything be done far away from here, and only at the right time."

In lieu of caddies carrying golf clubs, there were two crates of weapons nearby. Targets had been set up from twenty-five to a hundred meters from the teeing area, which would serve as the firing line. Beyond the targets, a bullet trap loomed like a prison wall. Before the activity began, Del Real wanted to get in a few practice shots. He unholstered his titanium gold Desert Eagle Mark XIX and took aim. The heavy handgun echoed all across his property, sending flocks of birds to more distant trees.

When Delgado and Flores arrived, they were surrounded by their security team. Their interest in the meeting was to make certain they'd be receiving a large influx of cash each month, the proceeds from the cartel's sale of guns and drugs in the United States. They were to launder these funds at their casino and pay them back to Del Real, less fifteen percent. It was to be a short-lived arrangement, however, since the reason Martinez was taking out the Hondurans was so that Del Real could take over the sex trafficking business and save himself that fifteen percent.

The teeing area of the first hole was where the seniormost circle of meeting attendees had been instructed to meet. When most of them had arrived, Del Real fired his gun in the air to get their attention. "Listen up motherfuckers!" he shouted. "Before we eat, we're going to have some fun." He pointed to the crates of weapons. "Take two each! One long and one short, and they're yours to keep."

Just firing his fifty-caliber into the air had made Del Real's hot blood run even hotter. In a flash, he imagined slamming in a fresh mag and murdering all his business partners. He'd have to pick them off before they reached the crates. He visualized their bloody bodies sprawled awkwardly on the grass, their mouths gaping, their stares blank. Frowning, he holstered his weapon, splashed water on his face, took deep breaths, and went back to playing the jovial host.

***

The sound of the cue ball colliding with the racked object balls reverberated in the billiards room like a gunshot in the night. Three balls dropped: two solids and a stripe.

"Nice shot," Martinez said, stepping close to whisper into Chucky Matón's ear. "This whole house is under video and audio surveillance. Be careful what you say."

Matón whipped his head around and glared at the only other person in the room: the bartender, who averted his eyes and found something to do.

"I said video and audio," Martinez hissed. "That means hidden cameras and microphones."

Matón nodded in understanding and stepped up to take his next shot. A series of strident cracks rang out as he cleared the table without affording Martinez a single opportunity. There was a real polish to his game. *Must be from so much time spent in biker bars*, Martinez reckoned.

Matón didn't celebrate the win. He didn't even smile. He slid out of his black leather jacket and hung it on a nearby chair, the short sleeves of his black T-shirt revealing his blended complexion. Half gringo, half Mexican, the leader of the North County Kings wasn't a hairy, hulking motorcyclist, nor was he a smaller man of bronze. He was somewhere in between.

Matón finally missed in their second game. Martinez chalked up his cue stick as he eyed the arrangement of balls. Then he stepped close, his voice barely audible. "I need your help. Later this afternoon we'll have to take a drive."

"How?" Matón whispered back. "Did you forget we flew here?"

Martinez removed his gray jacket and hung it on a chair like Matón had. Then he rolled up his sleeves. "You'll see," he said with a confident grin, proceeding to trounce Matón in the next four games.

The room began to fill up after lunch. Armando Jimenez Jr. sauntered in with three sturdy enforcers and a trio of dark-haired young ladies clad in dresses cut so short that Martinez didn't have to wonder whether they had panties on.

Jimenez Jr. was his father's only child. Forty years of age, he was big, with powerful hands, but his flab peeked out in places even his tailored suit couldn't hide. He must have just shown his entourage his personal vehicle since it was the topic of conversation as they came in.

"It's why I wake up in the morning," he was saying. "My pride and joy. It's armored to withstand high-powered rifles, and it's got undercarriage IED protection and run-flat tires."

***

As Walker sat monitoring the action with the rest of the team, his ears pricked up. He knew which vehicle was being discussed since he'd seen it on the video feed: the SRT formerly owned by Maldonado. Besides the accessories mentioned by Jimenez Jr., the black Jeep Cherokee SRT also sported ballistic glass, electrified door handles, a spike-drop feature, and a smoke screen device. Five years earlier, it had been a worthy adversary for Walker's supercharged Mustang. Not only that, but he'd been bound, gagged, and transported in a coffin-like compartment hidden under its second row of seats.

***

"But what's under the hood?" one of Jimenez Jr.'s enforcers asked.

"A 6.4-liter HEMI that makes 475 hp," Jimenez replied proudly, as if he'd built the engine himself. His lady friends gasped appropriately. He spent the next hour dominating every challenger who dared to lay down his minimum bet of five hundred bucks. "You lose again, Martinez," he sneered, draining his drink and setting it down.

Martinez placed his own drink on the same table, though it hadn't needed a refill since before lunch. He made a show of sadly handing the man-child a wad of dollars. Then, with feigned unsteadiness, he stumbled back to his barstool.

"Wannaplayforealmoney?" Jimenez Jr. asked with greedy eyes and a cocky smirk, quite drunk by then.

"Let's play doubles," Matón suggested immediately. He hopped off his barstool and drew a roll of bills from his boot. He and Martinez won a few, lost several, and soon the stakes were up to fifty grand, which Jimenez Jr. couldn't cover.

"I'llbetmyJeep. Itsworthseventy," Jimenez Jr. said.

Thus, in the final game of the afternoon, Martinez's eyes instantly regained their focus, his hands as steady as those of a sniper. In an attempt to distract him, Jimenez Jr. made a loud, abrupt comment just as he was about to shoot: "SoyourefromTenancingo."

"The devil's cave," Martinez replied as he lined up his shot. "The girls call it that because once they're inside, they can't get out. There's no one to help them. We're actually planning to take the bus there tonight." He sent the cue ball rolling toward the five ball at a precise ninety-degree angle, barely kissing it into the side pocket. Then he sunk the three easy shots he'd set himself up for.

"I hate riding the bus," said Matón from his stool.

This cracked Martinez up. Then he took a deep breath and banked the eight ball into a near corner pocket from across the entire length of the table, winning the game.

Jimenez didn't seem to realize he'd been had, but his enforcers did. They glared at Matón as Jimenez tossed him a car key. "Nowyoudonhavtotakethe-bus," the drunken gangster said. "Comeongirls. Mydad'llbuymeanewone." He staggered out of the room without so much as a glance or a word to anyone else.

This was one of two reasons why Toño Del Real had risen to the top at such an early age. With a grown child as his closest competitor, it was no wonder Del Real was the cartel's best hope for the future. The second reason was that he'd had his own family murdered.

***

At the golf course, waiters came and went while heavy bets were placed on shooting contests. After losing one such wager, Jimenez Sr. turned to Flores and handed over a stack of new hundreds secured by a banknote strap. "Im-sohappyforyoureagreatshot," Jimenez Sr. said with undisguised sarcasm. Flores smiled and thanked his fellow outlaw, then winked at Delgado, who'd been victorious in a similar challenge. Both Hondurans were glad they'd been keeping their skills sharp, and also that they'd opted to stay sober for the weekend. Of course, through their man on the Human Trafficking Task Force, they knew the meeting was being watched, but they were also beginning to suspect that their alliance with the Mexicans was a deadly charade. Besides the fact that Del Real and Jimenez hadn't been nearly as polite as expected for what was supposed to be a long-lasting joint venture, Carkas and Carli hadn't answered their phones in a week. This suggested that someone was taking out their men: possibly Martinez, Chasquas, Chucky Matón, or a hitman flown up from Mexico, if the cartel was responsible for it. The possibilities were numerous.

Flores and Delgado flew home with serious reservations about the Cartel del Norte. It was a quiet four-hour trip in the forward end with only their security detail in the rear. Flores cracked open a hefty tome on military strategy while Delgado poured himself a stiff drink and fell asleep in front of an action movie.

Matón and Martinez stayed behind. After a side trip to Tenancingo, they'd drive the SRT all the way back to San Diego.

But first they'd help Rogers smoke Park and Walker.

15

THE RAT

DAI Rogers had lied to Lieutenant Taylor when he said he didn't speak Spanish; it was his first language. Born to and raised by a Nicaraguan mother, Matt Rogers' real name was Matias Rodriguez. All he knew about his father was that he'd been an officer in the U.S. Navy who had cheated on his wife with Rogers' mother while on shore leave. When Rogers' mother later got in touch with the man to say she was pregnant, he sent her some money with the understanding that she would never make contact again. With those funds, she traveled to Mexico and got herself smuggled across the U.S. border in the trunk of a car. She settled in Arizona, where she gave birth to the future leader of the Human Trafficking Task Force. The rat.

***

"Stay away from her!" twelve-year-old Matias Rodriguez had shouted in as deep a voice as he could muster, fixing his stepfather in the sights of the man's own hunting rifle. Matias hadn't hated his stepdad, not much more than he disliked his own mother, but the boy had come out of his room to find the man towering over her, her eye swelling shut and blood dribbling out of her mouth.

"Put that down, boy," his stepfather said, but Matias pulled the trigger. For the past few years, his mom had been building him up as the real man of the house, describing his stepfather's unfaithfulness and abuse, saying that if anything ever happened, she'd hope Matias would step up and protect her.

It was the first time Rogers killed a man. He remembered being surprised at how much blood spewed from the man's wounds and how quickly he was gone. Two years after that incident, the police had come to their door, arresting and later deporting his mother in connection with various crimes including check fraud and drug trafficking. He never heard from her again.

As Rogers stood in the hotel room in Mazatlan with these bitter recollections, he doubted what his mother had said about his stepfather's abuse. His current theory was that she'd married the man just to get her green card, then set out to inherit his house and bank account. She'd probably loaded the rifle herself before instigating that fight.

His telephone vibrated in his pocket. Nodding to the rest of the surveillance team, he slid his cell phone out of his pocket, then stepped out of the room for privacy. The device looked deceptively simple and old-fashioned with its tiny, non-touch display, but in reality, its titanium housing hid military-grade hardware.

"*Dígame.*"

"I have good news and some very bad news," came Delgado's deep baritone. "Is the security switch on?"

"Yes."

"First the good. Seley, Hassan, and Sami are down."

"Roger that."

"Ha! Now for the very bad. Pat O'Connell and Lynn Peters just uncovered your juvenile record. They know who you are. If they haven't told Park or Walker yet, it won't be long before they do."

"Fuck."

"I'm not paying you the rest until the entire task force is down."

"Negative," replied the former leader of the HTTF. "That's not what we agreed for this contingency."

There was a long silence on the line. Supposing that Delgado was debating the matter with Flores, Rogers leaned on the second-floor railing to wait. Down at the pool, happy parents played with little children as the last rays of the sun slipped away. A teenager performed a back dive off the deck, arching his body in mid-air, slicing cleanly into the deep end.

"You win," Delgado boomed when he came back. "Take care of everything down there and we'll send the wire."

***

Delgado ended the call and made another, this time to Martinez.

"*¿Qué pasó?*"

"Security switch on?"

"Yes."

"There's been a change of plans," Delgado said. "You'll still assist Rogers but after that, you are to execute him as well."

***

Rogers was so upset that he didn't even look at Walker when the latter opened the door to let him in. Now his mission was time-sensitive; he drew a breath and ambled forward as casually as he could to where Taylor was sitting. "We've got enough to go on," Rogers said. "With these recordings, I'll be able to take down the Honduran Connection."

"And I've got proof that the North County Kings are working for the Cartel del Norte. That'll get them a federal indictment," Taylor replied, heaving himself out of his chair. "We'll get everything packed up and be ready to go by the time you get back. Sure you don't want me to go with you?"

"Thanks but no thanks. The site's abandoned. I don't think we'll have any trouble."

"Okay then."

Rogers looked to Park and Walker. "Ready guys?" he asked. "Turn off your phones in case we need to proceed with stealth. Or just leave them here."

On the flight to Mazatlan, when Taylor and Rogers had shown each other photos, discussed their overlapping investigations, and gone over the tactical plan for the present surveillance mission, Taylor had described the bloody battle that had taken place in Mazatlan five years earlier between his narcotics task force, Walker, Walker's wife, Park, Stare, Cowgill, and David Goode on one side, and on the other, several associates of the Cartel del Norte including Jack Cage and his private security force. When Taylor had mentioned that the cartel had sold the oceanfront complex where the firefight had occurred and that the site had been unoccupied ever since, Rogers had figured that a trip to the deserted property would be the perfect excuse to get Walker and Park alone. He'd shoot the detectives dead, receive his final payment from the Hondurans, and retire to the Caribbean, sipping adult beverages on white sand for the rest of his life. With this objective in mind, he'd risen from his leather seat and headed back to the aft end of the jet, where he struck up a conversation with Park and Walker about the incident. As expected, the detectives had offered to show him the site.

After a ten-minute drive from the hotel to the abandoned complex, Rogers eased the DEA van to a halt in an affluent neighborhood built on the side of a cliff. When the three men piled out of the van, they saw an eclectic mix of unfinished construction, vacant overgrown lots, and palatial homes in the bright white wash of the street lights. The fifteen-foot wall encircling the property they were about to enter was still in decent shape, though the front gate was stuck open. They switched on their flashlights and squeezed themselves through the gap in the gate. To the left, their roving beams fell on an empty guard house with broken windows and crude graffiti sprayed on the walls. Straight ahead was a circular driveway that served three clifftop residences. Rogers continued forward, but Park and Walker stayed where they were. He stopped and gave them a moment, assuming they were reliving the incident in their heads. He had to wait for Martinez and Matón anyway.

A few moments later, Park and Walker led him across the front grounds, stepping through several rainy seasons' worth of weeds and scrub before they came to the driveway and the houses. All three homes were large, modern, and finished in white stucco, but the one in the middle was a full-blown mansion.

They scaled a fence on the left side of the leftmost house, then followed a concrete walkway that took them to a sprawling pool terrace situated between the middle mansion and the Pacific Ocean. The pool was empty except for a few inches of dirty water, and what little grass remained around it was dead. They headed toward a low stone wall lining the ocean side of the property. *That would have been a terrifying drop to take*, Rogers concluded, peering down at the jagged rocks and the crashing moonlit surf. He felt he should ask a question about the incident to maintain the illusion of his interest, but when he turned to Walker, the blond detective's features were twisted with rage and tears streamed down his cheeks. Walker wasn't in a talking mood.

Park led Rogers away from the wall, training his flashlight beam on a large, reddish-brown stain on the concrete walkway. Oddly, the mark was marbled with an off-white color.

"Blood and brain," Park explained, jerking his chin toward the nearest rooftop. "A memorial to a scar-faced psychopath who also took a fall."

At that instant, the sound of a precision engine whirring to a stop reached their ears from the road outside the main gate. Park and Walker exchanged a glance and pulled their pistols.

"Plenty of pricey cars around here," Rogers said, waving away their concern. "It's probably next door or across the street. I'll go check it out. Be right back."

He jogged off before they could object.

16

HIDE AND SEEK

Walker wasn't alarmed. He agreed with Rogers that the sound of an expensive motor was not an unusual noise, considering the kind of neighborhood they were in. He certainly hadn't forgotten about the possibility of a traitor being on the task force, but he was naturally inclined to trust his team leader. If Walker suspected anyone, it was Hassan, while Park seemed more concerned about Ayla Sami.

Heavy surf pounded the rocks below as they waited for Rogers to return. They kept their pistols drawn with the muzzles pointed toward the ground. "Any news from home?" Walker asked. "I left my phone at the hotel."

Park fished his cell out of his tactical trousers, turned it on, and studied the screen for a moment, his features lit by the dim glow of the device. "Check this out," he said, passing the phone to Walker.

SELEY SHOT DEAD. SAMI AND HASSAN MISSING, THEIR CAR LEFT AT THE CASINO. ROGERS' REAL NAME IS MATIAS RODRIGUEZ, WANTED FOR MUL-TIPLE FELONIES AS A JUVENILE. CALL ASAP.

Walker handed back the phone. "If Rogers really is the rat," he said, "then the entire task force is gone except you and me. I bet he was waiting for backup and now they're here."

"We have to assume that's true," Park replied, already scanning his surroundings and tensing up for a fight. "Let's use the gate to our advantage, beat them to it if we can. You go left, I'll go right."

Walker sneaked through the shadows on the ocean side of the middle residence. As he turned the corner into an alley-like space between two houses, now heading toward the gate and the guard station, he spotted a figure coming his way through the weeds.

"There is a vehicle out there, but it's two houses down," Rogers called out, still at a distance, his pistol drawn but pointed down. "The driver got out of his car and went inside. What are you doing, Walker? Lower your weapon."

Walker saw no reason to comply. He had the advantage and wasn't about to give it up. "Make and model," he bellowed.

"Hummer H2."

That was an obvious lie. Hummer engines give off a deep grumble, Walker knew, while the motor he had heard was a higher-register scream, like that of ... an armored Jeep Cherokee SRT. "Drop it!" he commanded, sighting Rogers' center mass. "Don't come any closer!"

Rogers stopped walking, his expression strangely calm. He didn't let go of his pistol, but he didn't raise it, either.

With an echoing *crack*, a far-off shot rang out from the direction of the road, producing a searing pain in Walker's right shoulder. He flipped his Glock to his left hand, leveled it, and fired, but Rogers had flown around the corner of the middle mansion.

With his right arm dangling uselessly by his side, Walker ran after the rat as more distant shots rang out and bullets buried themselves in the ground near his feet. He figured the shooter was using night vision. Chasing Rogers to the gate, he fired as he ran, but none of the rounds struck their evasive target. Walker grunted from pain as he fit his gun's muzzle into his right armpit, seated a fresh mag, and racked the slide. This gave Rogers time to make it out to the road.

As he approached the gate, a firefight broke out on the other side. He slowed his pace. Could Park have reached the road so quickly, or were the bad guys shooting at each other? In the midst of all the popping shots, a door slammed shut and a large vehicle raced away. Walker peered through the gap in the gate, saw no threats, and squeezed himself through. It came as no surprise to see the black Jeep Cherokee SRT parked nearby and the DEA van missing. Rogers had escaped.

Suddenly dizzy and faint, Walker had to lean on the Jeep to steady himself. He turned and slid down to the gravel to keep himself from passing out.

"What now?" a distant voice called out from the other side of the SRT. Probably Matón.

"Let me think," said someone else. Martinez, Walker guessed.

Their crunching footsteps were coming closer. If they saw him, the best-case scenario would be a bullet to the head.

He'd never see Tina or Tina Michelle again.

He'd never meet Mia, the baby on the way.

Walker's mental gears whirred at maximum speed until he came up with a plan. It wasn't a great one, but he was out of time. He crawled to his feet, eased open the SRT's rear side door, got in, and quietly pulled it shut. Five years ago, the vehicle had smelled new. Now it reeked of spilled drinks and smoke. The leather upholstery was pockmarked with cigarette burns. He flipped a hidden switch, lifted the second row of seats, and climbed inside the coffin-like compartment, reasoning that Martinez wouldn't know about it, and if he did, he wouldn't think to look there.

Seconds later, he heard one of the rear doors being yanked open. There was some metal-on-metal scraping before it chunked shut again and all the locks were engaged with a subtle beep. His face felt warm and his ears were buzzing. Then, in a frightening rush, warm turned to hot and the buzz became a roar and that was the last thing he knew.

***

"Hide in there," Matón told Martinez, gesturing toward the guard house as they came through the gate. "They know who *you* are, but they won't recognize me. I'll walk in, say I need help with my car, and lead them back to you. It'll be easy for you to pick them off. Even easier since Walker's already wounded." Matón puffed out his chest and grinned triumphantly, seemingly proud of his plan, happy to have given Martinez an order for once in his life.

Incredulous, Martinez shook his head. He thought Chucky Matón might have been dropped on his head as a baby. Either that or all those beers at the biker bar had scrambled his brains. In any case, the man's reasoning was seriously flawed. "Exactly," Martinez sneered. "Walker's hit. So they wouldn't believe you even if they didn't recognize you. But they will, since they were watching us at the meeting."

Matón studied his boots and nodded sheepishly.

"Now listen carefully," Martinez went on. "The risky part is going to be the approach through the weeds and across the driveway, since the street lights will show them where we are. So we'll split up. You run around the outside of the house on the far right, and I'll go straight up the middle. Meet you at the pool."

Matón pulled his rifle's charging handle, cocking the weapon with a metallic *ker-chick*. Since both men wore ballistic vests and carried rifles with night vision scopes, Martinez reckoned they held a decisive advantage. Once the detectives were out of the way, he'd be weeks away from occupying either Flores' or Delgado's suite at the casino resort. He'd have to see the rooms for himself to decide which one he wanted.

***

"Let's try to use the gate to our advantage, beat them to it if we can. You go left, I'll go right," Park had told Walker, but, as he knew, plans often get scrapped after the first shot is fired, and that's exactly what happened. As Park crept past the pool along the concrete walkway, winding his way around the right side of the rightmost house, his trusty Sig Sauer at the ready, he heard shouting and a single gunshot. Quelling an urge to sprint across the grounds since he didn't know how many unfriendlies there were, he decided to take high ground. To his left was a side door. He shoulder-smashed it open and dashed up two flights of stairs. On the way up, he heard heavy gunfire from multiple weapons.

He burst out onto the third-story rooftop, now with a good view of the road and the DEA van speeding away. He crawled to the four corners of the rooftop, peering over the parapet to look for Walker. He didn't see him but he did spot Martinez and Matón slipping through the gate and running toward the houses in separate directions. He didn't fire, since his accuracy would be poor with a handgun at that range, and he didn't want to reveal his position if he was going to miss anyway. Instead, he sprinted back down to the ground floor. It was reasonable to assume that his enemies would continue to advance toward the pool, so instead of heading back out the side door or through the back doors to the terrace, he slipped out the front door. He ran left, past the front of the middle mansion, then past the north house all the way to the high wall surrounding the property.

His pistol leveled, he came around the corner to see a dark figure from behind. It wasn't Walker, he knew, since the man had long hair and carried a rifle. Aided by the moonlight as he approached, Park identified the enemy as Chucky Matón. He squeezed the trigger five times. When Matón went down, he scrambled forward to take the rifle, but stopped and straightened when a commanding voice rang out behind him.

"Drop your gun, detective. Hands up. Turn around, but not too fast."

When Park complied, he saw a man holding a rifle on him from a distance of about thirty feet. When the figure came closer, he recognized the man as Martinez.

"Where's your partner?" the gangster asked.

"He said he was going to visit your sister."

Martinez aimed close to Park's boots and fired. "Both of my sisters are dead. I'll ask you once more, and then I'll send you to meet them. Where is he?"

"Standing right behind you," Park retorted, but even Matón wouldn't have turned to look. He closed his eyes and wished Carla a long, happy life, hoping she'd stop taking those pills, earn her pilot's license, and find someone else. Someone who could get her pregnant.

"*¿Todo bien? ¡Escuché disparos!*" came a voice from the front gate.

Park guessed it was a worried neighbor asking if everything was all right after hearing shots fired.

At this, Martinez did whip his head around, just for a second, but that was all Park needed. He darted around the far corner of the house, which Martinez riddled with bullets, screaming as he chased Park across the pool terrace.

Park knew the complex very well. He had no trouble moving from cover to cover as he circled back to the north side of the property, where he found impressions in the dirt in place of his pistol and Matón. He cursed himself for leaving the man alive. After searching all three houses and then the grounds again, all while evading the two human traffickers, he could only hope that Walker had escaped. He hurried across the front grounds and out the gate. Thinking the crooks might have left their keys in the SRT, he tried the door handle but received an electric shock that sent him to his knees. He shook it off and ran several miles to a main street where he hailed a passing taxi.

Back at the hotel, he told Lieutenant Taylor and his men what had happened. Then, exhausted, he sat on the floor with his back to the wall, wishing he could call room service for a cold, emotion-suppressing six-pack.

"Let's start with what we know," Taylor said. "Martinez and Matón are in the SRT. Do we have any idea where they might be headed?"

Park looked up and right as he mentally replayed the entire video feed from the billiards room. "Yes, we do," he said.

17

—— • ——

THE DEVIL'S CAVE

In the early morning, the black SRT rolled in to Tenancingo, which, despite its tiny population of ten thousand residents, is the leading provider of sex slaves from Mexico to the United States. It is estimated that twenty percent of those residents are directly involved in the sex trafficking trade, an industry that generates one billion dollars per year in Mexico alone.

Between the nearest small town and his destination, Martinez counted thirteen "no-tell" motels renting rooms by the hour. Billboards advertising these establishments displayed images of very young women wearing lingerie and orgasmic facial expressions. Two blocks away from his home, a large canvas banner nailed to a wall told him and all other sex traffickers to stay away from the local girls, showing graphic photos of the vigilante justice that would befall anyone who failed to heed the warning.

Martinez knew that the conspicuous SRT had already been spotted by his lookouts. If he hadn't called ahead, it would have been reported as a suspicious vehicle, even at that early hour. "I bet you miss your bike," he said.

"Not here I don't," Matón answered from the passenger seat. "The roads are crap."

"Ever been to Honduras?" Martinez asked. "Mexican streets are paved with gold by comparison."

"So Mexico's a shithole and Honduras is worse," Matón retorted with a scowl. "Now tell me why we'll have spent forty hours in this car by the time we get back to San Diego, when we could have flown back with Flores and Delgado. You said something about valuables?"

"Remember when Jimenez told us about a secret compartment in the back? My father just died, so I have a store of cash that I need to get to SD, but I don't want the feds to find it at the border."

"I thought you meant human valuables," Matón said.

Martinez turned onto his pink mansion's driveway and glided to a stop. He couldn't have been happier that his brother would be taking his place, living there and seasoning the girls from then on. He couldn't count the number of times he'd had to take the new girls from that house, smuggle them over the border, and then drive all the way back again. It was a sixty-hour round trip. "No, not human valuables," he replied as he pushed open his driver's side door. "The compartment only fits one person."

Matón got out and stretched his arms and legs. "Wouldn't someone die down there? You know, from the heat and lack of air?"

"I think it's connected to the air conditioning system, so a person can survive down there for days."

***

But only if the driver turns on the AC, Walker lamented, lying face up in a pool of sweaty blood and piss. For the past ten hours, he'd been breathing through a crack while his wounded shoulder lit him up with pain. He'd been seconds away from crapping his tactical trousers when Martinez and Matón finally left him alone in the car. He scrambled out, concealed himself in a cluster of trees and bushes for a minute, then walked the streets hoping to catch a bus or a taxi.

The first vehicle to pull over was a Mexican police unit. Walker was beyond relieved that a fellow lawman had come to his aid.

"Are you all right, *señor*?" the officer asked through the open window of his 4x4. "You don't look too good. Uff! And you don't smell too good, either."

Walker cracked a weak smile. "Actually, I could use some help, *oficial*. My name's Jeff Walker and I'm a police detective in the United States. I've been shot."

The officer hopped out. "But your Spanish is so good," he said while inspecting the bloody wound.

"It's a long story," Walker replied, producing his badge.

"My name's Officer Timoteo De la Torre and you need a doctor. Come on, I'll take you."

***

After lunch, Martinez's brother brought out two duffel bags full of dollars. When Martinez went outside to store them in the hidden compartment, he stopped and stared at the bloody mess, deducing that Walker or Park—probably Walker since he was wounded—had joined him and Matón on the trip. *And he's probably still in town,* Martinez figured, pulling out his phone.

***

"Copy that," said Officer De la Torre into his cell phone, clicking it off as he drove along.

Beside him, Walker groaned. He hoped his shoulder wouldn't need reconstructive surgery.

Soon the big pickup jolted to a stop outside the police station. Four officers filed out the front doors. It took all of them to drag Walker inside.

"Don't worry. You won't be here for long," De la Torre said, relieving Walker of his Glock, his wallet, his badge, and his phone. Then he shoved Walker into a holding cell and slammed the door with a resounding clang. The cell was one of four in a back hallway, two on each side. Every detainee had brown skin, mostly of the dark variety. Walker's cell held four men. One eyed him warily, another with malice, and the third paid him no attention as Walker took a seat, leaned over, and lapsed into unconsciousness on the concrete floor.

"Get up *cabrón*. Time to move," someone said, prodding Walker in the ribs with a heavy, dusty boot.

Walker blinked his eyes open and wondered how long he'd been out.

"De la Torre told us that Alonso Martinez is on his way," the man said as he helped Walker to his feet. "Supposedly to take you to the hospital, but no one thinks that's true. Do you know who Martinez is?"

"I do," Walker replied. "Unfortunately." His gaze darted past the iron bars toward the front of the small-town station. De la Torre and several officers were sweeping and straightening things up. Their biggest donor was about to arrive.

"The name's Mauricio but my friends call me Banchis," said the man, offering a powerful, leathery hand. He looked about Walker's age, though his face was prematurely lined. His skin was rough and dark from hard, outdoor labor.

"Jeff Walker. I have to get out of here or I'm dead."

***

Park was fluent in Korean but knew no Spanish. Lieutenant Taylor, on the other hand, spoke the local language passably and had several contacts on the Mexican Federal Police force. When Park had searched his memory and said that Martinez and Matón were headed for Tenancingo, Taylor had requested authorization for Cowgill and Stare to land at an airstrip close to that small town. Two hours later, when they clomped down the airstairs, a pair of federal officers was waiting to escort them into the devil's cave.

***

"You're dead then," Banchis replied. "Because these pigs won't let you out, especially since they know Martinez is coming for you."

Walker bristled at the derogatory term, but he knew Banchis was right. The best time to try something would be after he was let out and before he was shoved into a car.

Banchis' indigenous features were distinctly Asian. As always, Walker was struck by such clear evidence of the ancient migration from that far-eastern continent to the one he was on. And it was so hot in that stinky cell that he jokingly reasoned that once the Asians got there, they'd wished they'd never come. "Your accent's not Mexican," he said.

Banchis shook his head. "Honduran."

"What are you doing up here, then?"

"I was looking for Martinez, actually, but I got picked up for stealing."

"And now he's coming to you."

Banchis nodded glumly. "My uncle searched for his missing sister for forty years, and just a month ago he found out who took her. Before that kidnapper took his last breath, he gave us the name and location of the person who'd paid him to do it. Miguel Angel Martinez, Alonso's father."

As Banchis said the words, his features twisted with wild-eyed rage. Walker suspected that the man who'd taken Banchis' aunt had suffered a slow and painful death, either at Banchis' or his uncle's hands. Or both. While his mind was on missing sisters, he wondered about Murci and Nayeli, hoping that the former was making progress and that the latter was okay.

Banchis slid a yellowed family portrait out of his back pocket. "My uncle was too old to make the trip so he sent me. Look," he said. "That's me as a baby, there's my uncle, and that's my aunt."

"I don't recognize—" Walker started to say, but he whipped his head around when the front doors of the station were thrown open and Martinez and Matón strode in. The local police fell in line behind them and the group headed straight for the holding cells, forming a semicircle on the far side of the bars with Martinez in the middle.

"Jeff Walker," the gray-suited mobster said with a smirk. "Pleasure to finally meet you."

"The pleasure is all yours," Walker replied. When he thought about how many young girls this slick pervert must have violated over the years, he gripped the iron bars with both hands and rattled the door as he stared the crook down. This caused a lightning bolt of pain to shoot from his wound to his brain. He had to hold on tight with his good hand to stay on his feet.

Martinez's dark eyes danced with amusement and his lips curled into a mocking grin. Banchis ran forward to grab him through the bars but the mobster took a smooth step back.

"*¡Hijo de tu puta madre!*" Banchis shouted, rattling the bars even harder than Walker had.

Matón put his hand on his holster but a glance from Martinez stopped him.

"And you are?" Martinez asked calmly, turning his smirk on Banchis.

"I am looking for my aunt, Maria Solorio Pardo. You'd better hope you don't know her."

Martinez's cruel grin widened. "Actually, the name does ring a bell." He nodded to De la Torre. "This one doesn't need medical treatment, per se, but a psychiatrist might do him some good. I'll take him, too."

De la Torre produced a heavy ring of keys. "Walker and Banchis, turn around with your hands behind your backs," he barked. "The rest of you line up along the back wall." He snapped handcuffs on Walker and Banchis through the bars. Then, covered by two other officers with guns drawn, he unlocked the cell door and turned the pair of prisoners over to Martinez and Matón, who led them out of the building into the blinding sunlight.

"Walk to the Jeep," Martinez said. As Walker and Banchis trudged along with their hands cuffed behind their backs, he and Matón followed them at a safe distance with pistols leveled.

Walker's squinting eyes guessed the distance to the SRT at thirty yards. It was now or never, but what could they do? If they ran, they'd be shot. If they tried to fight, they'd be shot. If they did nothing, they'd be shot later.

Banchis looked as desperate as Walker felt. "If you find my aunt, tell her about my uncle and me," he said.

"I will," Walker promised, with little hope that he would live to meet the woman. As they neared the SRT, he resisted the impulse to throw a back kick, thinking he might be able to break Martinez's leg just as the man had done to Lulu. Then Walker would snap each of the asshole's dirty fingers; he'd never touch a girl again.

A pair of federal police cruisers sped into the parking lot and ground to a halt. Four men piled out with rifles leveled, including Park and Taylor.

With the immediate reaction of a pair of crooks always ready to run, Martinez and Matón sprinted to the safety of their truck. Gravel pelted Walker's legs as the black Jeep tore out of the parking lot, heavy rounds slamming into the side of its armored panels.

The two federal lawmen chose not to pursue them. Instead, they radioed for assistance and took De la Torre and his men into custody. In the commotion, Banchis slipped away with a wink and a grin.

"Better to get your shoulder treated back home," Park told Walker once they were airborne and six hours from San Diego. He popped a cold can of beer. This time they occupied the forward recliners while Lieutenant Taylor and his men sat in the plush cluster of seats at the aft end.

"Mexican medical care is not that bad," Walker replied, holding an ice pack on his shoulder. "At least most people have access to health care, even if they do have to wait in line for days to get it."

As Park drained can after can, Walker recounted his experience. Then Park described what had happened on his end since the two of them had split up.

Park extended his fist. "You had me worried for a minute, partner."

Walker smacked Park's knuckles. "Thanks for coming to get me, bro."

18

MURCI TURNS NIGHT INTO DAY

With six new arrivals and six already there, the girls at King for a Day were sleeping two to a tiny room and eating half rations. At breakfast, all twelve were crammed shoulder-to-shoulder around a long plastic table. As punishment for non-compliance, two hadn't been served. They'd be eating dinner only and doing extra chores until Doña Mari decided they'd learned their lesson.

"Here," Nayeli said, pushing her untouched half bowl of beans toward her hungry friends. "I can't eat."

"You'll be fine," Cristi said. "Try to relax and it'll be over before you know it."

"Hurry the hell up!" Doña Mari yelled, hobbling into the room with the help of a cane. She was about Mama's age, but thinner. She'd pulled her gray hair back into a bun.

"She run away from pimp," Kati whispered. "Long time ago. He broke her leg with bat."

The girls finished quickly and rose to get ready for their morning sessions, all except Nayeli. While the two punished girls cleared the table, she put her head down and tried to take slow breaths. In a question of minutes, she would have to go all the way for the first time.

"*Sí señor*," said Mama into her phone as she entered the room. A male voice shouted at her on the other end of the line. "I will," she muttered, tears collecting in the corners of her eyes. She clicked off and made her way to the kitchen, returning with a bowl and a spoon. Then Mama plopped into a plastic chair across from Nayeli, who took another look at the big, hopelessly dejected woman and figured that's what she was going to look like after forty-five years in this business. If she lived that long.

"Are you okay?" Nayeli asked, with a measure of real concern. After getting to know her over the past few weeks, she'd realized the woman wasn't all bad.

Mama nodded, staring down at her meal as if it were a bowl of diarrhea. "It's my boss," she said, breaking her English-only rule by speaking to Nayeli in their native language. She wiped her cheeks dry. "He treats me bad sometimes, like Beto did to you."

Nayeli balked at the mention of her former handler. She felt better now that he was gone. Mama said nothing, her gaze downcast, her cold beans still untouched.

"And you, Nina?" the madam asked after a minute. "You going to be okay today?"

"I just want to go home."

"That will pass," Mama assured her, but the look in her eyes suggested that after half a century, her own desire to escape hadn't faded in the least.

Chasquas stuck his head into the room. "Your client's here, Nina," he said, his features intense. "Why aren't you ready? Dammit girl, he paid thirty times the normal rate!" With the family resemblance and the crude tattoos on his arms, hands, and face, Chasquas looked like a larger incarnation of his late cousin.

Mama patted Nayeli on the back, and the girl rose to her feet and followed Chasquas to the reception area, where her gaze fell on a man with greedy eyes. He attempted a disgusting smile that she couldn't have returned even if she'd wanted to.

"Well?" Chasquas snapped. "You know what to do."

Nayeli took the man's hand and started up the stairs just as the front door banged open. Chasquas turned to greet a man he must have assumed was a customer, but Nayeli knew better.

It was Murci.

"Nayeli!" her brother shouted, shoving past Chasquas, but the lanky Latino grabbed his arm and spun him around. "That's my sister, *cabrón*!" Murci roared, grabbing Chasquas by his shirt and slamming him into the wall.

Chasquas stayed calm and spun out of the hold, launching into a flurry of lefts and rights as Murci reached under his shirt. Murci took several punches on his mouth and chin before he brained Chasquas with a pistol, toppling him like a chain-sawed pine.

Murci bounded toward the stairs, but he was stopped by a deafening blast and a resulting hole in the wall behind him. Doña Mari stood in the open archway with a smoking shotgun leveled. She racked it with a metallic *click-clack* and blew another hole in the wall, then pumped the weapon once again. "Drop your gun and get the fuck out of here!" she shouted.

Murci complied with both demands. He met Nayeli's gaze before leaving. She knew he'd be back.

To Nayeli's extreme relief, the customer demanded a refund and left without getting what he'd come for. Thirty minutes later, however, three burly men bounced their bikes into the parking lot outside. Two stayed by the door and the other one went in to get her. He followed her out to his ride. "Sit down, hang on, and shut up," he growled.

They sped away from that awful place, which was exactly what Nayeli had been wishing for, but how would Murci find her now?

She hoped she wasn't being taken somewhere worse.

***

That evening, Doña Mari laid her cane on the table and eased herself into a seat across from Mama. Late evening at the brothels was always quiet, the girls physically and emotionally exhausted and the madams relieved to have made it through another crazy day. For the two brothel managers, every sunrise brought some unexpected confrontation or problem, and they'd been in the business for fifty years. If the girls were tired, they were dead on their feet.

"Flores sends his best," Mama informed her colleague reluctantly.

Doña Mari beamed at Mama cruelly, but the lines on her face soon faded back to their unhappy shape.

"He also said that starting tomorrow there'll be no more regular sessions, VIP only," Mama went on.

"Until when?"

"Until he gets things straightened out. Two weeks maybe."

"That's good news," Doña Mari replied, cracking open a diet soda. "By the way, Chasquas wants to party. Want to come?" A vulgar smile crept across her lips.

In Mama's opinion, it wasn't proper for Mari to be "partying" with a much younger man. She began to imagine her colleague's gnarled hands performing massage therapy on Chasquas' lower body. That led her to wonder whether he had any tattoos down there. *Probably not*, she concluded with a trace of a smile. "No, thank you," she replied primly as she rose, heading into the kitchen with her dishes.

"Your loss," Doña Mari called out. She grabbed her cane and went upstairs.

Mama switched off the lights. She was glad that she'd have Mari's room to herself for a while. As she headed for the stairs, she heard the popping grumble of motorcycles outside, but she wasn't worried. After that morning's incident, there'd be two men stationed by the door at all times. It was probably the end of the first shift, time for another pair of enforcers to stand guard.

***

Murci was kneeling in the same spot as when he and Seley had watched with binoculars from across the street. It had been a mistake to tell Chasquas that Nayeli was his sister. Now they'd probably moved her. Maybe they'd moved all the girls. He watched the two men guarding the door, wondering how he and Seley had been spotted last time, since with the trees and the bushes and the distance between them and the door, it would have been next to impossible to see them. Then he remembered having exchanged a glance with a shifty-eyed convenience store attendant when he and Seley had run back to their bikes and roared off to the freeway. Good thing he'd parked farther away this time. Plus, now it was dark and he wore a black jacket and dark jeans.

He'd made the necessary preparations, and now it was time to strike. Murci strode across the street in the crisp night air, his features twisted into a homicidal scowl. Slipping unnoticed between points of cover, he skirted around the edges of the strip mall until he was on the far side of the two sentries' bikes. This was the tricky part, or one of the tricky parts, he reckoned, unscrewing the valve stem cap on a tire. He let the air out slowly, praying he wouldn't attract the guards' attention. He didn't; as they leaned against the wall by the door, smoking and talking, they gazed straight ahead.

Murci retraced his steps through the parking lot and crossed the street again. He straddled Seley's bike and fired her up with the touch of a button. He made the sign of the cross and stomped the massive motorcycle into first, then let out the clutch and sped across the deserted road. When he bounced into the strip mall, he toed the machine into higher gears. The cold wind buffeted his body with increasing force as he shifted into fourth and fifth. Now he was flying, roaring past the pair of sentries, who scrambled onto their bikes and took off after him.

One of them didn't get very far.

The other chased him through the streets, nimbly matching his full-speed turns, but Murci cut into a dead-end alley, quickly killing the engine and slipping into an unlit alcove. When his pursuer followed him in, the man continued all the way to the dead end, braking to a stop in a large puddle that looked like water.

Murci stepped out of hiding and showed the man a lit Zippo lighter. "They move my sister?" he yelled, his face hot.

The crook held his hands up in surrender. It didn't take him long to decide what to say. By then he must have smelled the pool of gasoline he was parked in. "Yes."

"Tell me where or go to hell!" Murci screamed.

"The Castlefield Waterfront Hotel."

"Pass me the gun."

The trembling man did as he was told, setting his weapon down and kicking it over to Murci, who now had a tough decision to make: should he go back on his word and burn the man alive, thereby increasing his odds of saving his sister, or should he keep his promise and let the guy go? Unfortunately for the enforcer, Murci had run out of kindness and understanding by the age of twelve, and for all he knew, part of this guy's pay might be taking advantage of his sister. He tossed the lighter into the moonlit puddle and night whooshed into day. The screaming biker dropped to his hands and knees and blazed like a log.

Murci didn't look back as he sped away, but he did feel the explosion on his back when the gas tank ignited. He checked his rear-view mirror. A brilliant orange cloud bloomed upwards in the night sky. He accelerated around a winding on-ramp, heading south on I-5 back to the motel, still shaking from the adrenaline spike. This new machine wasn't as nimble as his old bike, but it had four times the power and didn't weigh much more. As he brought it up to speed, he was reminded of the brave man who'd left it to him. He'd never forget Agent Seley.

After two violent confrontations in one day, it took Murci several hours to fall asleep. As he tossed and turned, his mind took him back two years.

"Make me proud, son," his father had said, handing over what was left of his savings. Then Murci had nodded grimly and boarded a bus. When he arrived in Mexico City, he was taken to a private home instead of the U.S. Embassy for his picture to be taken. That should have been his first clue.

Streetwise but not yet worldly, Murci smiled proudly at the phony work visa he was handed an hour later. Then, along with a truckload of other desperately poor young men, he was driven across the border to North Carolina where he was made to build houses six days a week, twelve hours a day, rain or shine. And there was a lot of rain.

The one good thing about the job was that he always slept well, even if it was in a dormitory crowded with irritable peers. But the negative aspects of his situation far outweighed that one good thing: fees for breakfast, water, electricity, and taxes were deducted from his pay. If he wanted dinner, that came out of his pocket, and the same went for soap, razors, toilet paper, medicine, and anything else he might need.

At the end of the first week, his foreman, who was also Mexican, shot him a guilty look as he handed over thirty dollars. That remorseful flicker in his boss's eyes was the one thing about him that wasn't fake.

"That's it?" Murci exclaimed. "I worked sixty hours."

"It would have been more if you'd been here the whole week," the foreman replied.

The only day Murci had missed was the day he'd arrived. "What can I do?" he blurted out, now alarmed.

"If you mean running away," the foreman replied, "I don't recommend it."

The dormitory was located in a fenced-in complex, with a daunting amount of guards, guns, and dogs all around. He could try to make a run for it while at the construction site, but he'd heard horror stories about guys who died trying. And his passport and visa had been taken, supposedly for safekeeping. This left Murci with no safe choice but to keep building houses for fifty cents an hour, but that wasn't going to work, either. After the transfer fee and what he needed to spend on himself, he'd be sending home six hundred pesos a month, the cost of one of his father's doctor's visits.

"There is one thing you can do to earn some extra cash," the foreman said without skipping a beat. "On Sundays. But it's a little bit dangerous."

"I'll do it," Murci said. "I don't care what it is."

19

— · —

THE HEIR TO THE THRONE

The vista through the conference room windows was gloomier than ever before; the bay could not be seen through so much fog, and the chilly wind seemed to pass straight through the glass. Most of the eyes in the room were red and puffy. Park's were bloodshot and his head was killing him. He knew he reeked of liquor. It was then that he admitted to himself that he needed help. *Only when you're ready to help yourself,* his inner voice replied.

In the open doorway, Chief Deputy DA Pat O'Connell offered his hand to Lieutenant Taylor and to Taylor's detective sergeants, Moore and Erikson. He motioned toward the golden oak conference table occupied by Park, Walker, Lynn Peters, and someone new: Sean Choi. Choi was a technology analyst who'd been working on Hassan's team at the Sheriff's Department, and years ago he'd worked for Oceanside PD.

Except for the newcomers, everyone wore black, having come straight from Hassan's and Sami's funeral. Seley's would be held in his home state. "Good morning," O'Connell began as everyone settled into their chairs. "It wouldn't feel right to start without a moment of silence."

All eyes fell on the three flower bouquets set on the table in front of three empty chairs.

"Thank you," O'Connell said after a time. "As most of you know, there's a federal warrant out for Rogers' arrest. Any contact with the fugitive is to be made by or through the U.S. Marshals Service. I cannot stress that enough. No

one is to communicate with him without authorization. Are we clear?" Affirmative murmurings followed. "Good. Now, I know you're all wondering about
the future of the task force." O'Connell paused for a beat. "I am too." That got a
few laughs. "But we will proceed until instructed otherwise. Lieutenant Taylor
and his men have offered to pick up the investigative slack, while Sean Choi will
take over for Hassan. Are there any questions or objections?"

No one had any. Especially not Park, whose muddled mind swirled with
memories of Agent Seley. Yet another brother-in-arms killed in the line of duty.
Seley's death was one of the main reasons he'd stayed up late trying to drown
his feelings. A tear slid down his face as he stared at the empty chair across
from him. That's where Seley had been sitting when they'd argued over whether
MARTAC or BORTAC would be the better team to send in.

At a nod from Chief Deputy O'Connell, Sean Choi's current supervisor, and
another from Lieutenant Taylor, his former employer, Choi called his laptop
display to the overhead screen. His black hair was shorter than it had been five
years before, but it was no less disheveled, and he had that same sleepy look as
though he'd been up all night hacking away at the computer. "Morning, all,"
he said from his seat. "DDA Peters has briefed me on the case and I've gone
through all of Ali's notes. So I'm more or less up to speed, but stop me if there's
anything I need to know. First, we've finished going through the cloud data
from Chasquas' phone." He brought up his first slide, which contained two
columns of text messages. The word *Castlefield* appeared many times, usually
abbreviated as *C, CF,* or *CFW,* with a red circle drawn around each instance.
Then he hit a key, causing blue circles to appear around other words such as
Toño, Del Real, DR, and *cartel.* "We're still trying to track down the Castlefield's
current owners," Choi said, "but the property records are nebulous. The hotel
is still in the process of being sold." Then he pulled up a set of documents,
displaying them one by one as he spoke. "However, we were able to dig up
permits for recent construction work, signed by attorneys based in Mazatlan.
The renovations included several high-tech, high-budget security features." The
last of the digital documents was an invoice listing cost items including an access
control entryway and a panic room. "So the Castlefield Waterfront Hotel ap-

pears to be the Cartel del Norte's new headquarters on this side of the border," Choi concluded. "As for the casino resort, we've confirmed that its title is held by the same group of related shell companies as the IMBs and the crematorium."

"So now we know where the two gangs' home bases are," Taylor said. "We're going to need multiple SWAT teams."

"There's Thunder Road, too," Walker put in. "The biker bar. So that makes three home bases. But why are the Hondurans and the Mexicans working together in the first place? I wouldn't expect any cooperation between them."

"Maybe they're stronger together than they are apart," Park suggested lamely. "Laundering the profits at both hotels in case one gets shut down."

"Could be," Taylor replied. "But I think the cartel doesn't really want to join forces."

"I agree," Lynn Peters said. "Let's look at it this way: what does each group stand to gain from the partnership?"

"The Hondurans benefit from the cartel's larger cash reserve," Walker said. "That much is clear."

"OK, but what's the cartel's interest?" Peters returned. "They're already in league with the North County Kings, so why would they want to share secrets and profits with another small, local gang?"

The room fell silent.

"Exactly," Peters said. "They don't. They're planning to take over the Hondurans' prostitution business."

"Exactly," echoed Taylor, holding Peters' gaze for a moment. Their eyes smiled at each other even if their faces stayed grim.

Walker leaned back in his chair and crossed his arms over his chest. "So let's assume Del Real is about to take out the Honduran Connection. Or he's already in the process. He'd need someone on the inside before and after Delgado and Flores go down."

"Martinez," said Taylor. "The only Mexican in the Honduran gang."

"More importantly, the cartel still needs the Martinez family to supply them with human capital," Walker added. "Or sex slaves, though I hate to say it like that."

Several heads nodded.

"So Del Real's plan must be for Martinez to run the Hondurans' old operation for him," O'Connell said from the head of the table. "Let's talk about next steps."

"If Ayla were here, she'd remind us to keep our focus on the victims," Peters said, her blue eyes intense. "The most important thing is to save Nayeli Sanchez and the other girls."

"Where are they?" O'Connell asked. "King for a Day?"

"Nayeli's been moved," Walker said. "We know she was taken to the Castlefield, but we're not exactly sure where they're keeping her. The rest of the girls will probably be taken there as well now that King for a Day is blown." Walker went on to identify his source as Murci Sanchez, recounting how the young man had burst into the IMB, seen his sister on the stairs, fought Chasquas, and narrowly avoided being blasted in the gut.

"Do we have probable cause for the Castlefield?" Park asked, rubbing his temples.

"Not yet," Peters answered. "For the judge to sign the warrant, we need all the evidence collected in Mazatlan transcribed and translated by certified linguists."

"That could take weeks," Taylor said. "But the Castlefield's a public place. We can look around and talk to employees."

Everyone began to speak at once, but O'Connell held up a hand. "Lynn and I have already gone back and forth on this," he said over the din as they all quieted down. "Above all else, we need to build a solid case. So here's what we're going to do: Lynn and I have to meet with the marshals. Taylor, Moore, and Erikson, check out King for a Day and Thunder Road. Park and Walker, you've got the Castlefield Waterfront." He buttoned his blazer as he stood. "Let's see what shakes loose. Something always does."

***

"We have to assume that the task force has identified all of the massage parlors," Delgado said nervously. "The casino too." He and Flores occupied twin armchairs in his library at the Cumbres Casino Resort. The room was identical to the one in Flores' suite, except for the titles of the books on the shelves. "*Pinche* Rogers," he groaned. Flores pursed his lips and nodded in angry agreement.

As Matias Rodriguez, Rogers had been hired by the Hondurans when he'd moved from Arizona to California. He was a tough kid who'd started out as a soldier like Beto, but he was also bilingual and highly intelligent, so they'd bought him a new identity and helped him through high school and the police academy. Along with Rick Rivera, this gave them two powerful allies on the right side of the law.

Flores and Delgado enjoyed many lucrative years with Rogers as a vice detective and then head of vice, but lately the relationship had gone sour. Rogers had begun to question the morality of sex trafficking. This was a deal-breaker, of course, so it was agreed that their long-standing cooperation would cease after the merger with the cartel was complete. Yet things had gotten out of hand since that agreement was made, with several verbal altercations in which both sides had threatened the other with death.

At first, when Delgado had ordered Martinez to kill Rogers, he'd thought it was a good move, but now he realized it had been a mistake. And it had been especially foolish to trust Martinez and Matón with such a critical task.

Delgado's valet brought out a badly needed whisky and water for him and a gin and vodka martini for Flores.

"The Maras have agreed to send us twenty-five men," Flores said, savoring a sip from his cold martini glass. "Chasquas is looking for a couple of houses here in the valley."

Despite the powerful air conditioning, Delgado's forehead was dotted with beads of sweat. "Excellent," he replied, then downed half his drink and closed his eyes to take a breath.

"You know he's going to come for us," Flores said.

Delgado's eyes flew open. "I know. That's what I'd do," he said. "Who was the *pendejo* who shot at him before Walker and Park were down? Martinez or Matón?"

Flores shook his head to say he didn't know.

"Speaking of taking shots, it has to be the cartel that's paying someone to pick off our men," Delgado said. "But I don't think it's Rogers."

"I agree, and I'm ruling out Chucky Matón," Flores declared. "Both Carli and Carkas would have eaten that idiot for breakfast. If you ask me, it's either Chasquas or Martinez." Flores rose and crossed the soft crimson carpet, coming to a stop at a floor-to-ceiling window with a view of the valley and the distant mountains. He appeared to be lost in thought. Then he turned back. "I think it's Martinez," he said.

A modern bell tone sounded. As Flores went back to his armchair, the security team let in the Hondurans' most trusted lieutenant. They'd been working with the Martinez family for thirty-five years, and Alonso Martinez was the pride of that clan. The heir to the throne.

Once Martinez took a seat on a nearby settee, Delgado leaned in and leveled a withering gaze on him. "I don't trust you, Alonso," he said. "Swear to me you're not on Del Real's payroll."

Martinez flew to his feet with indignance. Delgado also rose. Flores stayed seated, but drew a pistol just in case.

"I swear I'm not on Del Real's payroll," Martinez echoed, backing out of the suite with his eyes on his former employers.

20

_— • —_

A HARD LESSON TO LEARN

M artinez and Matón rode the elevator in uneasy silence up to their new penthouse megasuite in the Castlefield Waterfront Hotel. The renovations were now complete, meaning the construction workers were long gone, both figuratively and literally, since anyone privy to the specifics of the new security system had been executed and cremated. They strode out of the lift into a short hallway that led to a single blast-proof door, the first of two. Martinez waved a key card across a sensor where a handle or knob would usually be. It slid open and they stepped into an anteroom just big enough for the both of them. Once the door had glided shut, Martinez held his eye to an interface that scanned his iris, then spoke his full name and a passphrase. Matón went through the same routine and only then did the second door vanish into the wall. They made their way through a carpeted corridor to reach a vast sitting room that had once been a six-hundred-dollar-a-night suite. As Matón admired the sparkling view of the bay, Martinez picked up the phone to order their breakfast.

***

Murci pushed a loaded service cart into the same access control entryway, waiting anxiously to be let in to the megasuite. When the second door slid open, a man with a long goatee and a black leather jacket inspected his cart and patted him down. Murci was beyond relieved that the biker had failed to find the two tiny microphones he'd taped under his sleeves, though it disturbed him to see, as the man led him down a carpeted hallway, that the patch on his jacket was the same one worn by the bikers who'd killed Agent Seley.

Buying the listening devices had been easy. Using them for illegal eavesdropping, however, was a different matter, one that Detective Walker had warned him against. But Murci wasn't worried about the bad guys pressing charges. If all went well, he and Nayeli would soon be back in Mexico. If not, he'd be dead.

An hour earlier, Murci had found his way to the hotel's kitchen and explained his situation to a waiter, a fellow Mexican, handing the man five crisp hundreds. Now he wore the Castlefield's wait staff uniform: black pants, a white dress shirt, a black bow tie, a crimson jacket, and a name tag identifying him as Horacio.

The sitting room was gigantic. It boasted a one-hundred-and-eighty-degree aerial view of the bay. Morning sunlight glittered on the sea as white yachts cruised lazily by. Forty floors down, a marina was full of boats, while Coronado Island lay straight ahead.

And there he was: Gray Suit, with his cruel mouth and slicked-back hair. His sister's handler lounged regally on one of several black leather sofas, his eyes on the glittering bay and both arms draped over the backrest. He didn't look up as Murci came in. As the biker settled onto a nearby couch, Murci uncovered the plates and set them on a coffee table between the men. "Enjoy," he managed through clenched teeth. With a sideways flit of his eyes, he saw Gray Suit appraising him curiously, as if the slick killer had recognized his waiter but didn't know where from. Murci went about his work as his heart pounded like a bass drum and Gray Suit eventually turned his attention to his omelet.

As the human traffickers were busy with their food, Murci was able to slip one listening device under the coffee table and another into the folds of a sofa.

"Wait a minute," Gray Suit said, springing to his feet.

Murci froze. At least he'd tried. Nayeli would always remember that.

"Your tip." Gray Suit handed over a folded pair of one-dollar bills.

"Thanks," Murci muttered, turning to push the cart out of the room. He wasn't bothered by the insultingly small gratuity; he still had thousands of Gray Suit's dollars back at the motel.

***

After breakfast, Martinez and Matón took a call from Toño Del Real, whose deep voice bellowed through the speakerphone. As usual, his words were carefully chosen, spoken in general terms as a kind of code.

"Let me know as soon as you take delivery," Del Real said. "And I want the beauticians and their managers taken to the basement." By "delivery" he meant the laundered two million minus the Hondurans' fifteen percent, and "the basement" was the living quarters just built in a subterranean part of the Castlefield. "They'll stay there until we get the new beauty centers set up, and some of them will remain after that time."

"Understood," Martinez replied, aware that the Castlefield would be offering its own call girls to VIPs. Including himself, obviously.

"I don't suppose you've taken care of the final lieutenant."

"Not yet, boss."

"I want that done by Thursday. That's when we're arriving, and you will pick us up."

"Okay. What's the plan?"

"We'll hit the casino very early Sunday morning. I suppose our rivals are holed up in their suites with heavy security all around?"

"They are."

"No problem," said Del Real. "Deregister all their men from your security system so they can't get in to the megasuite. We're also going to need weapons and demolition materials. Write this down."

***

Tina's and Carla's footsteps clicked and clacked on a polished concrete floor as they strode through a wide corridor to a door that led outside. "You got this," said Tina, pushing the door open. The pungent odor of gasoline blew in on a chilly wind.

"Thanks for doing this," said Carla, squeezing Tina's shoulder. "I really appreciate it." Then she headed out to her first solo helicopter flight.

Tina was so concerned about her current predicament that she had to double back several times as she wound her way to the aviation academy's cafeteria. She bought a cup of coffee and perched herself on a stool at a window with a good view of the airfield, watching Carla lift off, gain altitude, and gradually disappear. Only then did she allow herself to focus on the problem at hand, so intently that she forgot about her coffee and let it go cold.

When she and her cousin Toño were children, they had played together in San Diego and Mazatlan when their fathers went to visit each other. She, he, and all the other cousins would build sandcastles and play frisbee on the beach. Later, it was surfing, swimming, beers, and brawls. Then it was drugs and guns.

"I'm worried about you," Tina had told Toño one day when they were seventeen.

Del Real didn't reply. He just kept walking down the beach while she gaped at his bruises and scars.

"Okay, I'm more than worried. I'm scared," she admitted. "I watch the news. I know what you guys do and how risky it is."

"Don't worry about me," he replied. "I'm loving every minute of it."

In the following years, the two families drifted apart for a variety of reasons, not least of which was that Tina's father objected to his brother's involvement in what was then the Sinaloa Cartel. But Toño stayed in touch with Tina, wishing her happy birthdays and checking in. Deep down, she'd always known that something was wrong with him, but her sense of family loyalty kept her from severing ties, and later from telling her husband about him. Jeff only knew that she had wealthy relatives in Mexico.

Two weeks prior, when Tina had made the mistake of telling Toño that Jeff had been asked to join the Human Trafficking Task Force, a normal relative might have offered congratulations or sent a gift basket, but not Toño Del Real. Sensing an opportunity, he'd asked her to betray her husband and her city for a hundred grand. And now there'd been a new development. Just that morning, as she was getting ready to pick Carla up and drive to the aviation academy, Del Real had called again, this time with a threat.

"Hello?"

"Hey, cousin. What happened? You said you'd call me back. Have you made a decision?"

"No," she'd lied. After a fortnight of insomnia and tachycardia, she'd finally resolved to end her relationship with her mentally-ill relative, but she didn't know how to tell him, which is why she hadn't called. His temper was as bad as Jeff's. "I need more time."

"Well, this is my last call. If you don't give me something I can use, I'll be forced to do something I don't want to do."

"What do you mean something you don't want to do? I don't know anything about Jeff's work."

"You could have found out. And now we're out of time. See you soon."

Tina was terrified. She knew that Toño didn't respect the traditional prohibition against kidnapping and torturing his enemies' families. She'd even heard a rumor that he'd had his own father, uncles, and cousins killed in order to take control of the Cartel del Norte. She remembered her coffee and took a lukewarm sip, beyond worried for the safety of her husband, her parents, her sisters, and, most importantly, her two-year-old daughter. Then she came to a decision: if Toño were to show up in San Diego and cause her any trouble, then she, too, would be forced to do something she didn't want to do. She would tell Jeff everything. He'd be furious, but he'd forgive her. She hadn't done anything wrong.

Tina click-clacked to the counter to buy another cup of coffee and sat down with it just as Carla's helicopter came into view. At first, she was relieved that her best friend had made it back, but the chopper was approaching too quickly and in an unstable manner, pitching up and down and yawing back and forth. Then it began to spin parallel to the ground like the main rotor blade. For a moment, it seemed Carla might regain control, but the aircraft suddenly tipped to the side, dropped, and smashed into the tarmac. The impact snapped the tail off the fuselage and the rotor blade ate up the asphalt.

A former paramedic, Tina barged through a nearby door and sprinted through the dust and debris to the site of the crash. She found Carla slumped forward over the controls and bleeding from a head wound. She knew not to move her without spinal stabilization in case of a back or neck injury, but when she looked down at a spreading pool of gasoline and up at a shower of sparks shooting out of the smashed controls, she dragged Carla to safety as the gas caught fire. The heat from the blast singed her skin.

Hours later, at the hospital, after Carla's head wound had been stapled shut, Carla explained the reason for the crash. "I got drowsy," she said. "I knew it was the worst possible thing to do, and I fought against it, but I just had to close my eyes. I told myself it would only be for a second, but I fell asleep. When I opened them again, I was spinning out of control."

"Don't tell your flight instructor that," Tina replied with a frown. "And definitely don't mention the sleeping pills."

"I hadn't taken any."

"Doesn't matter. I'm telling you as a friend, from the heart. You have to be more careful with that stuff."

"I will. I promise. I don't know what to say."

"I love you, honey," Tina said, pulling Carla into a long hug. "You don't need to say anything."

Carla heaved and shuddered as she wept, soaking Tina's blouse with tears. It was a hard lesson to learn.

Later, as they walked through the parking lot to the car, Tina said, "You told my cousin 'no,' right? Has he called you lately?"

"No, not since that first time," Carla replied, a thin smile forming on her lips. "Which is good because I'd have had to cuss him out again."

21

—— ◆ ——

THE BASEMENT

"There is one thing you can do to earn some extra cash," Murci's foreman had told him. "On Sundays. But it's a little bit dangerous."

"I'll do it," Murci had said. "I don't care what it is."

It wasn't that there happened to be an opportunity on Sundays; rather, the entire operation was a funnel that pushed the desperate construction workers into the Sunday scam, making their handlers even richer while placing the laborers at great risk and depriving them of their one day off.

A rock-hard fist thundered into Murci's jaw, reminding him to focus on the confrontation at hand. The crowd went wild. He staggered back, re-assessing his situation. His opponent was a co-worker, one who'd been in North Carolina much longer than he had. The fellow was about Murci's size, but his body was even harder. There was little humanity left in his empty gaze.

Murci and his adversary faced each other with their hands up in the center of a thick circle of bloodthirsty spectators. All had paid for a ticket and most were laying bets. The winner of the bare-knuckle brawl would earn fifty dollars. The loser, a bag of ice and a pill. If the winner killed the loser, he'd get an extra hundred. The only rule was that a fighter couldn't bring or use any weapon except for what he found on the ground. And there was no limit to the number of contests they could participate in; fighters would often stay in the ring until they lost.

Both men picked up a large, conveniently-placed rock. Murci's opponent came quickly forward, eager to cave his head in. But Murci didn't advance. He took careful aim and hurled the small boulder into the man's jaw. Incredibly, his opponent didn't go down, but he did drop his rock as he reeled, and it was easy to take him down. Murci didn't kill him in this fight, his first, but he soon understood that it was better to do so, and not only for the bonus: it was common for deadly fights to break out during the week between adversaries who hadn't killed each other.

For two years Murci supported his family in this way, but somewhere along that span of time he became a different person. At first he'd had to cross a line to kill his challengers, but later, he began to enjoy seeing the light drain out of his enemies' eyes. And to him that's what they were: enemies. Somehow his desperation for money had warped his mind such that he felt hate for them.

He'd train all week, before and after work, staying limber and quick for the Sunday fights. Cardiovascular conditioning was key. He ate as well as he could and drank plenty of water, spurred on by the knowledge that his parents would get what they needed and Nayeli could stay in school. He never lost, but he was frequently injured. On top of that and more importantly, Murci knew he'd eventually be killed by someone faster, smarter, stronger, or luckier than he was.

Faced with this unsustainable situation, and since he was risking his life anyway, he figured he might as well risk it in an escape attempt. One night he slipped out of bed, snuck out of the dormitory, and strangled the armed guard posted outside the administration building. After finding a ring of keys in the dead man's pockets, he sneaked inside and recovered his passport and visa. Another one of the keys fit the ignition of a black motorcycle in the parking area, the same one he'd ridden over the border to look for Nayeli.

In addition to the money he'd been sending home, the experience had given him skills that were coming in quite handy in his present effort to save her. After listening in on what Del Real had said about the basement, he'd ridden Seley's bike down to the lower levels of the Castlefield's parking structure, where he discovered an unmarked sliding door just like the security doors to the megasuite upstairs. He squatted behind a truck and waited for someone to come along, in the meantime calling Walker and telling him what he'd learned.

***

A pestering suspicion distracted Martinez from his work until he finally figured out why he'd recognized the waiter: "Horacio" looked exactly like Nayeli Sanchez. They could have been twins. Martinez shook his head, chastising himself for the oversight. How could he have missed that crucial detail? He'd already known that Nayeli's brother was in town looking for her; that's why she was taken to the basement in the first place. So he sat at a bank of monitors in the megasuite and waited for the big brother to show up again.

He didn't have to wait long at all.

***

"Hello there," oozed a mocking voice. Murci's phone was snatched out of his hand. "Leave your gun on the ground, stand up slow, and face the wall."

As Murci complied, his gaze fell on black shoes, then gray dress pants, then the business end of a pistol, and finally a cruel face that made him wish for one more fight to the death. It was Martinez, whose name he had learned while speaking with Detective Walker.

Martinez shoved Murci against the wall and zip-tied his hands behind his back. When he searched Murci's pockets, he found the lock pick set, which he confiscated, and a plastic can of chewing tobacco, which he opened and sniffed with a disdainful frown but let Murci keep. Forgetting to search Murci's boots, he led him to the sliding door and waved a passkey over the sensor. They stepped into an anteroom identical to the one upstairs.

"Override thermal detection," Martinez muttered. He recited a passphrase and held his eye to a scanner. When the second door glided into the wall, Murci spotted his sister sitting up on a bare mattress, one of her wrists shackled to a chain on the concrete-block wall. She was the only person in the large, yet pitifully spare, living space. The only amenities were a sea of mattresses on the concrete floor, a couple of toilets without surrounding partitions, and a communal shower.

At the sight of her, Murci turned into a wild animal, kicking, biting, and head-butting Martinez, who took a simple step back and repeatedly pistol-whipped Murci in the head until he stopped fighting and fell unconscious.

***

"Murci!" Nayeli exclaimed, shaking him awake. "Finally," she whispered as she threw one arm around him. Murci couldn't hug her back since his wrists were bound.

"I need you to cut my hands free," he growled. "There's a knife in my boot."

Nayeli nodded, unsheathed the blade, and freed his wrists. Tears trembled in her eyes. She held his gaze for a moment, her face close to his, then lowered her eyes in shame.

"You came here to earn a decent living for your family," Murci told her softly. "You haven't done anything wrong."

A single tear traced its way down her cheek. Then she buried her face in his chest and wept.

Murci stroked her hair and growled like an animal. This was not how things were going to end.

***

Martinez felt better after realizing his mistake and locking the big brother up. He left the basement and drove his Alpina to King for a Day, where at the curb he met Matón in the black SRT and three North County Kings on chopper bikes. On cue, Mama, Doña Mari, and all eleven girls filed out the front door. Most of them climbed into the SUVs, but three of the girls hopped on separate bikes and hung on to a biker.

Chasquas pushed the front door open and stepped outside. Martinez gestured for him to come around to his driver's side window. "I forgot my gun. I need to borrow yours," said the gray-suited gangster.

Chasquas blinked uncontrollably as he drew his pistol and handed it over butt first.

Martinez wondered what sort of powder the illustrated Honduran had inhaled for breakfast. "Stay here until I get back," he said. "Chucky's boys are going to deliver a package."

Chasquas gave a barely perceptible nod, at which Martinez pulled away, Matón followed, and the three bikes brought up the rear. Before long, they all squealed down the winding ramps of the parking garage at the Castlefield. The large group entered the basement through the security doors two at a time.

Once inside, Martinez made his way over to Mama and Doña Mari. "Do you understand the details of this new arrangement?" he asked, towering over the older women.

"Yes, sir," Mama replied, anger showing in her eyes, but quickly switching to apparent submissiveness.

"Good," Martinez snapped. "Tell all the girls, then."

"Where will Mari and I sleep?" Mama asked.

Martinez's only reply was a single sideways jerk of his chin toward the bare mattresses on the floor. The fat woman made him sick and the cripple was as dumb as dirt. He turned his back on them and strode out with a contented grin, satisfied after a highly successful day.

22

THE NEW RIGHT-HAND MAN

C hasquas' uncontrollable blinking had indeed been the result of hard drug use, but his body was used to it. Since most of his associates knew about his habit and also because he didn't talk much, they assumed he wasn't smart, while in reality he was the brightest of them all. So of course Chasquas had been suspicious: all of his fellow lieutenants were presumed dead except for the one who'd asked him to hand over his gun and wait alone in the massage parlor. Actually, he was beyond suspicious. He assumed that Matón's men, instead of coming to deliver a package as Martinez had told him, would soon be arriving under orders to send him to meet his maker.

With no time to search for Doña Mari's shotgun, he raced to his locker and armed himself with a razor-sharp machete, the traditional weapon of the Mara Salvatrucha street gang. Then he bounded up the stairs and peered out the window. Watching. Waiting. In less than a minute, three bikers bounced into the parking lot and grumbled to a stop at the curb. They drew their pistols and stormed the reception area. Chasquas left the window and headed for the top of the stairs, peeking down at Matón's men. They were using hand signals to communicate. Figuring they'd split up to search the premises, he slipped into the upstairs office and pressed himself against the wall near the open door, ready to chop away at whoever stepped in first. Soon came the sound of boots clomping up the stairs, growing louder as one biker headed for the second floor. Oddly, the clomping stopped, so Chasquas risked a look. On the landing, facing away from him, was a man clad in black jeans and a black leather jacket, with the

Kings' skull-faced patch on the back. The biker was peering down a hallway that contained five massage rooms all in a row on the right side. Foolishly, the man let his gaze linger, likely recalling the happy endings he'd enjoyed there. Chasquas padded quickly and quietly up to him, raised his weapon, and attacked his shooting arm from behind. It took three chops to hack it off: one that sent the man to his knees and two more to sever the limb. The screaming biker's vital red fluid gushed and spurted from a stringy stump as Chasquas grabbed him by his long black hair and slit his throat. He tossed the machete to a corner, picked up the biker's pistol, heaved the dying man over one shoulder, and carried him into the second massage room as more heavy boots pounded up the stairs. He shut the door behind him and lowered what was now a corpse, using it as a shield. He aimed the gun at the door. With no delay, the second biker threw open the door and fired, but the few rounds he got off buried themselves in his dead comrade. Meanwhile, at such close range, it was easy for Chasquas to end the second biker's life with a bullet between the eyes.

The third biker hit the landing with his handgun blazing. Chasquas heaved his human shield at him while sidestepping and firing at the man's legs, since he needed him to stay alive. When the biker dropped, Chasquas lunged forward and snatched the man's gun from his hand. Now he had twin Sig Sauers. He jammed them into his waistband for the time being.

As the crippled biker begged for his life, Chasquas retrieved his machete from the corner. Without breaking stride, he returned, stepped on the man's arm to hold it in place, and chopped off his wrist in two swoops.

"Who sent you?" Chasquas demanded once the screams had died down to a level that allowed for interrogation.

"Ma . . . Ma . . . Matón," the biker blubbered, his eyes fixed on his gushing stump.

"I know. He's your boss. Who else?" Chasquas raised his short sword, ready to strike again.

"Alonso Martinez."

Chasquas lowered the long blade and nodded slowly, his suspicions confirmed. "Anything more to say?" he asked. "You're as good as dead, but I can make it fast or slow."

"Del Real's coming to San Diego to execute Flores and Delgado. He's on his way. That's all I know, I swear to God."

Chasquas was unmoved by the fear in his fellow man's eyes, but he did keep his promise. With the machete still in his right hand, he drew a pistol with his left, held it to the man's temple, and pulled the trigger.

He didn't have much time. Even if more members of the North County Kings weren't headed his way, the police certainly were. He undid two of the dead men's belts and pulled their holsters off, pleased that one of them was left-handed, because that meant he'd be able to carry a pistol on both hips. He also took a set of keys from one of them, then hustled down the stairs. When he came to the reception area, he took a final look around the room. He knew the establishment well and had even helped to build it, but a wave of disgust washed over him. He would freely admit he was a killer and a drug addict, but he would never have sex with anyone against their will. Hearing sirens in the distance, he threw the front door open and tried the bikes. His key fit the second one. As he roared out of the parking lot, Chasquas offered a silent prayer of thanks to Our Lady of the Holy Death for keeping him alive.

In under an hour, he was sitting in Flores' library with both of his Honduran bosses. They were sipping cold drinks in a cool room, yet all three men were visibly upset.

"This means war," Delgado declared.

Chasquas and Flores nodded in grim agreement.

"Here," Flores said to Chasquas, handing his new right-hand man a thick white envelope. "You've earned it."

"Thank you sir," Chasquas replied, wondering how long he'd last as right-hand man.

***

Walker's shoulder hadn't needed major surgery, just the removal of the slug and a few stitches. Even so, there wasn't much he could do at the moment but sit at his desk and chip away at the pile of paperwork that had amassed in his absence. Three mugs of coffee had made him more alert, but only briefly. Now he felt weak and sluggish. What he really needed was to move his body, but he wasn't cleared to do anything but walk.

"Feel like some fresh air, Walker?" asked Detective Sergeant Cheatham, poking his head into the cubicle. In his late fifties, Walker's new supervisor was relatively old to still be on the streets, but the former Army drill sergeant was a unique physical specimen. He'd been teaching the defensive tactics training classes for twenty years, and rare was the lawman who could get the best of him. He reminded Walker of Master Chang, his former combat instructor, though Sergeant Cheatham was black, not Asian.

As they walked through Spanish Landing Park with the harbor on the left, Walker's mind drifted from Rogers' betrayal of the task force, to the resulting deaths of four of its members, to Murci's and Nayeli's plight, to Carla's helicopter crash, and then to something new: Tina's recent evasive and withdrawn behavior. He was about to move on to the next topic, his buddy Tony Park, but his superior officer beat him to it, snapping Walker back to the present moment with his booming voice.

"You're aware Park's taking a personal day today," Sergeant Cheatham barked as they strode along side by side.

Walker had to hurry to keep up. "Yes, sir."

"Do you know why?"

Walker hesitated. A few days back, Park had confided in him about his struggle with alcohol, which hadn't been news at all, but Walker wasn't sure what, if anything, Park had told Sergeant Cheatham. If Walker said yes, that he did know why, he'd be questioned further. If he said no, it would be a lie. He concluded that the safest way to proceed was to say nothing.

"I know you're just looking out for your partner, Walker, and I respect that, but I need to know whether or not Corporal Park is okay. You know he was invited to try out for MARTAC, correct?"

"Yes sir, I do," Walker replied, feeling more alert and energetic being outside and close to the ocean. He took the first conscious breath of his walk. Now his stride easily matched that of his supervisor.

"I haven't spoken with MARTAC's commander about it," Sergeant Cheatham said, "but you can see how I'd be concerned about any of my detectives saying they need time off to get their head around a drinking problem."

"He's okay, Sarge. Park's been through a lot."

"I know."

"I think telling you about his bad habit was his way of clearing his conscience."

"That's what I thought. Not everyone can be squeaky clean like you, am I right?"

***

"Snap out of it!" Tina had hissed one morning when he'd returned at 5:30 a.m. "Do you think this is a game? Like we're kids playing house?" She'd rebuked him in a whisper so she wouldn't wake their daughter.

It was a losing proposition. With an average slots payout of ninety percent, the house always won in the end. At the card tables, the odds were better if you knew what you were doing, but in the long run, anyone without a photographic memory always left poorer than before. Walker had tried, many times, to convince Park to sit at the blackjack table with him, but he was too good a friend to agree.

As a law enforcement officer, Walker often thought about right and wrong, about the line that criminals cross in the commission of an immoral act. It was the same line that he himself stepped over every time he crept out of bed to drive to a gaming establishment. As he and his sergeant headed up the steps to headquarters, he wished he could turn back the clock and get a second chance.

"Be good to your good self, son," Sergeant Cheatham said with a knowing wink and an encouraging smile. "You've got a bright future ahead if you can keep it together." He held the front door open for his newest detective and clapped him on the back as he passed.

Walker strode to his cubicle and settled in with renewed energy, more determined than ever to make a positive change in his life.

23

TAKEN

MARTAC, short for MARitime TACtical team, is the San Diego Harbor Police's SWAT unit. All of its operators are assigned to regular, full-time patrol or investigative duties, so when Tony Park crunched to a stop in his blue 4x4 pickup at 4:30 a.m. outside the abandoned building where MARTAC trains, no introductions were needed. His welcome reception consisted of ten men standing at attention in a row under the dull orange wash of an old streetlight.

The commander, Lieutenant John Colbert, stood apart from the others with his arms folded over his chest. The thick-set veteran lawman was about forty, his lined face the only sign of aging. "Morning Park," he bellowed. "Are you ready?"

"Yes, sir."

At a nod, Sergeant Steve Ortiz and five others stepped forward, forming a rough circle of men around Park. The rest of the team took three steps back. Park hadn't been forewarned, but he knew this was to be an initiatory beat down. Common in fighting groups from military organizations to street gangs, this practice weeds out cowards before they get themselves or someone else killed. It also forms strong bonds, especially when told and re-told over adult beverages. Park had faced this ordeal once before, on his first day as a Navy SEAL, so he knew he would lose. That was the point. To see if the candidate is willing to fight even when defeat is certain.

Ignoring the sense of panic that made him want to run, he drew a breath and formed a plan. He'd take out the closest guy first, lowering the odds from six on one to five on one. It wouldn't matter, though; if by some miracle he began to gain the upper hand, Lieutenant Colbert would send in more men.

Park dropped into a fighting stance and spun in a slow circle, staring at each of his adversaries. None of them showed any fear. Several wore dark grins; apparently, it was their turn to inflict the punishment they had endured in their own try-out. The six men inched forward, tightening the circle. Park kept an eye on Sergeant Ortiz, the closest man, but he faced away so as not to reveal his plan. To Park's surprise, however, the men came to a halt and raised their hands in surrender. Scowls warmed into friendly grins, and a ripple of laughter rose up from the entire team, but it was too late for Sergeant Ortiz, whom Park dropped with a hard right hand before he understood the joke. At that, MARTAC's chuckles swelled into hooting, howling laughter. Park helped Ortiz to his feet and issued a profuse apology, which the sergeant waved away with a rueful grin.

In the next test, Park had to change into swim trunks, strap on a forty-pound weighted vest, and hop off the dock into the chilly bay. There he treaded water for ten minutes.

"Now with your arms out. Hold them high," Sergeant Ortiz barked with a hint of a smile.

Park used the eggbeater technique to stay afloat despite the double handicap, pushing one leg down at a time, almost as if he were pedaling a bicycle. When the ten minutes were up, he groaned as Ortiz tossed him an empty five-gallon water jug.

"Fill it up," Ortiz commanded. "Then hold it high, upside down, until all the water drains out."

Park's legs burned. By the time the jug was empty, he was a little out of breath, but he easily threw it back to Ortiz and he didn't need anyone to help him out of the water. A couple of guys clapped him on the back, offering encouraging words as if there were some question as to whether he would pass the test, but Park knew there wasn't. Nothing that he endured that morning even came close to what he'd had to go through in the Navy's twenty-four-week BUD/S training program.

Next, every man, including the leaders, ran five miles and performed one hundred push-ups. The final activity was to storm through maze-like corridors in teams of four, sticking close to the walls before clearing rooms in search of enemy shooters.

By eight a.m., anyone who hadn't known that Park would turn out to be a major asset for the team was well aware of that fact.

"Welcome to MARTAC, Park," Lieutenant Colbert boomed. "Congratulations."

Park walked down the line and each man offered him a handshake or a clap on the shoulder.

It was a great start to a terrible day.

***

"How did it go?" Walker asked after the morning briefing. He was out of the sling and cleared for regular duties.

Park shrugged on his sport coat and grabbed his keys. "Fine," he replied. "I passed. Let's go."

They were on their way to the Castlefield Waterfront Hotel to follow up on the information given by Murci, who'd told Walker that Nayeli was being held in the Castlefield's basement, that the entrance was on the lowest level of the parking garage, and that Del Real was coming to town that day, possibly planning to blow up the casino early Sunday morning.

Walker's phone buzzed in his pocket. He fished it out and held up a finger. "Hang on, man. It's Tina calling from home."

***

In a reverse version of the task force's trip to Mexico, Toño Del Real and company flew in his private jet to a small airstrip outside of San Diego. Martinez and Matón were waiting to pick them up in the Alpina and the SRT respectively.

As he disembarked down the airstairs, Armando Jimenez Jr. didn't seem happy to see the black Jeep Cherokee he'd gambled away. Del Real chuckled to himself. Jimenez Sr. had refused to buy his son a new one.

***

"Hey!" Tina exclaimed, pulling open her front door. "You're looking good." She and Carla exchanged a hug.

"Thanks," Carla replied. "Too bad about this gruesome head wound, though."

The women cracked up as they headed for the living room, where Tina Michelle was playing with her dolls on the floor. Tina had on jeans and a T-shirt while Carla wore a gray sweatsuit.

"Besides that, I mean," Tina said. She'd spoken honestly; Carla's curly brown hair and her makeup were well done and her eyes were clear and bright.

"Yeah, I've been eating more, and I threw those pills away."

The sunlight filtering in through the big bay window was strong enough to make Tina draw the curtains. "Can I get you some tea?" she asked.

"Sure," said Carla, dropping to all fours to play with Tina Michelle.

A minute later, Tina brought out two steaming mugs. "I have to ask you something," she said, handing over one of them before lowering herself into a brown recliner. She regarded her best friend with direct eye contact.

"Okay," Carla replied warily. She cradled her mug with two hands as she settled down onto the matching brown couch.

Tina took a sip of green tea, her favorite. "What made you decide to be a helicopter pilot? And what happened to our plan to buy Bella someday?"

"I don't know," Carla answered. Her tone was relaxed but her bouncing leg told a different story. "I guess I needed something new. Something fun."

Tina narrowed her eyes. "I don't think that's it," she replied, then rose and sat beside Carla, placing a hand on her arm.

"Um, well, it's that and something else," Carla said, the pitch and speed of her words increasing.

"Reeeally," Tina drawled incredulously.

"Yes. Really," Carla insisted. "I want to fly us on our trips instead of taking those long car rides. It'll be great! We can all go to Vegas. Or head up the coast."

That did sound great to Tina, but she knew bullshit when she smelled it. She raised her eyebrows and frowned, staring now.

"Fine," Carla finally admitted. "It was because your cousin Antonio said that if I made a few trips for him, he'd pay me a hundred grand. More if I could tell him what the Human Trafficking Task Force was doing. I agreed at first, but then I changed my mind. I really did cuss him out, though."

Tina nodded.

"And about our plan to buy Bella, nothing's changed, but I might not be working there after I get my license. Or maybe just part time."

"No worries. Hey, speaking of Bella, aren't you supposed to be at work?"

For a moment, Carla looked perplexed and even a little offended. Then she pulled out her phone and swiped her finger across the screen. "What do you mean?" she said. "You asked me to meet you here, saying it was urgent, so I got Cristopher to cover for me." After she showed Tina a text message seemingly sent from Tina's phone, the women locked wide eyes.

The silence was broken by a heavy rapping at the door.

Carla sprang to her feet and snatched up Tina Michelle, carrying the child to the back of the house. Tina fished her phone out of her jeans, pressed the button for Walker's cell, and kept it in her hand as she headed for the door and looked out the window to see who it was. She pressed her lips into a tight line and shook her head slowly as she stared into her cousin's dark eyes.

"*Buenos días*," Del Real called out from the other side of the door. He was just as big as Walker. Clad in black jeans, sharp-toe boots, and a black cowboy hat, he looked like a soap opera star, the one who always plays the villain. "Let me in," he demanded, his voice muffled by the pane of glass between them. "We need to talk."

"No way," Tina replied, feigning power she didn't have. "I'm on the phone with Jeff right now."

"Hello? Tina? Are you okay?" came Walker's distant voice.

"Perfect," Del Real barked. "Pass me the phone."

Tina's eyes flitted to an entryway table where they always kept a spare pistol, and the key to the drawer was in her pocket. She went for it. Her heart pounding, she inserted the key even as Del Real unholstered his massive golden pistol and fired two thunderous shots, destroying both locks on the door. She managed to slide open the drawer and get the gun out, but before she could seat the magazine, Del Real barged inside and headed straight for her, snatching the weapon out of her hands. Then he took her phone. She didn't resist.

He towered over her, glaring as he held the cell to his ear. "This is Antonio Del Real. Be here in fifteen minutes. Come alone and unarmed. If you don't, you'll never see your family again."

***

Walker couldn't believe his eyes. The criminal whom Lieutenant Taylor had been trying to take down for years was standing in his living room.

"Up against the wall," Del Real ordered him, gesturing with his gun. Then he patted Walker down. "Have a seat," the crook said once he'd completed the search.

By that time, Tina was in the brown recliner with Tina Michelle in her lap, and Carla occupied the matching couch. Walker sat beside Carla, but it was his wife to whom he turned. "So this is your rich cousin from Mexico. Thanks for the heads up."

"Don't talk about me like I'm not here," Del Real snapped, raising his weapon. "Just shut the fuck up."

Tina's voice trembled. "He said he'd hurt Tina Michelle if I didn't spy on the task force. That's why I didn't tell you."

Tina Michelle began to cry. Her curly locks were the same light brown color as Carla's, only shorter. As Tina comforted the child, Walker rose and locked eyes with Deal Real. He stepped up to the man with his fists balled. "You said you were going to do what?"

"Back up and sit down," Del Real replied calmly. "If you get up again, I'll blow your leg off at the knee." At the same time, a pair of meandering red dots appeared on Walker's pregnant wife and his baby girl. Another on Carla's chest. Walker looked down. There was one on him, too. Del Real must have stationed a squad outside. "This weekend you will stay away from the Cumbres Casino Resort and the Castlefield Waterfront Hotel," said Del Real, his eyes daring Walker to do something.

Walker kept his mouth shut and planted his backside on the couch, averting his eyes so he wouldn't take the bait.

"Also," Del Real went on. "I'm going to be coming to San Diego more and more, so we are going to have to learn to get along. For now, I'm going to take charge of Tina and Carla, leaving your daughter as a sign of respect. If you can control yourself until Monday, I'll bring them back and set you up with some cash. Deal?"

"I can promise not to show up at Cumbres and the Castlefield," Walker replied, without actually agreeing to anything. "And I can send the Harbor Police somewhere else. But I can't guarantee that every law enforcement agency in San Diego will stay away."

"Yes, you can. You can find a way. And don't even think about it," Del Real said when he caught Walker's eyes darting to the entryway table. He turned around to show Walker his own pistol tucked into the back of his jeans. "Let's go, cousin." Del Real pulled open the ruined door as the hovering red dots all leaped onto Walker's chest.

Tina and Walker kissed as she handed him her crying child.

Walker leveled a molten gaze on the mobster. "If you hurt them, I'll find a way to make you pay."

Del Real didn't seem concerned. He turned his gaze on Carla, who sprang to her feet and shot Walker a glance as she left. Del Real followed her. As he closed the door behind him, he looked Walker dead in the eye and nodded once, tipping his black cowboy hat. Apparently, he hoped Walker, Tina, Carla, and Park would form part of his crooked gang.

He couldn't have been more wrong.

24

WHO'S THE BOSS?

The lights of Downtown San Diego cast a multi-colored sheen over the dark, rippling waters of the bay. As he admired this nocturnal panorama, Toño Del Real filled his lungs with the salty air let in by the megasuite's open windows. Then he padded across the soft, white deep-pile carpet of the sitting room and made himself a gin martini at the bar. He also filled two tall glasses with ice water and carried them over to Tina, who sat uneasily on a black leather couch, and Carla on an identical sofa set at a right angle.

"Well?" he said, after settling onto a third couch that faced Tina's, with a coffee table in between.

Tina met his dark gaze, frowned, and shook her head in a definite "no." Carla did the same.

"Strike one, as my father used to say." Del Real sipped from his drink. "Before his tragic death."

Tina was consumed by a sudden urge to snap off the base of his martini glass and stab him in the eye with the jagged shaft, but even if she and Carla were able to overpower the muscular, seasoned street fighter, the armed guard standing nearby would shoot them dead.

"Just hear me out one last time," Del Real went on. "I can see that you're loyal to your men."

Carla nodded. Tina too, though she vowed not to be drawn into conversation with her cousin. Years ago, they'd been close, so she had to make an effort to ignore him.

Del Real drained his drink, set the glass down, and took his time rolling up his sleeves to expose his brawny, battle-scarred forearms. He leaned forward and placed his elbows on his knees, eyeing them in turn. "This can be a win-win for us," he said. "I don't think Walker will cooperate. But you and me, Cristina? We're family. I can give you more money than you can spend. Tina Michelle will go to the best private schools, and you'll never have to work again. All you'd have to do is report to me every once in a while. What do you say?"

When Del Real had first threatened Tina Michelle, Tina had decided she would not betray her husband for any amount of dirty money. And she was offended that her relative would risk his relationship with her to expand his criminal empire. Her gaze settled on the glass of ice water before her. She plucked it up from the table and drew in a large mouthful without swallowing it.

Del Real turned to Carla. "What about you, pretty lady? I heard you're having trouble getting pregnant." Carla hung her head. "My offer's still good," he said.

Tina had been able to keep her temper in check while Del Real was speaking to her, but as he stooped low enough to bully her best friend, she rose. Smiling sweetly to hide her intention, she stepped around the coffee table, sat beside him, and blew out all the water onto his face.

Del Real's wet neck, shoulders, and chest bulged like those of a bulldog, but he didn't strike back. His only reaction was to calmly whip out a white handkerchief and pat himself dry. "Strikes two and three," he said. Then he turned to the guard. "Take them to the basement."

***

The Cumbres Casino Resort was by far the largest business in the valley, towering over both a high- and a low-rent district. Chasquas had chosen two homes in the low-rent district to house the L.A. Maras, reasoning that the street soldiers' striking appearance would be less noticeable in such a place. Half of them were already at the casino working, and the other half stood before him in their rented house: two rows of six hardened fighters with crude, grisly tattoos all over their hungry torsos, arms, hands, and faces. With one exception, they looked like younger versions of Chasquas. Very much like Beto.

"Listen up, *cabrones*," Chasquas called out as he paced, staring at each of them in succession. He, too, had stripped off his shirt, so they could see he was one of them, and he wore a holstered Sig Sauer on each hip. "You're on your way to a fancy place, where you'll have to look and act nice for a few days. So in a minute, you will change into suits. But first I want you to burn these faces into your brains."

The lanky Honduran passed out large color photographs of Walker, Park, Lieutenant Taylor, Ex-DAI Matt Rogers, Antonio Del Real, Alonso Martinez, and Chucky Matón. "The one with the long goatee is the leader of the North County Kings. I know you've had problems with them in the past, so I expect you'll recognize Chucky Matón."

Several shaved heads nodded and angry mutterings arose as the prints circulated among the Maras. Chasquas continued to pace. "If you see these men or anything else out of the ordinary, you will report it to me immediately," he said, stopping to study the features of one man who was twice as old as the others. After a long staring contest, he moved on down the line. "Go get dressed. We'll leave in ten."

An hour later, Chasquas and his two bosses convened in Flores' library. The trio sat in deep, tufted leather armchairs beside a wall full of books. A pair of Maras in dark suits stood nearby, with two more in the hallway outside the door.

"I'm sure our girls are at the Castlefield in the basement," Chasquas told Delgado and Flores. "And I doubt Martinez and Matón remembered to deregister me from the security system."

"I wouldn't have forgotten," Flores countered.

"It's worth a shot," Delgado said. "We can give you four men. What will you do if you can't get in?"

Chasquas was ready with a plan. "I need a spoon," he said.

Flores gestured for his valet to bring over the mentioned item.

"I'll be back in a couple of hours," Chasquas told them on his way out. He and four Maras took several cars to the Castlefield's parking garage, winding down the ramps to the third floor below street level. Equipped with AK-47s, body armor, and ballistic helmets, the group marched to the unmarked door in the corner. Two of them spun around, took a knee, and guarded the rear while Chasquas sprayed black paint over the CCTV camera above the door and waved his passkey over the sensor. The first portal slid open, so he handed the keycard to one of his men and stepped inside before it slid shut. He held his eye to the ocular scanner and uttered his personal passphrase, but an on-screen message prompted him to wait for assistance.

Fuck. A security team was minutes away.

"Override thermal detection," he said quickly, then spoke a different passphrase, glaring at the second door, willing it to retract into the wall.

It didn't budge.

Chasquas pounded on the first door and it slid open. "Plan B. Move!" he barked as he charged into the garage and got to work.

Two Maras ran to the service elevator, knelt ten feet from its doors, and raised their rifles. The other two hustled to their car and brought out a spike strip, which they unrolled and placed on the ramp at a curve. They, too, assumed strategic firing positions. Meanwhile, Chasquas double-timed it to a different car, extracted an RPG launcher, and concealed himself fifty feet from the spike strip, ready to blow away a big group of bikers if it came to that, knowing, however, that if he killed them all, he wouldn't be able to access the basement.

Thirty seconds later, three North County Kings piled out of the service elevator, but they came to an instant, submissive halt.

"Drop your guns!" shouted the two Maras leveling rifles. The bikers set down their weapons.

Before long, four motorcycles sputtered down the ramp and blew their tires on the spike strip. Their riders awkwardly drew and fired their pistols, but missed by a wide margin as they struggled to control their bikes. Chasquas and the Maras quickly rounded up all seven bikers, ordering them to lie face down with their hands on their heads, all in a row. Everything was going according to plan.

"We don't have much time, so you motherfuckers better answer fast," Chasquas growled, pulling the spoon from his pocket. "Who's the leader here?"

None of the Kings made a sound.

"Who's the boss, guys?"

Silence.

Chasquas knelt over the first biker in the row. "Turn over," he commanded the shaking man.

One Mara held the biker's arms and another his legs while Chasquas dug into the man's eye socket and popped out his eyeball. He held it up for everyone to see. The long optic nerve was still attached, dripping blood onto the polished concrete floor.

Chasquas hurried into the anteroom and attempted to gain access. No luck. He ran back to the row of bikers and shot the one-eyed biker in the head, then knelt beside the next one in line. "Who's the boss?" he whispered.

Two minutes later, Chasquas and the Maras were standing in the basement after shooting each of the bikers. All twelve girls, along with Murci, Carla, Tina, Mama, and Doña Mari were either seated on mattresses or milling about.

"Everybody out!" Chasquas bellowed as he freed Nayeli's wrist. He and the Maras roughly assisted anyone who didn't move out quickly enough.

On the way back to Blossom Valley, Chasquas trembled from the rush. His hope was to fill Flores' shoes someday, though his interests lay in narcotics and weapons, not sexual slavery. He came up with a solution: he'd help to win the battle at the casino, making sure Matón passed away in the process. Then he'd take the biker's place as the leader of the Kings. He'd grown up on motorbikes and could ride as well as anyone, and he was certainly tough enough for the role. He grinned and cackled at the idea for over a minute, unable to contain his drug-fueled merriment and oblivious to the fact that the Kings would choose their new leader from among their own ranks. It wouldn't be Chasquas, even if no one ever found out that he'd just tortured one and killed seven North County Kings.

At the casino, the Maras locked all the hostages in a remote, permanently unoccupied wing of the fourth floor, while Chasquas led Mama and Doña Mari into Flores' suite.

"Good to have you back, ladies," Delgado boomed. "You'll be staying here in the blue room, and you won't be working since everything's closed right now. Think of it as a vacation."

"Let's hope your holiday isn't cut short," Flores remarked without looking up from a thick hardcover volume. For days he'd been devouring books on military strategy, single focused on the impending assault.

Chasquas had twenty-five men to lead, so he made a hasty exit. Flores went back to his book, Delgado placed a call, and Mama and Mari trudged back to the blue room and watched TV.

***

Two floors up, Nayeli, Murci, Carla, Tina, Kati, Cho, and Cristi had been shoved into one room and the rest of the girls were next door.

"We need a plan," Tina told them in a low voice. "I'm not just going to sit around and wait for my cousin to kill us." She alone was perched on the king-size bed, her back to the wall, given preferential accommodation due to her swollen belly. Everyone else was seated on the carpet or still on their feet.

"Phone is dead," Kati reported, replacing the receiver.

Carla tried the door. "It only opens from the outside."

Cho didn't know how to say "welded shut," but she pushed on the windows to no effect, shook her head, and everyone got the message.

"I have a plan," Murci whispered. He drew his survival knife from the sheath in his boot and unscrewed the pommel, pulling out a mini survival kit that included fishing line. Then he produced the flat can of chewing tobacco he'd swiped from the megasuite.

Tina's features twisted into a grimace. "That stuff will make you sick," she said.

"Exactly," Murci replied, stretching the transparent line across the middle of the room eight inches from the floor. He tied both ends to bolted-down furniture. "Listen. Two girls eat this. Get sick and call for help. Guards run in, trip, and die." Hate flashed in his eyes as he showed them his long, serrated blade.

"It's worth a shot," Tina replied, nodding slowly along with everyone else. "But I'm pregnant so I can't eat that crap."

Murci passed the can to Nayeli, who forced herself to swallow half its contents, pausing now and then to let her gag reflex settle down. Kati reluctantly followed suit.

Murci pressed himself against the wall beside the door such that he'd be hidden when it swung open. "Yell for help," he hissed. "Now!"

25

PEST CONTROL

Infiltrating the L.A. Maras hadn't been a problem; the gang was always looking for smart, tough men. Most of Rogers' contacts were unaware of the warrant out for his arrest, so after shaving his head and losing the mustache, he'd had temporary tattoos applied by a Hollywood special effects company, then pulled a few strings and been selected for the contingent sent to protect the casino resort.

He was posted outside room 405 when the hostages began to cry out.

"Help! Emergency!" shrieked a woman on the other side. Others followed suit and someone pounded on the door. Rogers exchanged a nod with his partner, who pushed the door open while he went in first, leveling his Glock and panning it from left to right and back again. His stomach dropped when he spotted Tina. She didn't seem to recognize him, but in time she would, so he backed out into the hallway, letting the door slam shut. The last thing he needed was for the Maras, particularly Chasquas, to find out who he really was. He held his ear to the door and listened in.

***

Murci's heart rate leapt up into the red zone. In the confusion of the Maras' entry, as one of them backed out, the other had stepped far enough away from the door that now he'd have time to turn and fire if he were to sense someone behind him. But he hadn't gone far enough to trip on the fishing line. Murci caught Kati's eye and nodded, prompting her to act.

"I need doctor," she moaned between acrid mouthfuls of barf, kneeling on the carpet beyond the transparent string.

"Help, please," cried Nayeli from the bathroom before heaving black chunks into the toilet bowl.

Seeing no danger, the Mara lowered his pistol and charged straight into the fishing line. When he stumbled, Murci flew forward and buried his blade in the man's neck, neatly avoiding his clavicle, shoulder blades, and his ballistic vest. He pulled it back out while encircling the Mara's chest with his other arm, to hold the man in place as he slit his throat from behind. The shaven-headed street soldier fell to the carpet, trying to call out for his partner, but his words were garbled by all the blood in his mouth. The panic soon drained out of his eyes.

Tina slid off the bed, dug in the dead Mara's pockets, and found a phone.

"Jeff, it's me," she said when Walker answered. "The girls and I are at the casino, locked in rooms four-oh-five and four-oh-seven. Murci's here, too."

***

Rogers was alarmed when he heard Tina's end of the conversation. He had to get that phone out of the room. Yes, she would recognize him, but if she were allowed to make any more calls, it might prevent him from executing his plan, which was to force Flores and Delgado to pay what they owed him, then kill them and escape before Del Real attacked.

He threw open the door to room 405 and picked up his late comrade's gun. He raised both pistols and pointed them at each of the six female hostages, most of whom sat on the floor. The stench was sickening.

Rogers' eyes dropped to the fishing line. "Nice try," he muttered, then stooped to snap it with a jerk. He walked over to the bed and snatched the phone out of Tina's hand. Then he turned back to the murder victim and scanned the scene with his practiced gaze. Something wasn't right. The Mara's wounds were deep, as if inflicted by someone large or powerful. He looked at each of the young women in turn. "Where's the knife?" he asked. At that instant, the door slammed closed behind him, yet all six hostages were still in his line of sight.

"*Hijo de su puta madre*," he swore bitterly. It had to have been Murci Sanchez. Rogers raced back out of the room, where at the end of the hallway he saw the stairwell door bang shut. He chased the sound of clomping boots all the way down to street level, but lost interest as he stepped onto the casino floor. It was so expansive and so crowded with patrons that Murci could easily hide and get away, if he hadn't done so already. Plus, there were more pressing matters at hand: Rogers' first priority was to take Chasquas out. He checked his watch. Due a break in five minutes, he crossed the gaming floor and exited through the rear doors, where he ran into a pair of Maras coming to take his and his partner's place. Like him, the younger men wore dark suits over a ballistic vest, with shaven heads and tattoos all over their faces and hands. All three men looked wildly out of place, to be sure, but it would only be for a day. The Maras looked confused as to why Rogers wasn't at his post, but made no objection when in fluent Central-American Spanish he said, "There's a mess in four-oh-five. Clean it up and call it in. And tell Chasquas I'm taking my break in the shooting range."

He crossed the pool deck, passing long rows of lounge chairs and a handful of luxury tents on his way to the shooting range, which was closed to the public at the moment. Once inside, he flipped on the lights, took a lane, and squeezed off a few practice shots, seeing Chasquas' ugly mug instead of a faceless black silhouette on the paper target.

***

Earlier that same day, Park, Walker, and Lieutenant Taylor had met at Taylor's house in Oceanside, forty miles north of Downtown San Diego. Since the dwelling was one block from the beach, Walker gratefully filled his lungs with fresh, sea-scented air as they gathered around a lowered fire pit close to the pool.

"We're up against two large contingents," Taylor began, "since by now Flores and Delgado will have bolstered their security force. So what have we got in terms of police power?"

Park set down his coffee mug. "First, there's MARTAC. Twelve men, not enough to deal with Del Real's bikers. Not decisively."

"I agree," Taylor replied. "They're about forty strong."

"And who knows what kind of team the Hondurans have put together," Park went on. "Maybe another thirty?"

"Sounds about right," Walker said, swiveling to face Taylor. "I'm told you have a solid relationship with the Sheriff's Department's SWAT team."

"We do," Taylor replied. "Their Special Enforcement Detail is good for at least fifteen men. We always call SED first in critical situations like this. The Sheriff's Department also has a Bomb/Arson Unit which won't be mobilized with less than four."

"Good," said Walker. "That means I can lead a squad of canine teams in liaison with the bomb unit. So we're up to thirty-five not counting animals."

Park gave a somber chuckle. His eyes were clear and his face fresh. Carla's crash had scared him into sobriety. With his hulking frame, massive hands, and the murderous scowl on his face before and after his brief reaction to Walker's joke, Park looked ready to storm the casino on his own. He said, "The two groups of bad guys will be shooting at each other, so we don't need a one-to-one ratio. And there's something else to consider. According to Chief Deputy O'Connell, the mayor can summon a special police force in emergencies or cases of public threat. Conservatively, that should give us another five for a total of forty, not counting animals."

"Then we're good," Taylor concluded. "Let's do it."

***

Rogers blasted a few rounds into the paper target, saving the rest of his ammo for the real thing. He did not congratulate himself when he slid the target closer to inspect his perfect shot grouping; excellence was expected. He switched out his magazine, racked the slide, and popped the mag out again to press in one more round, since he knew the extra cartridge might make the difference between a beach house in the Caribbean and a trip to the medical examiner's office.

While waiting, his mind drifted to the question of how he and the Hondurans had come to be enemies after so many years of conspiracy. As a vice detective, he had never been able to keep a steady girlfriend. He'd always chalked that up to heavy stress and long, irregular hours, but if Rogers was being honest with himself, the real reason for it was that he preferred the company of call girls, who offered little drama and near-constant availability. Thus, over the years, he'd gained an intimate understanding of the rotten life human trafficking victims were forced into by men such as Delgado and Flores. And after fifteen years of covering for those two, he had changed his mind, while Delgado and Flores were set in their ways. They had firm opinions about what was right. To them, what was right was usually the wrong end of a gun. *Not this time,* Rogers swore to himself. The Hondurans were the ones who'd be on the wrong end of a gun, and it was their own fault for withholding the final payment and ordering his death. After all he'd done for them!

The front door burst open. Chasquas scowled as he strode down a hallway toward Rogers. "What the hell happened up there?" bellowed the lanky Honduran from ten feet away. "And why didn't you look for me as soon as you took your break?" Now within spitting distance, he squinted with hazy recognition. "Do I know you?"

Rogers casually pursed his lips and shook his head as he turned back to the target and made like he was going to fire, but then he whirled around and fired twice.

Damn, Chasquas was quick. Like a running back dodging defenders, the lanky Honduran spun away, pulling both of his pistols at the same time and taking cover behind a polycarbonate partition. Chasquas remained on the far side of that clear bulletproof panel designed to protect shooters from stray projectiles while Rogers backed away toward the cigar lounge. Once inside, Rogers knew he'd come to a back door that led to the business room, and another from there to the souvenir shop. Then another that led to a long hallway and back out into the shooting range through a different door. He fired a few suppressive rounds as he slipped into the cigar lounge, then sprinted through the connected spaces. He flew through the long hallway that opened onto the shooting range. He assumed Chasquas wouldn't be familiar with the layout of this incidental outbuilding and would therefore either stay in the firing range camped outside the cigar lounge or follow him in. He hurried through the corridor, stopping briefly at the door at the end. He drew a belly breath and eased the door open a crack, peering through the narrow opening. When he saw no threat camped outside the door to the cigar lounge, he figured Chasquas had most likely followed him in, so he stepped out into the shooting range and leveled his Glock. Panning the pistol from left to right, he detected nothing amiss, so he took off toward the door to the cigar lounge.

***

Chasquas had absolutely studied the layout of the outbuilding, and he didn't consider it incidental at all. He had spent several evenings poring over the construction plans for every building at the resort, especially the shooting range, as Flores had said that control of the complex could prove decisive. In other words, Chasquas was prepared for this contingency, aware that Rogers might try to take advantage of the U-shaped passage through the cigar lounge, the business room, the souvenir shop, and the long hallway that led back out.

Thus, instead of following the rat into the maze, Chasquas took cover near the hallway door, waiting for him to wind his way through the rooms. When Rogers eased the door open and stepped out, he was a sitting duck. Chasquas popped up with both Sigs blasting, nailing Rogers to the wall with several rounds to his ballistic vest. When the woozy rodent slid down the wall to the floor, Chasquas stepped closer and shot him in the head.

"You're probably sick of all these cash bonuses," Flores joked in his library a few minutes later, handing over another white envelope stuffed with hundreds. Chasquas smiled, wondering if his boss had a stack of these envelopes ready to go.

Delgado offered Chasquas a beefy hand. "Well done. Looks like you've got a dark future ahead of you," he jested. Flores and Chasquas exploded into a fit of snorting laughter.

Nearby, perched on either end of a brown leather settee, Mama and Doña Mari did not appear to be amused. As their handlers chortled and guffawed, they rose and made their way back to the blue room, arguing in a whisper.

The three Hondurans soon settled down and went over the battle plan again. If their lives and livelihood were to have any chance of surviving the weekend, everything depended on careful preparation.

26

— · —

THE BATTLE BEGINS

Toño Del Real stood in the megasuite with his big arms crossed, gazing absently down at the marina as the afternoon sun sparkled on the bay. After working for two days straight, his brain was fatigued but his body was primed for action, his pulse quickened by adrenaline.

When Martinez had told him how and when Murci had bugged the sitting room, Del Real had moved the timetable forward, from early Sunday morning to Saturday, today, at six p.m. He was finally ready to take the casino resort, the IMBs, and the girls from the Hondurans. First, he'd paid an expert programmer to breach federal cybersecurity defenses and follow the convoluted trail of financial relationships that led to Flores' and Delgado's beneficial ownership of those assets. Then he'd drafted the documents he would need them to sign. But getting past the bolstered security at the casino and forcing them to do it wouldn't be easy. Especially not with the police swarming through the building like ants in an ant farm.

On Friday, in preparation for the attack, he'd sent Jimenez Jr. and his enforcers to the casino resort to pose as guests, unarmed and in ordinary vehicles. They had brought incendiary devices hidden in shopping bags, in automotive fire extinguishers, and in a pair of laptop computers. Also a briefcase with a false bottom hiding four blocks of C-4 and a set of detonators.

Simultaneously, Del Real had dispatched a large group of North County Kings to the same vicinity. On top of what they'd been sent to do, the bikers' sputtering presence near the resort was intended to distract the casino guards,

making Jimenez Jr.'s team appear more innocent by comparison. The ploy
seemed to have worked: Jimenez had reported no trouble clearing the security
checkpoint set up at the entrance. After registering under assumed identities,
Jimenez and his enforcers had made their way to strategically requested rooms.
They'd planted the C-4 inside the room safes and inserted the detonators, then
hung do-not-disturb signs on the doors and headed back to the ground floor.
There they'd dropped their shopping bags in secluded waste bins and gone to
the business center, where they hid the doctored laptops in a cupboard. Their
last stop was the backstage area of the theatre. They had no problems finding
unobtrusive homes for the fire extinguishers. Then they'd exited separately and
driven back to the Castlefield.

In fact, they should be arriving any minute now, Del Real noted, his eyes
lingering on what he knew might be his last glimpse of the gorgeous bay.

The bombs in the casino were the key. He had no desire to destroy such a
valuable piece of property, but the threat alone would give him leverage in all
sorts of contingencies. Now it was up to the bikers to do their part.

***

Thunder Road was a biker bar in Oceanside that was owned by the North
County Kings. It had served as their headquarters for many years, and it still did,
but Matón's old office was now a storage room. Martinez stood near the front
doors, poised to take his leave. He gave Matón a nod, then headed out to pick
up Del Real at the Castlefield Waterfront.

From the intelligence gathered by Jimenez's advance team, they knew the
casino resort was protected by ten regular, unarmed security guards and thirteen
Maras, leading them to suppose that another thirteen Maras were resting nearby
on a rotation. All public traffic going into the casino had to pass through a
temporary security checkpoint, where the guards were searching every vehicle.

The plan was for the North County Kings to go in first, but not on bikes.
They'd pass through the checkpoint clean-shaven and dressed as vacationers,
riding unarmed with their wives and girlfriends in ordinary cars. Once inside,

the havoc they'd wreak would make it easier for Martinez to barge through the checkpoint, carrying Del Real and his security detail in the black SRT. Jimenez and his enforcers would follow closely in the white Alpina.

Matón paced the bandstand that overlooked the barroom before whistling for attention. "This is it, assholes," he began, drawing chuckles from the thirty men below. Like him, they were transformed, freshly shaven and sporting bright touristy attire. "At six p.m. the charges on the back fence will go off. So after the ladies drop us at the lobby, we'll have fifteen minutes to get there and gear up. Nichols' team will take the shooting range and hold that position while mine will escort Del Real to the second floor of the main casino building." As Matón's deep voice traveled to every corner of the room, his men shouted back at him in chorus, like a football coach and his team before an extra-violent championship game.

"When will the bombs go off in the hotel and who's controlling the detonators?" snarled one biker when it was time for questions.

"Several of us can set them off," Matón replied. "You don't need to know who. But that won't happen until we're safely out, if it does at all."

Another bruiser flicked his chin to gain his boss's attention. He said, "Since we're getting dropped off, how are we supposed to get back? Steal cars?"

"No, Thomas," Matón replied irritably. "We've already gone through this. You'd better not be drunk or high. Beyond the back fence, your bikes and the weapons cache are hidden in a cluster of trees under large camouflage tarps. So be sure to bring your keys."

The barroom fell silent as Matón met his men's gazes one by one, nodding slowly, letting the gravity of their situation sink in. "Now," he went on, his voice rising with the emotion he felt. "It goes without saying that we might be a few men short when we get back, myself included. So Nichols will be in charge if I don't make it. And if you're like me, you're afraid to die. But y'all have to believe me when I say Toño Del Real's a brilliant man. This is a calculated risk we're taking, and it comes with a big-time payoff. I mean mansions for everyone and all the cash we can spend. We'll call ourselves the North County Cartel!"

At that, the bikers erupted into a collective roar and stampeded out the double front doors. Outside, their significant others waited near a nondescript collection of family vehicles in tennis skirts, hats, sun dresses, and a cloud of cigarette smoke. The women hopped in on the driver's sides and started the cars as the men piled in next to them. The whole biker family was excited to become a bona fide mafia.

But only one biker would make it back alive.

***

At five-minute intervals intended to avoid the conspicuous appearance of a large group, the North County Kings pulled to a stop at the portico by the lobby and kissed their wives and girlfriends goodbye. They crossed the grounds in small groups, meeting near the pool at five minutes to six. At exactly six, an explosion shook the property as a section of the rear fence was demolished by the devices placed in advance. The bikers' cover literally blown, they hurried through the defeated barrier and untied the tarps covering the crates of munitions and the getaway bikes. Minutes later, heavily armed and armored, they split into two teams.

After finding the health spa locked and apparently deserted, Nichols' team burst into the adjacent shooting range and cleared each room. In the long hallway that led back to the firing lanes, they came to a row of locked closets.

"Gun lockers," Nichols barked. "Look for keys. If we can't find any, we'll force them open."

The bikers ran back to the souvenir shop and rummaged around in every place they could think of. No luck. The larger business room took longer to search. It was decorated like a traditional English gentleman's club, with immense leather armchairs, wood-paneled walls, and a glassy-eyed stag's head mounted on the wall. As before, they turned up nothing, but in the cigar lounge they spotted a ring of keys left behind the counter—not set out in the open, but not hidden, either.

Nichols led his men back to the hallway, making no objection when his second-in-command stepped up to the first locker, stuck out his hand, and said, "I'll do it." Nichols passed the keys to the man, who inserted a key, turned it, and was torn apart by a fiery explosion.

Now several of the bikers were missing limbs. Worse yet, a raucous battle cry rose up from the health spa, announcing the immediate arrival of ten well-armed Maras. Neither Nichols nor any of his men survived. They all perished in the initial blast, in the ensuing shootout, or while hiding in one of the rooms where they were hunted down and executed.

Amid the celebratory chanting of his men, Chasquas knelt over Nichols' blackened corpse and relieved him of his radio and keys. Flores had been right on two counts: preparation had been critical, and control of the shooting range had turned out to be decisive. Chasquas ordered the Maras to take defensive positions and wait for further instructions. Then, as he strode to the business room, he pulled his phone from his pocket and called the other half of the Maras, instructing them to gear up and report to the casino. Finally, he settled into a deep leather club chair and blew out a long sigh, thinking he had a minute to take it easy, but he didn't.

In seconds, he'd be running for his life.

***

Martinez, Del Real, Jimenez Jr., and their respective security details showed up fifteen minutes after the bikers did, the result of a crucial bit of planning, since with a shorter interval, the gate would still have been heavily guarded, and with a longer one, the police would have already been on scene. Thus, with the SRT in the lead and the Alpina trailing, Del Real and his associates rolled to a stop fifty yards from the security checkpoint, where a motorized gate and only a pair of armed guards blocked their path.

"Should I ram it?" Martinez asked Del Real, who sat in the back with his security team.

"Not yet," the cartel boss answered. "Tell them to open the gate or they're dead."

Martinez relayed Del Real's ultimatum through the Jeep's PA system. Inexplicably, the guards neither opened the gate nor offered any reply. They ran out of the guard house toward the main building.

"Ram it," said Del Real. He and everyone else in the SRT wore tactical helmets and modular ballistic vests equipped with neck and groin armor, carrying M16 assault rifles and a variety of sidearms.

Once the SRT was up to speed and half a second from smashing through, a sudden explosion shook it like an airplane in the worst kind of turbulence. A ball of fire consumed the armored Jeep as they crashed through the gate.

Martinez checked his rear-view mirror and saw nothing but flaming wreckage. The blast had directly impacted his brand-new Alpina, killing Jimenez and his men. Del Real and his men followed Martinez's gaze but no one said a word as they sped on toward the casino.

***

A few minutes earlier, Matón and his team had assembled outside the lobby. They'd been watching the distant security checkpoint while waiting for Del Real to arrive. When Matón heard the bomb go off and the gunfire at the shooting range, he whipped his head around to see smoke billowing into the sky. "Nichols!" he shouted into his radio but received no reply. By that time, the main building's fire alarm was shrieking and frightened guests were fleeing the casino en masse.

"D, are you there?" Matón asked on the same channel, looking back at the checkpoint just as the SRT crashed through the gate in a ball of fire.

"I'm here," came Del Real's booming reply. "Twenty seconds from your position."

"There was an explosion and a firefight at the shooting range and Nichols isn't responding."

"I'll take care of it," Del Real said. "Nichols, if you're listening, get your ass out of there."

As the SRT raced toward the casino, a blast bigger than the sum of those at the back fence, the shooting range, and the front gate rocked the grounds. Matón gaped as the building that housed the health spa and the shooting range caved in on itself. Several chunks of concrete landed close to him, having been launched over the pool area by the massive blast.

On Friday, when Del Real had sent the bikers to place Bangalore torpedoes on the back fence and hide the bikes and weapons, he'd also told them to affix plastic explosive to the back wall of the shooting range. Flores wasn't the only crime boss on the premises who understood the importance of good prep work.

27

THE FOG OF WAR

Del Real had attacked ahead of schedule, so law enforcement was late to the party. MARTAC and the Sheriff's Department's SED had to scramble to deploy and as a result they were reduced in number.

MARTAC commander Lieutenant John Colbert and team leader Sergeant Steve Ortiz were old friends. Colbert was tall and lean, with short black hair, and Ortiz was one inch shorter, blond, and heavier set. Colbert rode shotgun in the front of the BearCat, while Ortiz and six other operators including Park sat in the back on two facing benches. The standard SWAT team vehicle was equipped with off-road, run-flat wheels, one-inch steel plate armor, shooting ports, and a gunner hatch on the roof. Every man knew the tactical objectives, his role, and the primary and secondary infil and exfil routes, so nothing needed to be said over the grumble of the 6.7-liter turbo diesel engine. Park focused on deep breathing while triple-checking his gear and making wisecracks to ease the tension.

The BearCat was in the second position of a five-vehicle convoy. Already rumbling to a stop at the lobby portico was the Sheriff's Department's enormous armored truck. It carried a force of eleven men, including a pair of tactical emergency medical technicians.

In third position was a canine van carrying Walker and Lulu—whose leg had healed—and two other canine teams.

The fourth vehicle was the Sheriff's Department's BombCat. Similar to MARTAC's BearCat, it was designed for bomb detection and disposal. Fitted with a video command center, a radio jammer, and highly sensitive detection equipment, the BombCat was operated by two tactical bomb experts and carried several disposal robots.

The final conveyance to charge through the ruined checkpoint was the Sheriff's Department's mobile command center, a custom forty-foot trailer that would serve as the incident command post. Riding inside were Incident Commander Lieutenant Michael McEvoy of SED, who was in charge of the entire joint operation, as well as Lieutenant Taylor of the Oceanside PD Narcotics Task Force and two non-combat technicians to assist with the operation of the MCC. Boasting quad-band radios, an onboard server, satellite communication equipment, food, a large water tank, and a built-in generator, the mobile command center was designed to operate autonomously regardless of infrastructure or availability of resources.

The rotor beats of a transport helicopter were audible even over the explosions, the gunfire, and the arrival of the law enforcement vehicles as it touched down on the roof of the ten-story hotel. Five men wearing black gear and full-face masks piled out: the mayor's special tactical force.

The massive armored truck ground to a halt outside the lobby and SED poured out, storming through the front doors in three squads. MARTAC's BearCat did not stop. Along with the rest of the convoy, it rolled on toward the rear parking lot. There, Lieutenant Colbert hopped out and joined Lieutenants McEvoy and Taylor in the mobile command center, while two MARTAC operators sprinted to high ground to serve as snipers/observers. The remaining six members, including Park and Sergeant Ortiz, entered the casino building through the rear doors by the pool area, while Walker, Lulu, and the other canine teams awaited instructions in their van.

Every operator wore body armor and a tactical helmet along with eye protection, a communications headset, a rifle, a pistol, and different types of grenades. The only exception was a pair of breachers armed with shotguns loaded with special rounds designed to destroy door hinges.

IC McEvoy had gone over the tactical plan one final time before the convoy had rolled out of Sheriff's Headquarters. "SED's first objective is to localize and neutralize human threats while evacuating any remaining civilians," he'd barked gruffly but slowly, taking time to look them all in the eye. "This will free up MARTAC to locate and extract the hostages. Once Lieutenant Colbert and I have made contact with the barricaded suspects, we will tell you how to proceed. The mayor's tactical unit will provide support, starting from the roof down while we work our way up. Once the casino is controlled, we'll sweep the premises with the detection canines. Good luck and stay safe."

***

With Park on point protected by a ballistic shield and Ortiz running the show from the middle of the line of men, MARTAC climbed the south stairs to the fourth floor. At the landing, Park cracked open the door and peered into the corridor. Three security guards were posted in the hallway about halfway to the far-side stairwell.

"Police!" Park shouted.

It was thought that the casino guards, as official employees, would not be armed, but they drew pistols and opened fire, so Park threw open the door and MARTAC advanced in a dispersed stack formation while responding with well-placed rifle rounds. Bullets pinged off Park's shield as the three security guards crumpled to the floor.

As MARTAC continued toward rooms 405 and 407, a large man dressed in black tactical gear and four similarly outfitted operators emerged from the door on the other end of the hall. "Same team," the leader called out, his hands held high, his features concealed by a full-face mask. "Jim Crisman, Mayor's Special Tactical Unit. Nice shooting," he said once the two teams had come together.

MARTAC's team leader stepped forward. "Sergeant Steve Ortiz, Harbor Police Maritime Tactical Team. Where are you guys out of?"

"We're a private company," Crisman replied. "Ex-special forces, mostly." With their blacked-out visors and built-in respirators, the mayor's men looked like a human-sized swarm of killer insects.

"Ready?" Ortiz asked him. "We'll take four-oh-five and you guys take four-oh-seven." On Crisman's nod, Ortiz inserted a master keycard into the reader slots on both doors, one at a time.

MARTAC turned to focus on their own door, but the mayor's unit did not. Instead, Crisman's team trained their rifles on them and fired into the back of their necks. Only Park and Ortiz made it inside.

Park kept his cool even as bullets slammed into the door, cracking the wood but not passing through. His first thought was to secure it from the inside, but the swinging latch was missing, so he and Ortiz split up and knelt in separate corners, aiming their rifles at the door. They fired when the door swung open a foot, but it was quickly pulled shut. Two smoking tear gas canisters bounced across the carpet.

"Ortiz to command!" the sergeant bellowed into his headset, tears flowing down his cheeks. "We've located the hostages in rooms four-oh-five and four-oh-seven, but—" Stricken by a coughing fit, he was unable to go on. The only word he could clearly pronounce after that was "mayor."

Since the canisters were designed for riot control in outdoor situations, Ortiz, Park, and the rest of the hostages in room 405 suffered severe effects, even those who made it into the restroom. Their respiratory tracts were seized by searing pain and their crying eyes squinted shut involuntarily, so it was child's play for the mayor's unit to disarm Park and Ortiz, strip them of all their equipment, then bind everyone's wrists and ankles. As their black shapes moved efficiently through the fog and back out into the hallway, their respirators mechanically distorted and amplified their cyclic breathing sounds.

Ten minutes later, although the caustic smoke had dissipated into the ventilation system to some degree, Park still coughed and hacked, heaving for the toxic air. Once again he had seen his fellow soldiers give the ultimate sacrifice. Tears streamed down his face, now more from grief than from the gas. His hands formed fists and his muscles strained against his bindings. Anger rose up within him. Despite it all, he was glad to see his wife, Carla, his good friend Tina, and to finally meet Nayeli in person along with the other girls. The hostages scooted together and tried to bite through each other's zip ties, but it was impossible:

the heavy-duty plastic was too thick. A frightened silence settled over the room, the only sounds being gunfire and grenades on lower floors. Park met each of their gazes in turn. He knew what they were thinking: the bombs could go off at any moment, causing tons of concrete to come crashing down on their heads.

It would be a horrible death.

***

Lieutenant Taylor sat in the communications end of the mobile command center near the drone control station, conversing with a young drone pilot whose questions, it seemed, would never come to an end.

"How does the BombCat block remote detonation of bombs while still allowing the operators to communicate?" the young man asked. "Wouldn't all radio signals be disrupted?"

Normally glad to discuss technical minutiae with a colleague, Taylor was not presently in the mood for such queries. Unaccustomed to sitting at a command station, the former special forces soldier was itching to gear up and support the tactical squads, busy trying to decide how best to get outside and help. Even so, he drew a breath, forced a smile, and launched into what he swore to himself was his final explanation. One more question and he would tell the kid to shut up.

"Our tactical headsets use a variety of anti-jamming techniques," he replied. "And the RF jammer on the BombCat is programmable, so by using those two technologies together, the headsets can be over ninety-nine percent effective while the BombCat's jammer can still block remote detonation by cell phone, satellite communication, walkie-talkie, and other means."

"Thank you, Lieutenant," said the drone pilot with an appreciative grin.

"You got it, man," Taylor said, suddenly swiveling in his seat when Lieutenant Colbert opened the door to the conference room.

"Taylor," snapped MARTAC's commander. "We've got Flores and Delgado on the line."

Taylor strode into a separate room on the other end of the trailer, where Incident Commander McEvoy sat at a gray table with a conference speakerphone in the center. He and Colbert joined the IC, who leaned forward to address the Hondurans.

***

Flores and Delgado were holed up in Flores' panic room, safe for the time being. They, too, sat at a table close to a desktop telephone on speaker. Flores leaned toward the device and said, "We are being attacked, McEvoy. It is your duty to protect us."

"You *are* under attack," came McEvoy's voice. "I'll give you that. But are you aware that Del Real has planted explosives all over your casino? The smartest thing you can do is to let the hostages go and turn yourselves in. We can protect you from Del Real, and you'll get a much lighter sentence."

Flores didn't need to look at Delgado to learn what he was thinking, but he did so out of respect. The big man shook his head. Thinking fast, Flores concluded that the truly smart thing for them to do would be to draw Del Real and the police into his suite at the same time. The two forces would kill each other while he and Delgado could slip out through the trapdoor in the panic room. Recalling that Murci Sanchez had already escaped, Flores turned back to the telephone. "Deal," he said. "We'll tell our men to stand down, but we can't let go of all our leverage. As a show of good faith, we'll release one hostage now. The brother. Escort us out before the bikers arrive and we'll let the rest of them go. We're in suite two-oh-one."

***

Lieutenant Taylor knew Flores was lying. If captured, the Hondurans would spend the rest of their lives in a federal prison even with the minimum sentence. They were no more likely to turn themselves in than the City of Oceanside was to pay him for all the voluntary after-hours work he put in. It did occur to him, however, that Murci's extraction would be the perfect excuse to gear up and get in to the casino building. "I'll go," he told McEvoy and Colbert after the call had ended. They agreed, and Taylor added that he'd like to take Walker with him since they'd worked together in the past.

He donned an army-green tactical helmet and a ballistic vest with the word "SHERIFF" emblazoned on the front in yellow letters. He opened a gun locker and grabbed an M4 carbine assault rifle and three spare mags, rendezvousing with Walker near the canine van. The two men punched each other's knuckles and hustled across the parking lot to the casino.

Night had fallen, but with the casino building's exterior lighting they spotted a rocket-propelled grenade launcher peeking out of an open window on the fifth floor. They stopped short of the rear lobby doors and could only watch in horror as the RPG operator fired an explosive warhead at the mobile command center. The projectile hit the trailer near its fuel tank, causing an explosion that no one could have survived. Taylor and Walker raised their rifles, but the shooter went down before they could fire. MARTAC's snipers had beaten them to it.

The destruction of the MCC presented two problems: for one, their capacity for communication with the outside world was now extinguished, since all cell phones were jammed and the casino's phone lines were down. Much more worrisome, however, was the fact that the RPG operator had been wearing all black and a full-face mask, unlike any North County King, Mara, cartel member, or tactical operator on the premises. He had almost certainly been a member of the mayor's special unit.

Taylor had heard Sergeant Ortiz's most recent communication. Through all the coughing, he'd only understood that Ortiz and Park were in 405 or 407. Now he suspected that Ortiz had been trying to inform command that they'd been taken hostage by the mayor's men. Or worse.

"Taylor to SED," he growled into his headset.

"Roger, Sergeant Ragasa here."

"Someone just took out the command center with an RPG. He's down, but he looked like one of the mayor's men. I wouldn't count on any of them being friendly. Walker and I are at the lobby doors and headed your way. What's your position?"

"South stairwell at the second-floor landing. We just cleared the casino floor, with no sign of Del Real. Over."

The casino floor was lit up by too many chandeliers to count. Row after row of unattended slot machines played their percussive, bubbly chimes on an incessant loop, yet the sea of gape-mouthed bloody corpses that Taylor and Walker had to sprint past on their way to the stairs cast a heart-wrenching shadow over the sprawling room.

"Glad you could make it, guys," said Sergeant Ragasa once they'd reached the second-floor landing. He was a short and stocky Filipino with hard eyes. The ten SED operators crowded around him offered somber nods. They all wore army-green uniforms and helmets and the same ballistic vest Taylor had on.

Taylor noted the irony of his life having been saved by his desire to enter the battle. He felt a rush of sadness as he thought back to the young drone pilot who'd been so eager to learn, who had clearly looked up to him. Then there was the Incident Commander, Lieutenant Michael McEvoy of SED, MARTAC's commander, Lieutenant John Colbert, and the two non-combat technicians. He hoped they hadn't suffered.

Now that MARTAC wasn't responding, it was up to Taylor and Walker to locate the hostages and bring them to safety. But once that was done, Taylor was going after Del Real, whom he'd been chasing for years.

It was going to be a tough day for the Cartel del Norte.

28

HORSESHOES AND HAND GRENADES

Del Real had arrived at the casino at the perfect time. When he and his security detail plus fifteen North County Kings along with Martinez and Matón—a total of twenty-one heavily armed men—first stepped into the lobby, the only defensive force between them and the Hondurans' suites was a group of ten ordinary casino guards and one Mara. Most of the fighting took place on the casino floor. Del Real's crew attempted to reach the south stairwell while the security guards tried to prevent them from doing so, hiding behind slot machines and popping out to fire their pistols, only to be cut down by the bikers' rifles or blown apart by grenades. In the end, Del Real lost only one man, while all the security guards lay dead or dying on the blue-and-burgundy carpet.

Del Real's contingent charged up to the second floor and made short work of the few guards in the hallway, keeping one Mara alive as bait. The shaven-headed street soldier pleaded for his life. "Let me in! Please!" he shouted, pounding his fists on Flores' door.

To anyone peering through the peephole, the young man would have appeared to be alone, since Del Real and all the rest were waiting around the corner. All except Martinez, who had gone back down to the first floor as a precaution against what might occur in a few minutes. However, Flores and Delgado knew it was a ploy, as they were monitoring multiple camera feeds from the panic room, with an unobstructed view of the entire hallway.

Flores felt the blood drain out of his face as he watched Del Real's men gun down the Mara and go to work on the door. With shotgun blasts to the hinges and a manual battering ram, they smashed it down in no time. On entry, they fired at the pair of guards stationed inside, who fought back, dropping three bikers before they died.

With rifles panning, Del Real and his men moved through the rooms, searching for and finding the hidden switch Martinez had told them about. A wide bookcase turned on hidden hinges, revealing the blast-resistant door to the panic room.

***

"Time to go," said Flores to Delgado. He'd been hoping the police would come to defend him against Del Real, but apparently law enforcement had been too incompetent to make it up a single flight of stairs.

"What about Mama and Mari?" Delgado asked as he rose. The women had taken cover in the nearby blue room, its door easy to breach.

"Hopefully the rest of the Maras will get here in time to save them," Flores replied. "There's nothing we can do."

The Hondurans pulled open a trapdoor and lowered themselves into a crawl space, which they would scramble across, then drop down to a secluded corner of the casino floor close to an exit that opened onto the executive parking area.

Despite the fact that *delgado* in Spanish means "thin," the heavy-set man had some difficulty in the passageway, while his slighter counterpart breezed through the narrow space. When they came to the far end, Flores pushed out a panel. It fell to the carpet with a muted clatter. He was about to jump down when a familiar voice made him swear under his breath.

"Toss me your guns, turn around, and crawl back up," said Martinez, who stood by a ladder under the secret exit. He held an M16 on his former employers, who did as they were told. Martinez followed them up and forced them to open the panic room door.

The cartel leader's features burst into a wide grin when the blast-resistant door swung open. Covered by a small army, he didn't even raise his rifle. He swept his gaze over Delgado's dirty suit and said, "Looks like you had some trouble in there, Skinny."

In his prime, Delgado had been even stronger than Del Real, but that was thirty years in the past. Even so, his wrinkled fists could still fracture skulls. "Easy for you to say with a gang behind you," Delgado retorted. "I'll fight you right now. Hand to hand."

"Take us to your suite," Del Real came back calmly.

The bikers hustled the Hondurans down the hallway to Delgado's door, which the big man had no choice but to unlock. Then they pushed Flores and Delgado over to a table and down into chairs.

"Sign these papers right now or you won't like what happens next," Del Real ordered them, slapping down a short stack of documents.

"You'll never make it out of here," Flores spat out as his eyes scanned page after page. "This place is full of cops and the rest of the Maras are pulling up as we speak."

Del Real stepped over to the wall and leaned his rifle against it. Then, as he walked back, he unholstered his huge golden gun and pressed its muzzle into Flores' temple. He pulled the trigger as calmly as if he were activating the windshield wipers on his way to work. What was left of Flores' head tipped backward and his body slumped in the chair. A viscous blend of red and gray poured out of Flores' head onto the carpet.

Del Real turned to Delgado with a hard stare. "I only need one of you to sign. Do it and I'll let you live."

Delgado didn't need to read the papers. He knew Del Real's intention was to take everything he had, including his life. A fighter to the end, the big man leapt to his feet and with both hands ripped the massive pistol out of Del Real's grip, but Martinez had his M16 ready; he pulled the trigger twice and dropped Delgado like a dead tree blown over in a hurricane.

Del Real's face grew bright red from anger but he recovered quickly. Whipping out his cell phone, he swiped his thumb across the screen and punched in a series of numbers.

"We've got eight minutes to get to the bikes," he said.

***

"Glad you could make it, guys," said Sergeant Ragasa, whose operators offered Taylor and Walker grim nods. "As you know, Flores' and Delgado's suites are in the hallway just past this door. Since most of the unfriendlies will be here on floor two, I'll take six men while Deputy Wise will lead you and three others upstairs to locate the hostages. And MARTAC if you can," he added. "The mayor's unit is to be considered hostile until proven otherwise."

"Let's go," growled Deputy Wise, a barrel-chested man with sharp eyes. Wise, Walker, Taylor, and three SED operators headed up the stairs in a wedge formation that provided three-hundred-and-sixty-degree coverage.

"Sheriff's Department!" roared Wise, the first to have spotted a black-clad team above them in the same stairwell.

As the mayor's unit retreated onto the fourth-floor hallway, they sent a pair of tear gas canisters clattering down, one below Wise's team and one in their midst, encouraging them to continue upwards. Thus, with major respiratory distress and burning eyes, Wise's team came to the fourth-floor door. Wise swiveled to face them and gave a nod that was so slow and deep that it was more like a bow. Everyone lined up their sights on the door. When Wise threw it open, he was shot in the eye. Killed instantly.

One side of Walker's face was splattered with warm, sticky goo. He hugged the wall to dodge a barrage of rifle rounds that would have hit him like a tractor trailer at three thousand miles per hour. He tossed in a flashbang and pulled the door shut again, wondering whether they should charge forward, incapacitated as they were, or climb the stairs and try to find somewhere safe to recover. With Wise down, no one made the call. Not even Taylor, who shook with rage and frustration as he rubbed his eyes. By the time the flashbang exploded, Walker had made up his mind. He was about to shout "Follow me!" then lead everyone upstairs, but one of the SED operators beat him to the decision. That deputy pushed open the door and charged in a semi-crouch, firing blind at the hazy shapes in the corridor, giving Walker and the rest no choice but to follow him.

The mayor's men's darkened visors had protected them from the flash—but not the bang—and they had positioned themselves to repel the coughing, crying tactical team. Even so, it was a fatal shootout for almost everyone. Seconds later, Walker and Taylor were the only members of Wise's team still on their feet.

Walker was so incapacitated by the tear gas that he didn't know what was going on around him. At first, he thought that all the mayor's men were down, but when his rifle was ripped from his hands and he was struck squarely in the jaw with its butt end, he knew there was at least one left. Taylor suffered the same fate.

"You almost got us, I'll give you that," came a deep, distorted voice followed by mechanical breathing sounds.

Walker's eyes, throat, and lungs were on fire. He'd fallen to his knees from the blow. As his awareness faded even further, the voice spoke again. "You were close, soldiers. But close only counts in horseshoes and hand grenades."

***

Two floors down, the gunfight on the second floor unfolded just as badly for Sergeant Ragasa and the other six members of SED. When they stormed the hallway, they encountered Chasquas and thirteen Maras. Like them, the Maras wore ballistic vests and carried rifles. The two forces exchanged fire from either end, with men screaming and dropping fast on both sides. SED shot better than their adversaries, but the Maras' superior numbers forced Ragasa and the last two operators to retreat to the stairs. Only Ragasa made it out.

***

Half an hour earlier, Chasquas had been the only man to escape from the explosion at the shooting range. Forewarned by Del Real over Nichols' radio, he'd leapt up from the deep leather club chair and sprinted out an emergency exit just in time.

Now surrounded by a nauseating number of corpses in the second-floor hallway, he peered past his sights at the far door for a moment in case the cop came back, but time was a key factor. He had to find and protect his bosses, so he and the two remaining Maras entered Flores' suite, clomping over the smashed-in door to do so. The living area was deserted except for a handful of bloody corpses and the library and the blue room appeared to be empty. The panic room had been left open at both ends.

"You in here, Señor Flores?" Chasquas called out loud enough for anyone in the suite to hear, but there came no reply. "It's me, Chasquas!"

Hearing nothing, he hustled down the hall to suite 202, where he found Flores slumped in a chair with his brains blown out and Delgado sprawled on the floor in a similar state. Fighting a growing sense of panic, Chasquas motioned for the Maras to follow him. Silently, they moved toward the back rooms in complementary directions, covering each other as they cleared the luxurious flat. In the master bedroom, they found a trophy case swung open to expose Delgado's panic room. Inside, a clean-shaven Chucky Matón was preparing to drop through the trapdoor. He looked out of place in his strident golf wear.

Their rifle reports echoed loudly in the small space. Matón grunted and groaned as he crumpled to the floor with crimson liquid leaking from a number of vital points. Chasquas took aim at the biker leader's head, gazing into his panic-stricken eyes, then fired once more with a resonant crack.

Chasquas searched Matón for his keys, his only regret being that he hadn't run into Martinez. He bowed his head and prayed to Our Lady of the Holy Death that he'd catch the bastard on the way out. He'd kill him slowly, firing into his knees and the rest of his joints before sending him to a life worse than his current one. In case that wasn't possible, Chasquas implored the dark female deity to let Martinez suffer at someone else's hands for murdering his cousin Beto as well as Carli and Carkas.

"Let's go!" he ordered his men as he straightened.

It was over. Now more sober than before, he'd come to the realization that his dream of leading the North County Kings was just a fantasy. But he could still steal another one of their bikes.

29

FINALE

Toño Del Real pushed out the panel at the end of Delgado's crawl space onto the blue-and-burgundy carpet, which by then was more burgundy than blue. He dropped feet first, with a half twist so as to land facing danger. But there wasn't any, not that he could see, anyway. His intact three-man security detail followed, then eleven North County Kings.

Del Real scowled and shook his head in anger as he and his crew came to the rear lobby doors. He'd been looking forward to owning the resort. Furious with the Hondurans for choosing not to sign, he was eager to see their casino go down in a pile of dusty rubble. Regardless of who was in it at the time.

They stepped out into the cool night air and ran three hundred yards to the hole in the back fence. On the way across the pool area, high-powered rounds snapped past their heads, drilling into the concrete deck and shattering a nearby planter. The delayed report told Del Real he was dealing with snipers on the hill, and he knew they had to have been using night vision. His detail formed a tight triangle around him and they all returned fire, albeit blindly. Every man kept his head down and they ran even faster, but many bullets found their mark. By the time they reached the getaway bikes, the group was much smaller, ten out of eleven bikers having been killed or wounded and left to die.

Last time he'd checked, Del Real's phone had shown five minutes before the chain of bombs would start their sequence, and it seemed like a long time had passed since then. Critically, the explosive devices would only detonate if he disabled the bomb disposal vehicle before the timer hit zero.

They stopped short of the bikes to delve into an open weapons crate. Del Real emerged with an anti-tank missile system, which he hefted up onto his shoulder. His men followed suit, but two of them went down simultaneously, meaning there were at least two shooters.

Now flanked by only one bodyguard and one biker, Del Real could see clear as day through his optics. He targeted the snipers and loosed a warhead. When its explosive impact caused a landslide, the hillside shooters scrambled away to safety.

His men did the same to the BombCat and the BearCat, reducing the armored vehicles to orange clouds mushrooming up from fiery wreckage. Del Real dropped his weapon system and brought around an M16, which he'd kept slung over his shoulder. He scanned the grounds for enemies through the night vision scope. The police teams were still inside the casino. *Perfect.*

The scent of roasted flesh hung thick in the air as the trio advanced in a run toward the canine van and riddled it with auto fire. As they hustled back to the fence, no barking or any other sounds came from within.

His phone made an alarm sound. The timer had hit zero. He grunted with pleasure, knowing they'd taken out the jammer just in time. As the bombs in the casino building began to explode, they stomped their bikes into first and shot forward in formation, racing back to the airfield on the heavy black machines. Del Real's pilots were already running through their pre-flight checklist.

***

Martinez had dropped into the crawl space while Matón, the last in line of all Del Real's men, held the trapdoor open for him. Martinez hadn't been on his knees for more than five seconds when sharp cracking gunfire made him glance back over his shoulder. Matón grunted and groaned as he crumpled to the floor of the panic room, letting the trapdoor slam shut as he fell.

Martinez snapped his head forward again and crawled much faster, as if he'd been whipped in the rear end. He took the drop to the casino floor and hurried to the front doors, where he'd parked the SRT behind the Sheriff's

Department's massive transport vehicle. A pair of police officers stood nearby. It wasn't worth the risk. He hustled across the casino and burst through the rear doors, where he knew Del Real and the bikers would be. He spotted them far ahead, already past the pool. Determined to reach them before they left, he sprinted like an Olympic athlete through a series of sniper rounds that missed his head by inches and buried themselves in the lawn.

Martinez's stomach turned in on itself as he ran. With only a few hundred yards to go, he gave it everything he had, focusing only on the distant fence, not the poolside tents he was heading toward. Consequently, he failed to detect a blur of motion flying out of one of them like a bat from a cave. Martinez felt his legs kicked out from under him while strong arms pushed him down. His head slammed into the concrete pool deck and he screamed from nauseating pain. His attacker shoved a knife deep into his neck, right where it meets the shoulder, expertly avoiding the surrounding bones. When he regained consciousness, he was in the pool, being held under by the same strong arms. Jolted back to life by the need to breathe, he fought like a cornered animal, but it was too late. Against the wishes of every cell in his body, Martinez inhaled deeply, taking in a quart of water.

***

Three hours earlier, after killing the first Mara who came into room 405, Murci had caught the door as the second one entered, then slipped out while the man's back was turned. His objective hadn't changed, of course; it was still to save his sister, but Murci's reasoning was that he'd have a better shot if he were free. The first thing he had to do, then, was find better protection against a team of armed men in tactical gear than a knife and a T-shirt. He'd also need a passkey to gain access to room 405 again.

He raced through the hallway and clambered down the stairs, hearing someone behind him all the way to the first floor. He hid and watched his pursuer, the older Mara, exit through the rear doors and walk across the pool area, making for a large building on the other side. Murci wondered what to do. Should he find a phone, call Walker, and assist in the coordination of a rescue attempt? No. Walker, Park, and many more policemen were on their way, and they'd have already made their tactical plan. Murci figured his best move was to isolate one of the guards and strip him of his gear. Preferably a Mara, since they were better equipped. He forced himself to slow his gait and appear unperturbed as he headed for the large building his pursuer had stepped into, but as he reached the pool area, another Mara came his way. *Even better.*

***

Juan Carlos Hernández Mejía crossed paths with a fellow Mara, an older one he didn't know, on his way back from the shooting range. Chasquas had encouraged them to take their breaks there, saying it was preferable that they stay out of sight and improve their skills instead of smoking in the parking lot and scaring the customers. He nodded to his elder comrade and continued on toward the casino, where he would return to his post in the second-floor hallway. But as he approached the pool area, he spotted someone who shouldn't have been roaming around: it was Murci Sanchez walking out the rear lobby doors. Juan Carlos recognized him as one of the hostages he'd helped transport when Chasquas broke into the basement. He quickly drew his pistol but kept it on the far side of his body.

Honestly, he had no issue with his fellow Latin American, who he knew was only trying to save his sister. Like Chasquas, Juan Carlos wasn't a fan of sexual slavery, but he would certainly defend himself from a man who looked ready to kill for some equipment.

***

Even better, Murci thought. *Who knows what I'd have found in that distant outbuilding, but I can get this guy alone in a poolside tent, take him down, and be back in room 405 before the bombs go off.* The shaven-headed guard in the dark suit seemed to pay him no attention as they both strode casually closer to each other, but then the Mara whipped his arm out from behind his back and leveled his pistol. Murci's blood crackled into ice in his veins.

"Hands up," the man barked in Spanish. "Take another step and you're dead."

As the Mara unclipped his radio from his belt, Murci took another step. Many of them. It was the only chance he had, now while his hands were free and he still had his knife. He was already barreling forward when the Mara dropped his eyes for a fraction of a second to find the talk button. As Murci juked left and right, bullets zipped past him, shocking his heart into overdrive, but in a flash he was inside the Mara's reach.

The fight took them into the closest tent. Murci scrambled atop his adversary into a mount position, but he still didn't have control of the gun, which went off in the growling struggle, piercing his hand and stunning him. This allowed the Mara to slide out from under him, stand up, draw the pistol back, and smash it into the side of his head.

It was dark when Murci opened his eyes. Electrifying pain shot from his wounded hand to his temple, then multiplied into fireworks behind his eyes. Groaning, he climbed to his feet, unable to believe that the Mara had left him in the tent. He was even more astonished to find his knife still in his boot.

Then a miracle occurred. Astonishment gave way to wide-eyed incredulity as Murci saw Nayeli's handler burst through the lobby doors and sprint straight toward him. As he ran, Martinez flattened his palms like he thought he was a track star, dodging bullets that pounded the grass by his feet.

When Martinez was close enough, Murci flew out of the tent and swept the distracted crook's feet out from under him, adding to the effect with a well-timed shove. When the human trafficker slammed his head into the pool deck, Murci buried his knife in the bastard's neck just as he'd done to the Mara up in the room. He dragged the unconscious criminal into the pool, held him under, and waited for the convulsions to stop. Then he let go and watched him sink. The pool no longer shone in the night with a pleasant turquoise hue. Now, as the underwater lights filtered through the blooming cloud of blood, they cast a crimson glow into the surrounding darkness.

Just then, one after the other, two thunderous explosions echoed throughout the valley. Murci darted his eyes up to the casino building, gripped by a surge of dread, fearing it was too late to make it back to his sister. He sucked in a breath and dove down to search Martinez's pocket for a passkey, found one, then swam to the side where he heaved himself up and out. Dripping wet, he took off for the lobby but suddenly stopped when giant chunks of concrete and sheets of glass began to rain down all around him. The ten-story building swayed wildly, forcing him to spin on his heels and run for his life as the casino came tumbling down into a pile of rubble the size of a city block.

***

Mama and Doña Mari had been hiding under the bed in the blue room while Chasquas and his men had looked around the suite for Flores. The brothel managers blew out sighs of relief when the men left. It wasn't that Mama thought Chasquas would do anything to hurt her. Rather, she had a plan that she hoped would change her life, but she needed to be left alone for it to work. Her nose grazed the underside of the bed frame as she turned to face Doña Mari. "Grab the biggest handbag you've got and follow me," she whispered.

They scooted themselves out and clambered to their feet. Mama hurried into Flores' office and made a beeline for a large framed painting mounted on the wall behind the desk. "Help me with this," she said.

Together, she and Mari lifted the picture off the wall and set it aside, revealing a gray safe with a keypad. Mama entered an eight-digit sequence but nothing happened. She paused for a moment, turning the options over in her mind. Then she took another educated guess. Wrong again. With only one attempt left, she mulled over the various birth dates and other personal information she'd tricked Flores into telling her, his mother's name and so forth, but in the end she went with the numerical equivalent of her own name: Ana Maria.

The door popped open.

Mama's jaw dropped when her gaze fell on the tall stacks of bundled hundreds, a row of thick white envelopes, four polished wood boxes, and a pistol. They set to work straight away, pouring jewelry, diamonds, and other precious stones from the boxes into their handbags. Then Mari held each bag open so Mama could use both hands to stuff in the cash.

The safe completely looted, they zipped up the big purses and slipped them over their shoulders. Mama gripped her new pistol with familiarity, smoothly ejecting the magazine to make sure it was loaded, then racking the slide like a pro.

"How did you know the combination?" Mari asked on their way out.

"Got lucky, mostly," Mama said, hurrying past five dead men on the floor. "I've been trying different combinations since we got here."

"Do you think we'll ever see them again?" Mari asked as they came out into the hallway.

Mama had heard Del Real tell Delgado to take him to his suite, then gunshots down the hall shortly after. "No, I don't," she replied, shooting her friend a sad smile.

They were only one floor from freedom, but Mama headed upstairs instead of down. Wisps of acrid smoke still floated in the stairwell.

"Where are we going?" Mari called out between coughs, supporting herself on the handrail as she did her best to keep up. The first of the explosions made her yelp with fright.

"The girls don't deserve to die," Mama said, breathing more easily in the toxic fog than Mari. She figured it would be the only time in her life that her smoking habit would prove useful. When they came to the fourth-floor landing, Mama readied her pistol and pushed the crash bar forward. In the middle of the hallway, she saw three men. One of them, dressed in all black, was standing over and training his rifle on the other two, who were face down on the floor. She recognized one of the downed men as Detective Walker, the well-mannered Spanish-speaking policeman who'd interviewed her in her office.

Out of her mind with rage after years of abuse, Mama glared through her sights at the man in black. She knew who he was and what he stood for, since

Flores had told her about Mayor Rivera and his special unit. For her, it was a difficult shot with a handgun at twenty yards, but she steadied herself and fired twice, blasting the man in the neck and face, careful to avoid his ballistic protection. He went down but Mama was just getting started. She bulled forward while shooting at his legs and pelvic region, concentrating mainly on the pelvic region and stopping only when her trigger pull produced a click.

***

Walker and Taylor climbed groggily to their feet, aided by a woman Walker recognized as Mary Baretta, the manager at Western Nail Spa. She and the other lady looked nervous and they also had suspiciously heavy handbags slung over their shoulders, but Walker wasn't concerned about the contents. Not after she'd saved their lives, and especially not while the bombs all around them were going off with increasing frequency and proximity.

Walker rooted around in Crisman's pockets and came out with a hotel keycard and a heavy ring of keys. He stepped over a pile of bloody corpses to enter room 405, identifying several of them as MARTAC operators, fellow Harbor Police officers killed in the line of duty. Park was not among them.

"Jeff!" exclaimed Tina, who was sitting on a bed near a couple of people Walker knew well and many others he'd never met. He caught Park's eyes but said nothing while freeing Tina first. Then he hurried over to his anxious partner, who released Sergeant Ortiz, who set Carla free, and so on until all the hostages were ready to go, including those in room 407. It was a sizeable group, made up of Tina, Carla, Nayeli, Sergeant Ortiz, Walker, Taylor, Park, Mama, Doña Mari, and eleven other girls. Twenty individuals.

Ortiz and Park looked sadly down at their fellow operators and they both pried a rifle from a dead friend's fingers.

As the blasts continued, the ceiling started to come down in massive chunks, blocking their path as they sprinted to the stairwell, so they had to turn back toward the north stairs. When Walker pulled the door open, it could be seen that the way down was impassable, plugged up by fallen rubble.

"The only way out is up!" Park shouted over the explosions. Judging by the puzzled looks on nearly everyone's faces, it seemed counterintuitive to the group, but they all followed Park and Walker up to the roof, Taylor with Doña Mari on his back.

"It's going to be baptism by fire, honey," Park barked over his shoulder as they passed the eighth-floor landing. "You ready?"

Carla met his gaze and nodded with determination.

Park handed her Crisman's keys as they burst through the roof access door. She climbed into the cockpit of the mayor's transport helicopter while everyone else crowded into a fuselage designed for six soldiers. The main rotor spun slowly, then faster and faster with a heavy *whup-whup-whup*. Walker heaved the side door shut from the inside.

The swaying rooftop crashed down ten feet as the individual floors began to cave in, taking the chopper with it. Then it dropped again, rocking the bird as it lifted off. Finally, the whole building crumbled into a cloud as Carla fought to keep the chopper airborne.

"Are we going to make it?" Tina shouted, looking at all the passengers crowded around her like fans in the front rows of a rock concert.

Park swiveled to face her from the co-pilot's seat. "This is a Bell UH-1Y Venom!" he boomed over the rotor noise. "I saw the spec sheet once! Its empty weight is eleven thousand eight hundred and forty pounds, but the max takeoff allowance is over eighteen thousand five hundred!"

Tina frowned. She clearly wasn't in the mood for math, so Park did it for her. "That's a positive difference of six thousand six hundred and sixty pounds!" he hollered again. "If we assume an average of one hundred and fifty pounds times the twenty of us, that's three thousand, so even if the fuel tank's full, we'll be fine!"

Tina and Walker turned to grin at each other, cracking up as Carla brought the helicopter down in the rear parking lot. Park helped everyone out while Lieutenant Taylor and Sergeant Ortiz patrolled the area, marching with rifles at low ready through the smoldering remnants of the police vehicles.

"Hey!" Taylor barked. Walker followed his gaze. Past the ruined fence, in the wash of the streetlights, three black choppers sped away.

"We'll hold it down!" Sergeant Ortiz shouted, just as his snipers made it down from the hill.

There was no shortage of dead bikers for Taylor, Park, and Walker to search for keys. They sprinted past the fence, trying bikes until their keys fit the ignition. Then they gunned the big engines and roared off after the fleeing perps, following them at a distance. The chase took them all the way to Alpine, to an exit that led to a private airfield. One of the suspects didn't turn off. He sped past the exit and disappeared.

They rode as fast as they safely could, hitting one hundred miles per hour on a paved road that widened into a much broader stretch of tarmac, a runway on which a jet awaited up ahead.

"We've got him!" Taylor roared, pumping his fist in the air. Now they were close enough to the bikers to ID them under the bright lights of the airfield. It was Del Real and another rider they didn't recognize, presumably a member of his security team.

Park and Walker pulled their pistols and fired, missing Del Real, while Taylor gave his bike all the throttle it had left. Pulling up alongside the bodyguard, he grabbed the man with his left hand, ready to rip him off his bike. But Del Real, riding on the far side of his bodyguard, fired his golden fifty-caliber into his own man's gas tank. It exploded, killing the rider and knocking Taylor's bike to the runway. Both Taylor and his bike slid, scraped, rolled, and bounced for a hundred yards while Park and Walker swerved, struggling to maintain control.

Del Real had bought himself enough time to escape. As he rolled closer to the plane's lowered airstairs, he hopped off his bike while still in motion, his boots catching the tarmac in a run. He clambered up onto the jet and pulled the door closed behind him. Park and Walker skidded to a stop, averse to being hit by jet blasts.

"Don't worry. He's not going anywhere," Taylor told them, breathing hard after running to catch up, but the scraped-up former soldier's grin was as wide as if the three of them were sitting at a swim-up bar. He obviously knew something they didn't.

Sure enough, the airstairs swung down again and Del Real descended wearing full restraints, closely followed by Agents Stare and Cowgill.

"It took a while, since he'd covered his tracks, but Sean Choi finally found the flight plan. Just a few hours ago, in fact," Taylor explained.

"Looks like it's finally over," said Park, offering Walker and Taylor a knuckle smack.

"Yep," said Walker, his heart still racing after weeks of frantic action. "It's been great to work with you guys again."

Park's features clouded over and tears welled in his eyes. "Back atcha, man. By the way, I think you're ready for MARTAC. We've got plenty of spots open," he noted, without even a hint of a smile.

***

After Park, Walker, and Taylor took off after Del Real, and Sergeant Ortiz and the snipers went on to patrol the parking lot, Mama and Doña Mari took the twelve girls to where no one could see them. The human trafficking survivors glared at the women with icy disdain.

"I never meant to hurt you," Mama began. "And I know Mari feels the same way."

Doña Mari nodded remorsefully, then lowered her eyes.

Mama's eyes stung, brimming with tears. "That's how we were treated, so we did the same to—" Her voice broke, and she had to draw a quivering breath before going on. "To you. But that's no excuse, so please accept my deepest apologies." She hung her head and covered her face with her hands as she wept.

Even after Doña Mari spoke similar words and shed tears of her own, none of the girls stepped forward to comfort them. But many of the survivors cried for the first time since they'd been liberated, beginning to process their abuse. Once most everyone's eyes had been wiped dry, Mama and Mari divided the cash and jewels among the girls, keeping nothing for themselves.

On the way back to the parking lot, Nayeli ran to catch up with Mama. "What are you going to do?" she asked.

Mama's mouth broke into a loving smile for the first time in much too long. "I'm going back to Honduras, sweetie. I don't have any family there anymore, but Mari does, as you know, and she's kindly offered to take me in."

When they'd all been locked in the Castlefield's basement, having heard it from Walker, Murci had told Nayeli, who'd told Mama about Banchis, the prisoner who'd showed his family picture to Walker in the Mexican jail. As it happened, Banchis was Doña Mari's nephew.

"What about you?" Mama asked. "What are you going to do?"

"I'm leaving for Mexico tomorrow," Nayeli answered with a thin smile.

"I figured that, but do you have any plans for the future?"

"I'd like to go to college. I'm good with numbers."

"What a coincidence," Mama said. "I like math, too. *Que Dios te bendiga*, Nayeli."

"God bless you too, Mama."

Fire trucks, ambulances, and multi-agency law enforcement began to arrive, all with urgent matters to attend to, which gave Mama and Doña Mari a chance to steal away. Park and Walker also rolled up, but Taylor had stayed at the airfield to manage Del Real's placement into custody.

"Any sign of Chasquas, sir?" Walker asked Sergeant Ortiz. Now that his adrenaline spike was wearing off, his voice came out muddled due to the sharp pain in his jaw where Crisman had hit him.

"Yes, but he's gone," Ortiz replied. "He was seen running past the fence with two other men." Ortiz jerked his chin toward the distant rows of motorcycles, several of them missing.

Walker's mouth tightened in frustration. Chasquas could be halfway to L.A. already. Then Ortiz and Park fell into a personal conversation about Commander Colbert and the rest of the fallen MARTAC operators, so Walker quietly excused himself and made his way to where Tina was. He found her kneeling next to Sergeant Ragasa, telling the paramedics what she'd observed in her examination and what kind of treatment she'd given the man.

"Where'd you get the first aid kit?" Walker asked, extending a hand for her to grab as she rose.

"From the canine van," she replied. "Let me check you out." Tina led him to a bench and palpated his jaw with her fingers, feeling for abnormalities.

Walker winced from the pain. To his right, a team of EMTs was treating the other two canine handlers. Both lay flat on their backs.

Tina followed his line of sight. "Two non-fatal GSWs each," she said.

Walker wondered what had happened to them, but when he saw the side panel of the canine van riddled with bullet holes, he didn't have to ask. Tina hadn't said anything about Lulu, so he feared the worst. His mind prepared him for the shock by showing him a vision of his canine partner dead in the back of the van, but he heard paw steps and then the big black Lab trotted up unscathed.

"Hey!" Walker cried out, kneeling to hug and kiss the noble beast. She licked his face with her massive tongue, then sat on her hind legs, her features brightening in what could only be described as a smile. "What about the other dogs?" he asked, still stroking his dog's thick fur.

"They're fine, too," Tina said. "The other handlers let them out as soon as Del Real fired at the first of the police vehicles." She rubbed his shoulders for a delicious moment. "I don't think your jaw's broken, honey. Let me go see about the others." She placed a lingering hand on his shoulder before hurrying off.

Most of Walker's muscles were already aching, which didn't bode well for the next day. With difficulty, he rose to greet a surprising number of people lined up to speak with him. The first was Murci, whose arm was draped over his sister's shoulders.

"I don't know how to thank you, *hermano*," the young man said, offering his hand for as long as Walker would shake it. "You've got a friend for life if you ever need anything."

"Same here, brother," Walker said. "A recommendation for police work, maybe? And anything else, any time." He pulled out a key from his pants pocket and handed it over. "I know Seley wanted you to have his bike. It's parked in my driveway and the papers are under the seat. I have to stay here, but I can have someone give you a ride if you want."

"No thanks. We've got plenty of money for a taxi," Murci replied, exchanging a sly glance with Nayeli. "If you could just text me the address."

Nayeli's features warmed just a tad when she heard Murci and Walker speaking in Spanish. Walker thought it might have made her think of home, where she'd be in a couple of days. In any case, she stepped forward and threw her arms around Walker, shuddering as she cried. He comforted her for as long as he thought proper, then guided her into her brother's arms.

As Murci led her away, he looked back over his shoulder, offering Walker a final expression of gratitude. Walker raised his arm in farewell and held it high, long after Murci had turned forward again.

30

— • —

EPILOGUE

Six months later, on the way home from work, Walker took his supercharged Mustang on a detour over the two-mile Coronado Bridge, with the bay sparkling below on both sides. When he came to the island, he wound his way through a couple of streets and emerged onto Silver Strand Boulevard, heading south on a seven-mile peninsula only three hundred yards wide. Otherwise known as California State Route 75, the scenic highway had been the only way to reach Coronado Island by land until the bridge was finished in 1969. With the bay on the left, Walker passed the Naval Amphibious Base to the right, followed by a beach on the Pacific Ocean. Named for the tiny silver seashells that line its white sands, Silver Strand State Beach was where Tony Park had undergone much of his brutal SEAL training.

It was the end of another gorgeous day in sunny San Diego. A massive, slowly-sinking orange fireball cast a cozy glow onto the clouds, scattered across the sky in a warm, hazy canopy. Walker eased off the gas and relished the salty air coming in through the open windows. As the two-lane highway stretched on and on, his breathing slowed and he felt at peace.

"I'm home," he announced, closing the door as his first-born daughter ran to throw her arms around him. Then Tina added to the embrace, making it a group hug. Their house wasn't large and it wasn't in a fancy part of town, but it did boast a back yard with a patch of grass, a swimming pool, and, best of all, a gas-powered grill—Walker was hungry. As he felt the loving warmth of his family around him, his mind turned to the criminals he dealt with every day, many of them violent, deranged, perverted, or all of the above. Those crooks occupied much of his mental space, much of the time, but how many of them could say they came home to something like this?

Tina was in her element. A consummate hostess, she'd laid out two types of homemade salsa, fresh guacamole, corn chips, and vegetables, and she'd prepared the meat so all he had to do was grill it. Tina Michelle, now three, got busy at two round outdoor tables, setting napkins and silverware at each place. Mother and daughter wore colorful dresses, cute shoes, and their hair was done up just so. Carla was seated at the indoor dining table holding Mia, the newest member of the Walker-Garcia family. The baby girl brightened every room she was carried into, and someone was always asking to hold her. Walker kissed the precious child before heading up the stairs.

After a badly needed shower, he went out to the poolside grilling station carrying a tray piled high with marinated steak. Tina put on the patio lights as well as festive music that played through outdoor speakers. He cracked open a cold can of club soda, took a long, satisfying pull, and fired up the grill with a *whoosh*. Before long, the guests began to trickle in.

Park showed up first, stopping to chat with Carla and Tina in the kitchen before joining him outside. The sturdy detective leaned against the brick wall by the grill, facing the pool as he, too, sipped from a can of sparkling water. Park looked good. Strong and healthy. Ready for the next mission. Walker turned his attention back to the sizzling meat, its juices dripping onto the flames, filling the yard with a scrumptious aroma.

The next guests to ring the bell were Lynn Peters, Lieutenant Taylor, and Chief Deputy Pat O'Connell. Lynn was stunning in a black spaghetti-strap dress. Her shiny blond hair spilled far past her bare shoulders, matching her gold jewelry. Dom Taylor held her hand as they stepped inside. Both Taylor and O'Connell looked like they'd come straight from work, Taylor wearing slacks and a polo shirt, O'Connell in a navy-blue blazer over khakis. Walker was pretty sure O'Connell had needed to hire a tailor to fit those biceps into his sleeves. Then came Tina's younger sisters, Maggie and Dulce. Maggie's date was an old friend of Walker's and Park's named Marcus Crawford, a San Diego lifeguard sergeant and now the leader of the dive rescue team. Dulce was escorted by Sean Choi, who gave a cheery grin as he pushed her wheelchair up the ramp, into what was fast becoming a lively party. Walker had known about Crawford and Maggie, but if Choi was dating his other sister-in-law, it was news to him.

Everyone loaded their plates with steaming steak, refried beans, red rice, and Caesar salad, then found a seat at the outdoor tables. Little Mia charmed them all and Tina Michelle played happily in the pool.

Midway through the meal, Chief Deputy O'Connell rose to lift his glass. "I'd like to propose a toast," he boomed. The happy chatter slowed, then stopped. "First to Tina and Jeff. Thank you for the invitation to this delicious feast." Every guest echoed the sentiment, clinked their glasses, and took a sip of whatever they were drinking. "Now on a serious note," O'Connell went on after a time. "Since this is the first chance we've had to get together since the events at the casino, let's take a moment of silence to honor those lost in the line of duty."

Walker bowed his head, his first thoughts centering around Ayla Sami and Ali Hassan. He hoped they'd found each other in the next life. Then he shook his head at the memory of Agent Seley, who he hoped was cruising through the clouds on an even bigger bike. His mind next turned to Lieutenants Colbert and McEvoy, to DAI Peña, and all the other heroes who'd died in the service of their fellow humans. And how could he forget about poor Marcela? He felt certain she'd gone on to a better world.

As Walker lifted his head again, Lynn Peters met his gaze. Her sly smile made him think she knew something he didn't.

"Thank you," O'Connell said. "Now I'd like to pay homage to the living, to those of you who contributed to what some people are calling a successful operation at the casino. Despite the tragic loss of life, we did take down the human trafficking ring we'd set out to dismantle, as well as a major smuggling operation on both sides of the border. But if we're going to toast to something, let's drink to the girls making it home to their families and fully recovering from what they survived."

Again the invitees brought their glasses together and took a drink, but this time there was no happy chatter.

Finally, O'Connell cracked a joke. "This is a lot of toasting," he said. "We're going to need refills before I wind this up." His tight-lipped smile turned the mood around. "Carla, we couldn't have done it without your skill and bravery."

Carla beamed.

"And Tina, we would have lost many more if you hadn't been there to help." Tina studied the deck as if to de-emphasize her contribution.

"Choi, you too. If you ever need a job, give me a call. And speaking of employment," O'Connell went on, eying Lieutenant Taylor. "I know you're needed up north, Dom, but you've got a standing offer in the DA's Office. It'd be an honor to have you aboard."

"For me too, sir," Taylor replied, raising his glass as he met the man's gaze and the partygoers burst into applause and shrill whistles. Then O'Connell held up a hand, his speech rising in speed and volume as he came to the climactic revelation of happy news. "Finally, let's congratulate Tony and Jeff, who've been awarded generous bonuses by the city council for exceptional service to San Diego!"

At that, a major celebration ensued, with much clinking and drinking and standing hugs.

Carla stood up from her chair and took her husband's hands in hers. Park gazed into her brown eyes and said, "I found out yesterday, but I wanted everyone to be surprised. It's enough to cover a good down payment on that house we loved." His eyes went moist as he stepped closer, gathered her into his arms, and held her for a full minute.

The warm expression on Tina's face told Walker she'd forgotten about the past and was proud of him again. It was worth more than any amount of zeros on a check. Naturally, however, he was dying to know how generous the city had been, so as they embraced, he peered over her shoulder and prompted Park with raised eyebrows and an inquisitive jerk of the chin. Park came back with a series of numerical hand gestures. While not sufficient to clear all their debt, the money would be enough to set them on the right foot again.

Later that evening, Walker crossed the backyard grass to where Chief Deputy O'Connell sat alone on a bench, his gaze settled on the night-lit pool. Fragrant trails of smoke wafted from the end of his cigar.

"What's next for you, sir?" Walker asked as he took a seat.

O'Connell blew out a puff of sweet smoke, away from Walker's face. "Well, buddy, I've got five years left before I can retire," he said. "So I'll be running for mayor in the special election. I'm sure you know Rivera has been stripped of office and is facing multiple felony charges."

Walker was aware of that fact, but he also knew O'Connell was independently wealthy and didn't need to wait for his pension. The man was too modest to say that what got him out of bed early and into a tie every day was his commitment to serving his city. He'd make a great mayor.

Later still, after Park and Walker had cleaned up the patio and the grill station, Walker closed the barbecue lid. "Did you get enough to eat?" he asked, stooping to feed Lulu a massive handful of leftover steak.

Park leaned over to rub the black Lab's head. "Too much, bro. I'm so full it's going to take me ten shits to feel normal again."

Walker cracked up as he slid open the sliding glass door and they both went inside.

"So you get to keep her?" Park asked.

Walker slid the door shut behind them. "Yep. She'll live out her last years here with us."

The weary detectives tried to gain their wives' attention, but they were coolly ignored. Carla and Tina were perched at the kitchen bar amid raucous guffaws and deep-throated belly laughs. With them were the two couples: Maggie Garcia and Marcus Crawford, Dulce Garcia and Sean Choi. Crawford's deep tan and his long, sun-bleached hair made Walker more than a little jealous.

Once Crawford had tuned up Tina's acoustic guitar, a hush fell over the room as he launched into his first number, a love song he'd written for Tina's sister. His lyrics brought tears to Maggie's eyes and earned him a kiss when he was done. Then he segued into a complex limerick-like tune, also an original composition, followed by hearty applause and cheers all around. Crawford tried to hand the guitar back to its owner, but the group begged him for an encore, so he relented and lifted his voice once more. This time he belted out "La Bamba," inviting everyone to sing along at the chorus.

"Bam-ba-bamba," the delighted group crooned. "Bam-ba-bamba!"

The party in general as well as its musical finale made for an evening Walker wished would never end, but like all good things, it eventually did. Before long, he found himself sweeping the kitchen floor while Tina put the girls to bed. With the house back in normal order, he grabbed a pair of towels, turned off the outdoor lights, shed all his clothes, and slipped into the bubbly heat of the jacuzzi. The night air was cool and all the stars were out.

When he heard the sliding glass door open and close, he turned to see Tina on the deck stripping naked. He forgot all about the stars, but he did have the presence of mind to help her down into the hot, heavenly water. The bubbles came up to her belly button, so he was treated to the sight of her perfect breasts before she hit him with that incredible smile of hers. Then he resumed his seat on the bench and she straddled him, their mouths meeting in a long, slow kiss.

***

FOUR YEARS LATER

The brilliant Mexican sun had to pass through a layer of tanning oil before it soaked into Murci's mother's still-perfect skin. She lay on a lounge chair, refreshed after her daily swim, closing her eyes behind dark designer sunglasses. The delicious coastal breeze and the rhythmic crashing of waves below the private poolside veranda lulled her into what her yoga instructor referred to as an alpha state.

Murci stepped quietly out of his parents' master suite, easing shut the sliding door so as not to let the air-conditioning escape. He set a piña colada on the table beside her.

She stirred, stretched, and took a drink. "Thank you, son," she said with a smile.

He sat beside her in silence for a while, relishing the incomparable view of the coast at Cabo San Lucas, Baja California, Mexico. As a cruise ship chugged across the horizon, the sunset infused the shifting clouds with its red and orange rays, painting a kaleidoscopic masterpiece.

The sliding door behind them opened and shut again as she asked, "How was work today?"

"He's the best detective on the force," Murci's father said. "He'll be chief someday, mark my words." With a contented grin, the patriarch plopped down onto a third sun chaise. He wore only swim trunks and a wide-brimmed hat, looking and feeling nothing like his former self. His trim, strong body showed the difference that good health coverage and a light workload can make, especially to an older person. With a large staff to support him, Papá spent only a couple of hours a day in the executive office of their new oceanfront resort. He drew a breath, let it slowly out, and settled his gaze on the waves rolling in.

"I've got a date," said Murci, rising to leave.

"Not so fast, brother," came a melodious voice behind them as Nayeli emerged onto the veranda. She was dressed in fashionable attire suitable for the private university she went to, and her shiny black hair was cut shorter than before. One could no longer describe the confident young woman as a girl. "Can we take a picture first?" she asked, drawing a large smartphone from her purse.

The Sanchez family crowded excitedly together at the railing against the glittering backdrop of the Pacific Ocean. Nayeli held up her phone, making sure everyone was included, and snapped a happy photograph that would adorn their new home for many years to come. The lines on their faces, though deeply etched, were finally curving up instead of down.

THE END

READERS CLUB

Hello! I hope you enjoyed this second installment of The Park and Walker Action Thriller Series. If you did, I'd appreciate it if you left me a review on Amazon. It helps me as well as other readers. Just a line or two is fine. If you scan the following QR code, you'll be taken to the review page for this book.

 By signing up for my readers club, you'll not only receive an award-winning Park and Walker prequel short story, but from time to time you'll also get spam-free emails from me, in which I may send my personal book or author recommendations, let you know about any discounts or new Park and Walker books I have written, or possibly deliver another exclusive short story. You can unsubscribe at any time and I won't sell or share your email address.

A Hell of a Spring Break: A prequel short story to Book 1: *The Mazatlan Showdown*

In this award-winning short story, beach lifeguards Jeff Walker and Tony Park are sent on a week-long exchange program to the North Shore of Oahu, where a serial killer strikes twice. Are they to be the next victims? And which of their colleagues is the North Shore Thrill Killer? Read this gripping prequel to find out!

If you scan the following QR code, you'll be able to download your free short story and sign up. I'll never sell or share your email address and you can opt out at any time.

ABOUT THE AUTHOR

I first made my living as a professional musician, then as a licensed teacher, next as a commercial translator, and now as an award-winning thriller writer. My favorite authors are Lee Child, David Baldacci, and Clive Cussler. I live with my wife, our children, and four dogs. You can find me on Facebook at faceb ook.com/PatrickWeillAuthor, on Twitter @Patrick_Weill, or on my website at www.patrickweill.com.

My very best,
Pat Weill
February 2023

Made in the USA
Monee, IL
20 March 2023

30007580R00142